SILENT

By D. M. Mitchell

Max
Silent
Mouse
Blackdown
The Soul Fixer
Flinder's Field
Pressure Cooker
The Domino Boys
The King of Terrors
The House of the Wicked
The Woman from the Blue Lias

The First D. M. Mitchell Thriller Omnibus
The Second D. M. Mitchell Thriller Omnibus
The D.M. Mitchell Supernatural Double Bill

SILENT

A Novel by D. M. Mitchell

_____

SILENT

A novel by D. M. Mitchell

Copyright © D. M. Mitchell 2013

The right of Daniel M. Mitchell to be identified as the author of this work has been asserted by him in accordance with the Copyright, Designs and Patents Act 1988. All rights reserved.

All characters and situations in this publication are fictitious, and any resemblance to real persons, living or dead, is purely coincidental

Agamemnon Independent Publishing

ISBN-13: 978-1494794866
ISBN-10: 1494794861

Cover illustration, *Castle Dragutin*, painted by D. M. Mitchell

In memory of the late, great James Herbert.
He inspired me to want to become a writer.

All things are sold. The very light of heaven
Is venal; the earth's unsparing gifts of love,
The smallest and most despicable things
That lurk in the abysses of the deep,
All objects of our life, even life itself,
And the poor pittance which the laws allow
Of liberty – the fellowship of man,
Those duties which his heart of human love
Should urge him to perform instinctively –
Are bought and sold as in a public mart
Of undisguising Selfishness, that sets
On each its price, the stamp-mark of her reign.
Even love is sold.

Queen Mab
Shelley.

Part One

Hollywood 1927

1

Meat

He reckoned his days fell into two basic categories. Some are good. Some are bad. Today was definitely a bad day. As bad as it gets. It started out bad, it had a bad middle section and it sure as hell was going to end bad. So bad, in fact, he felt the stink of it would drive away any good days for a long time to come.

He also knew from experience that bad days always started with a phone call, a telegram or a letter. Three harbingers of doom, like the witches in Macbeth, and to make matters worse it was just his luck to get two out of the three of them that morning. The first was a letter from the studio. Cutting out the corporate lawyer bullshit, he summarised it thus:

Dear Mr Mason,

Latest release shit. No way are we renewing your contract. You're screwed. Have a nice day.

Frank Gibson

Managing Director
Prima Motion Picture Company.

Rick Mason sank down heavily onto the flimsy, moth-eaten mattress of his pull-down bed, the springs groaning in sympathy. He read and re-read the letter. He had to concede there was no way he could make its contents look any better, no matter which way he read it.

He ran a hand through his hair, glossy and black with hair oil.

They can't really mean this, he concluded. Someone's made a mistake. Some goddamn secretary or something had screwed up big time. They can't throw Rick Mason out onto the scrapheap by letter, without warning, without even so much as a face-to-face discussion, discard him like so much unwanted trash. By fucking letter! Hell, that cuts a man up real bad.

As if his agent had been reading his mind the phone rang.

'What the hell's going on, Victor?' Mason bawled into the mouthpiece.

'You've heard, then?'

'You knew about this, Victor?' he said. 'You damn well knew about this?' Mason thumped the hollow wall on which the phone hung and it vibrated.

'To tell you the truth, Rick, I've been fighting your corner for a few weeks.'

'Weeks? This has been going on for weeks and you never thought to mention it to me? You're my agent, for God's sake; you're supposed to have my interests at heart!'

'You're like a son to me...' said Victor Wallace, looking aimlessly out of his poky little office in West Los Angeles. The view was a brick wall. The room was sweltering. The window was open, the fan blowing on high, but the sweat still streamed down his back. He mopped his brow on a handkerchief.

'And you haven't seen your real son in ten years, Victor, so don't give me that line again. What's going on? I've got another eight months left to run on my contract with Prima. That asshole Frank Gibson is threatening to ditch me.'

'It's not a threat, Rick. I'll tell you what's wrong, *Dust of the Sahara*, that's what's wrong. It's an unmitigated flop, and you know what, I can't argue with them, because I've seen it. Tag on the other two flops and we end up in the current situation.'

'So they're blaming me for *Dust*?' said Mason. 'The plot was abysmal, the direction appalling, the editing shoddy and the amount of money they threw at this motion picture was too small even to call peanuts. They're blaming me for all that?'

'You're the movie's lead, Rick, remember? They don't think you have what it takes to draw them in. Not enough charisma, maybe even too short. Hell, Fairbanks could stick his name on a two-minute short advertising hair cream and he'd pack the theatres out.'

'Douglas Fairbanks? Want to know something about Douglas Fairbanks? He's short. He's not a six-footer like he looks up on screen. He's only a couple of inches taller than Chaplin, that's how short he really is. It's the slick camera work that makes him look tall, something they sure don't have at Prima. Anyhow, I'm not short! I'm taller than both Chaplin and Fairbanks!'

'Forget the short, Rick. Wished I hadn't brought the damn thing up. You gotta face it, Rick, they don't know where to pitch you. You're not as pretty as Valentino, and there's no way you can make it as a heavy. You're like an ornament they know deep down is good but can't find a shelf for.'

'An ornament?' He thumped the wall again and someone on the other side thumped back and hollered for him to can it or get a fist in the face. 'I can do a Fairbanks,' he protested. 'He's nothing special. Get on the phone to Gibson, plead my case, do what agents are supposed to do.'

He sighed. 'Plead? I've practically been on my knees to the man asking for one more chance for you. He was on the phone to me for an hour last night. I gave him all I had, Rick. He said he'd think it over. Guess he'd already made up his mind.'

'I've got another eight months left to run on my contract...' he opined.

'You've got two options, Rick; you either sit out the eight months with no picture to work on, or you take the money he's offering you, cash your chips in on the contract and walk away from Prima Motion Picture Company.'

'So what's he offering by means of a severance?'

'Three-hundred bucks, minus my cut.'

'What?' he burst. 'Three-hundred measly bucks? He's having a laugh!'

'We both know Frank Gibson doesn't have a sense of humour,' said Wallace. 'It's a dead end, Rick. Trust me, I've been down a few in my time. My advice is to take the money and we'll try to land you another contact, somewhere.' The way he said it didn't sound too hopeful.

'Call yourself an agent?'

'I got it upped from two-hundred!' he retorted indignantly. 'You'd better watch your mouth. I've worked my balls off running around this town on your behalf. Who agreed to take you on when every other agent slammed the door in your face? Victor Wallace. Who landed a contract for you at Prima when all the other studios didn't want to know anything about you? Victor Wallace. Who managed to get you an extra hundred bucks?'

Rick Mason rubbed his eyes and took a settling breath. 'Yeah, I'm sorry, Victor. I know you've been good. It's not your fault. But Frank Gibson can ram his three-hundred where the Sun don't shine!'

'Yeah, well, I'd sleep on that, Rick. Think it over carefully.'

'I've done my thinking, Victor; I'm heading straight on down to Prima studios and I'm going to tell Mr high-and-mighty Gibson to his face what I think!'

'That's not wise, Rick,' he said. 'Tell you what, why don't you come over to my office instead and we'll talk things over? Plan where we go from here.'

So that was a good example of a bad start to a bad day. And from where Rick Mason was standing he could see where he was going from here and it wasn't anywhere scenic. All you had to do was take to the streets of Hollywood to see what the future held for a nobody. Douglas Fairbanks? There were so many people thinking they were the next Fairbanks a producer could walk all the way from his office to the bank stepping on them and not touch the ground once. The place was teeming with young hopefuls washed in on one tide and swept away disappointed and dejected on the next. Like him they'd read their well-thumbed copies of *Variety*, or *Moving Picture World*, pored over articles on Mary Pickford, Lillian Gish, Rudolph Valentino, Charlie Chaplin, Greta Garbo, and a hundred other such movie stars, and hankered for a taste of the rhinestone glamour their touched-up photos exuded.

Rick Mason wasn't his real name. It was Stjepan Gjalski. He came over from Europe with his mother some fifteen years ago, still had a strong accent, though it was becoming softer now. That had been changed to Steven Gallis at Ellis Island, to make it easier to pronounce by those who processed him, and to Americanise it somewhat. But even that had been changed following Victor Wallace's advice.

'Nobody uses their real name in Hollywood, kid,' he'd said. 'Everyone here is pretending they're someone else and looking to land a career where they get paid big bucks pretending to be someone else. It's all baloney and bullshit – that's the first thing you gotta remember, kid. Never ever forget that. It's like a meat grinder. I've seen what it can do to people who don't make it – and also to a few that have – and for every hopeful that lands a contract there are a thousand who'll never be anything bigger than waitresses and waiters. So, first thing I'll do it work my ass off to help you because I know you've got talent; the second is never to bite the hand that feeds it; the third is to ditch that God-awful name, get yourself something more swanky, and take some kinda lesson to smooth out that European accent. America is the fastest-growing breadbasket in the world but those at the back of the queue tend to have a foreign accent; the fourth, you keep your nose clean, stay clear of the bottle and the broads and maybe you'll stand half a chance, because the first time you land yourself in trouble with the law Victor Wallace is walking away from you. You got all that, kid?'

He got it OK. He knew the ropes. Rick Mason had been doing the rounds in vaudeville for ten years or more, since he was aged about fifteen. He didn't have a father, just his mother. They'd come over to America from Slavonia before the war, to escape the grinding poverty and the Austro-Hungarian oppression that kept them there, so his mother used to rant when she was angry, which was most always. Millions of other immigrants flooding into America had similar stories, every one of them hoping to find a better life, and millions like him and his mother exchanging rural rat infested hovels for urban rat infested tenement blocks.

His mother, however, could sing beautifully. Sad songs usually, of a faraway home; songs that squeezed tears from her; songs that made her want to be alone. Mason had been able to play the fiddle, so they took to the stage and scraped a living that way, till drink got the better of her and he had to support them both, change his act to accommodate. She went into a fast decline, her attitude towards him aggressive, abrupt, hurtful, claiming she wanted nothing to do with him, that he was a burden she had had to bear for far too long. She wanted to go back home and it was his fault she could not.

She died of cancer of the throat, ending her days angry and bitter, and was buried in an unmarked pauper's grave. Mason was left to make his own way. Like thousands of others, if he had a spare dime he'd go to the nickelodeons and it became clear to him early on that film was his future, not strutting about a stage for an audience of five. He wanted to be a part of the new motion picture industry, so he packed his case and tossed a coin to see whether it was to be New York or Los Angeles and Hollywood. Los Angeles was the lucky winner, so he got a job swinging a broom in whichever studio wanted him and tried to force his big break, but no one was interested. At night he'd tread the boards to earn enough to keep him out of the soup kitchens, and up on stage that's where Victor Wallace first saw him. Saw something in the young man that nobody else had, and eventually his new agent managed to land him a contract with Prima Motion Picture Company.

Prima was headed by the formidable brother partnership of Luke and Carl Dillon. Prima had been one of the first studios to open in Hollywood, on the northwest corner of Sunset Boulevard and Gower Street, and had been building up a successful motion picture business for the past ten years or so. They were looking to move away from the one-reel shorts they'd been churning out every week and into the lucrative feature market where there were huge profits being made. As early as 1915, when Prima was only two years old, *The Birth of a Nation* had grossed a staggering $10 million, and there'd been a succession of big hits like *Ben-Hur* and *The Gold Rush*, which confirmed to the Dillons that's where the main direction lay.

Except Prima's ambition didn't match its ability to raise the massive investments needed, so they aped their betters by doing it on the cheap. They couldn't attract big names, for one thing, and investors saw them only as a factory turning out inconsequential shorts, so they had little money to splash around on their features.

As far as Rick Mason was concerned, from the very beginning *Dust of the Sahara* had all the hallmarks of someone dressing a hobo in top hat and tails whilst failing to hide the smell. And he'd finally paid the price for what he considered to be the studio's cheapskate shortcomings and cutbacks.

Well Rick Mason didn't consider himself to be meat in anyone's grinder, no matter what Victor Wallace said. Ignoring his advice he drove straight on down to Prima studios and pulled up outside the huge twin gates of stout wrought iron painted in glistening white, each bearing the name Prima in gold letters. There were two uniformed men standing in front.

Rick dropped the side window of the old Ford. A smell of gasoline fumes wafted in.

'Hi, Jake,' he said to one of the guards, who ducked down to the car's window. 'Let me in, will you?'

'Sorry, Mr Mason, no can do.'

'C'mon, Jake; you know me – let me in. I gotta see Frank Gibson.'

'You got an appointment?'

'Yeah, sure I've got an appointment. Just let me in, huh?'

Jake's sun-baked face, brown as a creased leather armchair, cracked a smile, but all the same he told Rick to wait. He went over to a box on the wall, cranked a call and spoke into the mouthpiece. He nodded a couple of times, hung up the phone and shut up the box. He ambled across to the car, hitching up his pants as he did so. He bent to the window again.

'Sorry, Mr Mason, you ain't got an appointment.'

'Then let me in and I'll make one at the office.'

'Can't do that either.'

'You've known me two years and more, Jake. I gave you birthday cards. Let me in. I've got to see Gibson. It's urgent.'

'Well Gibson's made it plain he doesn't want to see you. My advice, turn around, don't make a scene.'

'I tipped you plenty, Jake!' he said, thumping the steering wheel.

Jake's face steeled. 'You tippin' me don't buy me, Mr Mason.' He left the car, took up his place by the gates and looked away.

Ah, fuck, thought Mason. Maybe a guy is a piece of meat whether he likes it or not. He drove away, fuming inside.

* * * *

2

Luke Dillon

An old Nantucket sailor once told him that a ship went down in three stages: first, it hit the rocks; second, it broke its back; third, it sank beneath the waves.

Turned out the sailor was just an extra pretending to be from a Nantucket whaler, so the origin of this seafaring nugget was somewhat debatable. Still, it stuck in his mind, and Rick Mason saw frightening similarities to his own predicament. Sure, he'd hit the rocks hard. And right now the two men who were taking his car had threatened to break his back if he stood in their way.

'But you can't do this!' he protested as they made themselves comfortable inside. 'Get out of my car! Get out of Lillian!'

'Lillian?' said the man behind the wheel, dragging the brim of his hat down to shade his eyes from the early-morning sunshine slanting in through the windscreen. 'You gave your car a name?'

'Screw you!' returned Mason. 'Just get your filthy butts out of my car!'

'Listen, buddy, the thing is never to give anything a name till you've finished paying for it. You don't keep up on the instalments, we take it back, that's the deal. You pay what you owe and you'll get little Lillian back.'

'Hell, guys, have a heart! You can't take my car. She's all I've got. An actor needs a motor in Hollywood or he ain't an actor, you know that.'

The other guy in the passenger seat leant across the car's new driver. His nose had been broken, giving him the appearance of an ex-boxer, someone you'd think twice about messing with. 'Actor?' he said, his lip twisted into contempt. 'I don't see an actor, do you?' he asked his companion. 'Last time I read about Rick Mason someone said he was a man whose acting was so wooden, if someone yelled "timber" he'd fall over.' They both laughed.

'That's so fucking funny, almost as funny as the fact you bozos can read. You morons know nothing about acting. Just get out of my car.' Seeing it wasn't working, he softened his approach. 'C'mon, guys, do me a favour. I'll get you the money by the end of the week and I'll throw in a little bonus for you. How's that sound?'

The man at the wheel furrowed his brows in thought, turned to his partner. He nodded in response. 'OK, Mr Mason, you got a deal. We ain't as hard as you think. We'll give you your car back if you promise to get the money by the end of the week.'

'Mason bent down to the window. 'Really? Thanks, I owe you big time.'

'You fucking kidding?' He gave a loud guffaw. 'Now that's acting, sucker!' he said, stepping hard on the gas and driving away. 'Timber!' he shouted through the window, giving Mason a wave.

Mason ranted angrily and scuffed the dirt with his shoes in protest, but it did little except draw stares from passers-by.

The Palm Club. It's where they all hung out. All the big names. Anyone who was anyone in Hollywood went at some time to eat in the Palm. They used to joke that it was so exclusive even the President of the United States couldn't get a table. Little wonder, then, that Rick Mason had never been allowed through its gilded doors, but that wasn't going to stop him tonight. He knew Luke Dillon ate there every Friday night, and if he couldn't get into Prima studios to see that asshole of a managing director Frank Gibson then he'd go straight to the head honcho himself.

He'd scraped together his last few dollars, emptied his meagre bank account and pawned his watch and radio so he could hire out a fancy tuxedo. He also knew this guy who worked as a chauffeur down at Universal who agreed, for a price, to drop him outside the Palm Club in a borrowed limo. It was actually a 1923 Moon 6-58 touring car, in glistening light-blue coachwork, black fenders, whitewalls, cream leather seats and soft-top, the full works. When the car turned up, freshly waxed and gleaming in the club's many lights, and the uniformed chauffeur got out to open the door for Mason, it did the trick and fooled the two bullnecked bouncers, who didn't say a word as he strolled up to the doors. He waited whilst the doors were opened for him and breezed into the joint like he owned the place.

He was asked if he had a reservation.

'I'm with Luke Dillon,' he said, whipping off his white silk scarf.

There was a smell of money in the air. Good food, cigar smoke, expensive perfume. The women were some of the classiest he'd ever seen, floating around the place like sinuous sirens, their heels silent on the plush blue carpet. There was a cocktail bar that wasn't preparing cocktails, a nod to prohibition, but he knew there'd be cocktails somewhere. A band was playing, a woman crooning silkily into a microphone, her dress a figure hugging cocoon of shimmering green silk. He was momentarily overawed by it all.

'Mr Dillon didn't inform me he was expecting a dinner guest,' said a stiff maitre d' coming up to him. 'Your name, sir?'

'My name? It's the one in lights, dear boy! The one in lights!' He motioned to the sky. 'Don't worry yourself; I've spotted Mr Dillon, I'll see myself over.'

The maitre d' protested quietly, but Mason ignored him and threaded quickly through the sea of tables, their white tablecloths looking like a broken-up ice floe. He sat down at Luke Dillon's table, opposite him. The man looked up from the piece of blood-red steak he'd speared on his fork which had been poised to enter his mouth.

'Who the fuck are you?' He had a chain-smoker's gravelled voice. Dillon had been born in Brooklyn, the scar near his right eye, a permanent reminder of some barroom brawl or other, was testament to the fact that he didn't hail from the smartest side of town. His neighbourhood had been redwood-hard, and the Dillon family reckoned to be the knottiest part of this particular plank. His family had been dirt-poor, sodbusters who came over from Ireland over seventy years before, forced out of the country by the potato famine that killed a million. They say Luke Dillon's family hadn't eaten a potato since. But the two brothers, Luke and Carl, had made good, the origins of the original investment to set up Prima Motion Picture Company might have been acquired via dubious but never proven ways, but the venture had bought the Dillons a lucrative business and Hollywood respectability. They said the brothers still had all manner of people in their pockets, from police chiefs to politicians, and uncomfortably cosy connections with the Los Angeles underworld, but Hollywood can be very forgiving and blind, thought Mason, with the right amount of influence and money. Mainly money. The Dillons lived the high life in Mediterranean-style mansions up on Whitley

Heights, on the hills overlooking Hollywood Boulevard. Some of the biggest stars in Hollywood lived there too.

'I'm sorry to burst in on you like this, Mr Dillon,' Mason began, unaware that trouble in the form of an irritated maitre d' and two thickset heavies were massing behind him like a storm blowing in from the desert. 'Hear me out, please. Just a couple of minutes, that's all I ask.'

A meaty hand was slapped hard on his shoulder. 'This man bothering you, Mr Dillon?'

'I don't take too kindly to being interrupted when I'm eating,' said Dillon, putting down his fork and swiping his napkin across his mouth. Gold rings on his fat fingers caught the lights and appeared to spark like they were afire.

'You're a difficult man to pin down,' Mason said. 'This was the only way I could get to see you.'

'You've seen me, now fuck off.' He signalled with the tiniest of eye movements to the man behind Mason, and the grip on his shoulder tightened uncomfortably.

'My name is Nick Mason,' he said, trying to shrug the hand away.

'Let's not make a big fuss,' said a harsh voice at his ear.

Dillon shrugged. 'The pleasure is all yours,' he said. He picked up his fork and raised the lump of meat to his mouth.

'*Dust of the Sahara...*' he said. 'I'm the lead...'

Dillon raised a finger and Mason felt the hand slip away from his shoulder. '*Dust of the Sahara*,' he echoed. 'You know what you do if you get dog shit on your shoe, Mason? You wipe it off as soon as you can. *Dust* was shit on my shoe. You were part of that shit.'

'You can't blame me for the entire movie.'

'I blame everyone concerned with the movie.'

'But you don't blame Frank Gibson...'

'Look, you've got one minute to say what you gotta say, which by my standards is one more minute than I'd give other second-rate punks like you.'

'Give me one more chance, Mr Dillon. Just the one. I could be good for you, with the right movie, the right script, the right producer and director. I could make you millions.'

Dillon rolled his eyes. 'Sure you could. So now you're telling me you know better than the people I got working for me; people I hired, people who know their job backwards. You're an actor, Mason – no, wait, scratch that; you're not even an actor. You're a nobody. Except you're worse than that; you're a damn foreign nobody. You don't look American, you don't speak like an American, and if it hadn't been for Frank Gibson owing Victor Wallace a favour from way-back-when, you wouldn't have got a look-in at Prima. You've had your chance and blown it, end of story. Now fuck off back home to Europe where you belong and stop sucking off the American tit.'

'I've got eight months left on my contract with Prima…'

'No you don't. You got nothing with Prima.'

'I'll sue Prima.'

The man grunted and managed to crack a wry smile. 'Sure you will. Go ahead. You ain't got a dime to scratch your ass with, and if you decide to sue I'll even take your ass so you won't have anything left to scratch.'

The two men grabbed Mason's arms and yanked him out of his seat. 'You'll be sorry you ever said that to me, Dillon!' he said. 'Some day I'm going to be big and I'll make you eat every last word!' People looked up from their meals at the fuss. 'I'm Rick Mason – remember that name!'

'You ain't ever going to be anybody in this town,' said Dillon evenly. 'Loud mouthing me like that is the worst thing you could have done. I'll see to it that nobody will give you a job, ever.' He looked up at one of the heavies. 'The steak could do with tenderising,' he said. The heavy nodded.

The men dragged Mason swiftly outside, then instead of throwing him out onto the sidewalk as he expected, they carried him further, down into a back alley where they proceeded to rough him up with steel-hard fists and rock-like leather boots. Job finished, they straightened their suits and left Mason on the floor coughing out blood.

He got shakily to his feet. He looked over his ripped tuxedo. 'Ah, shit!' he said, knowing there was no way he'd ever get the deposit back on it now.

* * * *

3

Betsy Bellamy

Victor Wallace was certain he had a heart condition, which his wife told him wasn't possible given the fact she thought he didn't have a heart. If he didn't have one, he felt pretty sure he was close to getting one. His success – the meat on his table – depended upon the success of others. Finding the right material and hoping they'd perform, like a stable chooses its horses and its riders. Get it right and there was happiness; get it wrong and there was only misery. Truth was, he wasn't sure what he had with Rick Mason. It was like looking at a thoroughbred that should, by rights, take on any challenger and win, but put him in the field and that potential just didn't come to the fore. Yet he couldn't give up on him. Something inside – gut instinct, maybe – told him Mason was a winner in the wings waiting to happen, waiting for the right race to prove himself. That's why he couldn't cut and run on the guy.

'Maybe if you hadn't gone and opened your big mouth at Dillon's table I could have helped you!' he said, ramming a cigar into his mouth and failing to locate a match in any of his pockets. 'Not only are people closing their doors on me,

Rick, they're putting the bolts on them too. Rick Mason are two of the dirtiest words in Hollywood right now.'

'He doesn't own everyone,' said Mason sullenly, looking out of the window at the brick wall. Just like the one he'd run into, he thought.

'Well he owns plenty, believe me!' he puffed energetically at the unlit cigar. 'So what is it you expect me to do, huh? Walk on water?'

'I need work, Victor. They took Lillian.'

'Lillian?'

'My automobile. I loved that automobile.'

'Forget the automobile. What is it with you, Rick? You've got talent. You're a nice guy...'

'So wooden an actor that if anyone yelled "timber!" I'd fall over – that kind of talent?'

He waved it away. 'Stop moping. I know guys who got called hammier than pork joints and they're doing OK for themselves. Everyone's a critic, Rick. Everyone can do better, even though they spend their time talking about it and never ever doing it. Never look at press cuttings. Big mistake. They said Lon Chaney would never make more than a hundred dollars a week and look at the man now. That's critics for you. They know Jack shit. Me, I know talent when I see it and you've got talent. You ended up in the wrong production with a half-assed, two-bit studio, that's all.'

'Victor, you put me there, remember? You got me the contract.'

'Better than nothing, damn it!'

Rick Mason shook his head. 'Look, Victor, us bickering gets us nowhere. What am I going to do? Go back to the stage?'

'You gotta let me think about this a while. What gets me is the way Prima has been cutting back on things lately. Doesn't make sense. I know they've always struggled because they haven't got the amount of cinemas other studios possess, they pay through the nose for distribution and they fall foul more than most of the bluenoses down at the National Board of Review. The Dillons would have you believe this last thing is evidence of their business being spiked, and there may be some truth in that. But the thing is, the Dillons have the dough. Their finances are healthy, they've got a hefty reserve and could easily stump up for bigger, better features if they had a mind. So why act the cheapskate? Talk is that they're holding back for something big. The Dillons have got wind of something they want their hands on and they're getting ready to bring the big-money guns to bear on whatever it is when the time is ripe.'

'All good and well, Victor, but what about me? My own reserves are threadbare. A man's got to eat.'

'The Dillons might have their fair share of friends, but they've also got their fair share of people who hate their guts. Jealous people. People they've wronged. People who'd like to see them taken down a peg or two. They know that too.'

'And that benefits me how?'

'The way I figure it, there are those out there who might look kindly on the way you stood up to Dillon at the Palm Club. They might even take you on simply because it would be a snub to Prima, making a show as to how they're not in the Dillon's back pockets or afraid of them. It might even open doors that may have been slammed in my face before you landed the contract with Prima. But you gotta have patience and leave me to do my job. The best thing you can do is keep your nose clean for a while and I'll see what I can do. I still have connections around here, though you're not helping them any.'

Mason allowed himself a smile. 'You've been good to me, Victor. I'll never forget that.'

'Good to you? You're a commodity, Rick. If I thought you were a lame duck I'd dump you tomorrow. The only reason I'm sticking with you is there's money for me in it eventually, when you finally come through.'

'Yeah, sure you would, Victor,' he said.

'So what are you hanging around here for?' he asked, his cigar wagging up and down like a dog's tail as he spoke. 'I got work to do.' He indicated a desk full of papers. 'You're not the only horse in my stable, you know.'

'You couldn't lend me a hundred bucks, could you? I'm all out.'

'A hundred? Are you joking?'

'I haven't even got the fare back home, Victor…'

Wallace reached into his trouser pocket and took out a fat leather wallet. He peeled it open and pinched out a few crumpled notes. 'There's thirty. It's all you're getting so don't go giving me those puppy eyes of yours; they may work on the dames but they sure as hell don't do anything to me.'

Mason thought he'd better not push it so he gratefully accepted the loan. 'I'll pay you back,' he promised.

'You bet you will, Rick, with interest.' He put a fist to his chest. 'I've got a heart condition, you know that? And you ain't helping it any. Now please clear off if you don't want to kill me.'

Mason had to admit he was feeling a lot more positive after his meeting with Wallace; right up to the moment he saw his trunk at the bottom of the stone steps leading up to his apartment block. A couple of kids were sitting on it.

'What are you doing with that?' he yelled. 'Get the hell off it!'

'The guy inside told us you'd give us a quarter each for watching your trunk till you got back. Told us to make sure nobody made off with it,' said one of the kids. He had a mean look in his eye. Penitentiary fodder in a few years time.

'Scram!' said Mason, pushing them off the lid of his trunk.

'Where's our money?' the other kid snarled. He looked ten-years-old going on thirty, thought Mason, his companion's cellmate in a few years time.

He relented and tossed them some money. The door opened and his landlord stood at the top of the steps, small, round, fat and bald and none too pleased. 'I told you, Mason,' he shouted. 'No rent, no stay.'

'Luigi!' he pleaded, his hands spread out in appeal. 'One more week, that's all I ask. Look, I'm signing a contract tomorrow. The money's as good as in the bag. One more week, eh? You know I'm good for it.'

'You bring me what you owe in back rent and then I'll let you have your rooms back.'

'But I haven't anywhere to go!' said Mason.

'That's not my problem!'

'I'm going to be a big star one day. I won't forget the favour…'

'You know how many times I've heard that?' he said, shaking his head. He went inside and made a point of slamming the door so it rattled.

Rick Mason sighed. It came from a deep pit of despair inside him. He lifted the lid of his trunk to check over the contents, then closed it and sat on it. He fumbled for cigarettes, lit one, pushed back his hat and thought over options. It didn't take long; there were precious few on the table.

'You look like I feel.'

It was a woman's voice. Mason looked up to see a tall, slim figure standing in front of him. Young, pretty, with large expressive eyes any camera would love to get on close-up. She wore an off-white, short-sleeved cotton dress, shapely legs dropping out of it ending in light-green shoes that didn't sit well with the outfit. She had a small beaded clutch-bag grasped in both hands.

'Do I know you?' he asked.

'Not yet,' she replied. 'Had a bad day?'

'Had better,' he said. 'You gloating?'

'To gloat you've got to be in a better position than those who are the subject of your gloating, I would think. I'm afraid I don't occupy such an elevated position.'

'So that means what?'

'I'm not gloating.'

'Glad to hear it,' said Mason. 'What can I do for you, Miss...?'

'Bellamy. Betsy Bellamy. Can you spare a cigarette?'

Mason looked about him at the many people walking the street. 'Out of all this choice you picked me to ask? What is it you really want?'

She came over and sat on the trunk beside him. 'A girl asks a fella in the street for a cigarette they get the wrong idea. I ask someone like you, who, the evidence would suggest, doesn't have spare money to splash around on – what shall we call them? – costly pleasures, and all he's going to think is I want a cigarette. That's what I thought, but guess I thought wrong.'

'So that's all you want?'

'You're very suspicious. We share similar orbits, you and I, Mr Mason; we're both spinning a little too far away from the Sun and feeling the cold.'

'You know my name.'

'Sure, I've seen you on the big screen a couple of times. Never thought to see you sitting outside on a big trunk. You looked like you had it made.'

He tapped a cigarette out of the pack and held it out for her to take. She popped one in her mouth and he put a match to it. 'Appearances can be deceptive,' he said. 'Let's say Prima and me had contractual differences we couldn't sort out. Let's say I gave Prima the big elbow.'

She laughed, puffed out smoke. 'Sure you did. Same as I told them they could stuff their audition this morning. And the one before that.'

'So you're an actress,' he said. 'Hard to find someone who isn't.'

'I would be if I could land the right part. Till I do I'm a hotel chambermaid borrowing cigarettes because being a hotel chambermaid isn't paying too good. I think I need to change my agent.'

Mason nodded slowly. 'I see. You suppose I might be able to help you out. I didn't think it was just the cigarette you were after.'

She laughed again and he found himself warming to the sound. 'Don't kid yourself, Mason. Have you looked at yourself recently? You're obviously flat broke, kicked out of your apartment, your cigarettes are cheap, and all you own is this single trunk. A gravy train you most certainly are not.' She rose to her feet, held the cigarette up between index finger and thumb. 'This is all I wanted from you. It's been a pleasure talking to you, Mr Mason, but I've got to go prepare for another audition for a part I probably won't get because I refuse to lie on my back on the casting couch. Goodbye, and I hope your luck changes.'

'Wait, Betsy,' he said, rising from the trunk. 'I didn't mean to come over rude. Betsy Bellamy – is that your real name?'

'It's real,' she replied.

'You eaten recently?'

She blinked, averted her gaze. 'Not recently, no.'

'You want to grab a bite to eat some place?'

Betsy Bellamy took a long, thoughtful drag on the cigarette and the end flared. 'I'm not that type of girl, Mr Mason. I told you that.'

'And I'm not that kind of man,' he countered. 'A piece of pie, coffee, just two cold, lonely planets in the same orbit coming together for a little while, that's all.'

'You paying?'

'Get it while you can,' he said. 'What little I've got won't last long!'

* * * *

4

Aim High, Sink Low

'I've got another fifteen minutes and then I've got to be going,' she said, pushing away her plate and grabbing the coffee cup. Betsy Bellamy had made short work of the blueberry pie. She noticed him staring at her from across the table. 'Times have been tough for Davey and me,' she explained, turning to look out of the plate-glass window of the diner.

'Davey?' he said. 'Who's Davey?'

'He's my brother.'

Rick Mason felt relief wash through him. He'd hardly been able to take his eyes off her the whole time. Something about her had sunk its soft hooks into him and when he started to find the way she ate her pie mildly fascinating, he knew something was wrong. Or right, depending which way you looked at it.

'Your brother's here too?'

'Yes. He's a writer, or trying to be. He'd like to be a novelist but nobody's interested so he's trying his hand at writing screenplays.' She smiled. 'He's my unofficial chaperone.'

'You have a chaperone?'

'Yeah, quaint, I know. He's older than me by a few years and insisted he come out to Los Angeles with me, make sure I don't fall in with the wrong sort, that kind of thing. I guess it's been kinda good to have him around. Hollywood's a lonely place.'

Her eyes were blue, he thought. The blue you get in a swimming pool in bright sunshine, the kind you want to dive right on into. Her skin was flawless, one side of her face edged by a fiery band of sunlight from the window.

'So where is your Davey?' he asked.

'He washes dishes three days a week, works as a mechanic in a motor repair yard three days, writer at night and on a Sunday. It's Tuesday so he's washing dishes.'

'Is he the protective kind when guys come around you?' He stirred his coffee, putting the spoon into his mouth and sucking it dry.

'All the time,' she said. She glanced at the clock over the counter. 'I have to go soon.'

'What part are you aiming for?' he asked.

'Young woman with a dog,' she said. 'Walk on, walk off.'

'Exciting.'

'I'll take what I can get. We can't all be as lucky as you to land a lead in a movie, even if the movie was *Dust of the Sahara*.'

He winced. 'Why do you do it?' he said. 'I mean, you seem like a nice girl, you've obviously not eaten properly in a long while and you're putting yourself through the audition mill with nothing guaranteed except sunshine.'

She put her coffee cup down. He noticed it didn't make a sound, the movement was that slow and deliberate. 'You know why, Rick. It's like a drug. It gets into your system. Ever since I was a kid at school, stepped up onto a stage and got my first rattle of applause, I knew I had to be an actress. I'll do whatever it takes to make it.'

'What if you don't make it?'

'That's not an option,' she said, those blue eyes looking like cold metal. He saw a strong streak of determination in her and liked her all the more for it. 'But I don't need to tell you that, because you already know.'

'What does brother Davey say about his little sister trawling the streets of Hollywood looking for her big break?'

'It's easy to cheapen it or make it sound dirty, Rick.' He could tell she was a little annoyed by his question. 'Men trawl the streets too, looking to make it; ever think of saying the same to them? No, bet you don't. What I want is no different to anyone else's ambitions – we're all looking for our big break, every one of us, wherever we are, to lift us out of the crap that's our ordinary, unexceptional lives. Mostly we don't find it. But some do. Those are the ones who don't give up trying. That's the American way, isn't it, to aim high? Become the next President, if you want to.'

'Principle and reality are two different things. Where I come from it's social class that gets you to the top rungs of the ladder. If you start out at the bottom, you ain't ever going to make it to the top. Over here it's money. Money is America's class system, but it doesn't want to admit that.'

'But over here you're free to make that money, no matter who you are. That's why you came over, isn't it, for that freedom? Europe is full of socialists,' she said, eyeing him. 'See the mess they're making.'

A shadow loomed over the table. 'You can't leave that there,' said a tall black guy who was waiting tables. 'Your trunk is blocking the aisle and someone is going to fall over it. You gotta shift that thing.'

Mason apologised and said they were about done. He watched the man's back as he trudged away. 'Take that waiter,' he observed. 'If he wanted to get a part in a motion picture it would probably be as a primitive native, slave, servant, waiter or farmhand. End of choice. Me, I could try out for a cowboy, Roman, polar explorer – everything real life ain't. But him, even in Hollywood he can't escape what's laid out for him. I just think that no matter where we are, America or wherever, we all ought to have the same chances in life.'

She rose from her seat. 'I didn't create the rules, I just play by them. So are you a socialist? Leftist revolutionary? If so, you're in for a hard time and I'd keep those kinds of things to myself if I were you.'

'None of the above. Just a guy who wants to see fairness.' Mason got to his feet. 'All I'm saying is don't let this game poison you. Hollywood can suck out the decent person you are and replace it with something else if you let it. No amount of ambition is worth sacrificing basic humanity. Acting, yeah, well it can be a wonderful thing, I guess, but it can be a curse too. What's the sense of aiming high if you've got to sink low to do it?'

She laughed. 'I've got to go now or I'll miss my big break.'

'Can I come along with you?'

She frowned. 'I don't know. It would mean you hauling that trunk a few blocks.'

'Not so much in it,' he admitted. 'Most of what I had is down at the pawn shop.'

'It's your back you'll be breaking. Why put yourself out over me?'

'Because one day I'm going to marry you. That's why.'

Her mouth hung open a fraction as she drew breath. Her brows lowered, eyes narrowing. 'I really should dump you now,' she said. 'You're a crazy socialist.'

Crazy about you, he thought, grinning. 'I'm an actor; we're all crazy!'

'Well don't let Davey hear you talking like that. He's liable to land you one in the sucker.' She left him to settle the bill, walked out into the harsh Californian sunshine and crossed the road. She heard him calling out from behind her, and turned to see him stood outside the diner, holding onto the trunk's handle. 'I can't wait for you!' she called.

'Where's the audition?' he shouted.

'Nestor's!' she hollered back.

'I know it; not far from Prima. I'll see you there.'

'Suit yourself,' she said, leaving him to lug the trunk across the road. She shook her head and smiled to herself. He was kind of cute, she thought, but she doubted he'd keep his word. Those sorts of guys were like flies around shit out here. And actors were the worst kind of fly.

'I can walk however you want me to walk,' she said, shielding her eyes against the bright light that swamped the impromptu stage they'd set up in one of the outside lots at Nestor studios. 'Tell me what I did wrong.' Betsy Bellamy still hand her arm crooked, pretending to hold onto a dog lead.

'We ain't here to teach you how to act, lady,' said one of the two dark, shadowy forms from the chairs out front. 'You were OK but not what we're looking for.'

'Was I too quick?' she asked. 'I can do it slower.'

'We're busy,' said the man. 'Get your ass off the stage so we can get on with this. We have other people to see.'

'I need the work,' she persisted. 'Just tell me where I went wrong and I can fix it. I can dog-walk a hundred different ways.'

'I'm sure you can, but not for us.' He motioned with his hand for her to leave. She hesitated. 'Don't make us kick you out,' he warned. 'Next!' he yelled, and a stick-thin woman clattered nervously onto the stage. They took one look and before she'd even opened her mouth to speak, shouted 'Next!'

Betsy grunted her disappointment but kept her head, and only let off steam once out in the street again. She kicked a fire hydrant. 'Bastards!' she said. She heard applause and looked up to see Rick Mason sitting on his trunk by a wall.

'I take it that didn't go well?' he said.

'All they need is someone to walk a dratted pooch across a scene. Four or five seconds max. That's it. And I have to go through all this to hear I can't walk a dog for four or five seconds the way they want it. You know what that does to a person's confidence?'

'I've had worse,' he admitted. 'Tell you what, though, when they want someone to come along and audition for the part of a woman kicking the hell out of a fire hydrant, it's a part you were born to play.'

Her face coloured, got all heated up. 'That supposed to be funny?'

He shrugged. 'I guess.'

'Well you thought wrong, Mason! Jesus, I hate this town.' She went over to the trunk, sat down beside him.

'Cigarette?' He offered her one. 'Don't worry, you'll get your chance. I know it.'

'Oh yeah? How come you're so certain?'

He put his back against the wall, tipped back his hat and folded his arms. He stretched out his legs, all relaxed like he was on a sofa in front of a log fire. 'Because I'm going to help get you that chance, that's why.'

'So speaks Mr Big-Shot sitting on everything he owns. Correction – most everything; the rest is in hock.'

He laughed. 'It won't always be like this. Life never stays the same. Things change. You and me, we're gonna make it big!'

'You and me, huh? So now we're a twosome?'

'Sure we are. And it's gonna be bigger than big. We'll be able to tell the kids how we moved from a cramped old trunk out on the sidewalk to a mansion up on Whitley Heights.'

She flashed her bright eyes at him, her mood already lighter. 'Now we have kids?'

'Three. Two boys and a girl. And a couple of dogs, too.'

'I prefer cats.'

"That figures,' he said. His face fell thoughtful. 'Can I ask you a question?'

'Fire away.'

'Have you got room at your place for a guy to bed down for a night or two till he gets straight? A man with a medium-sized trunk? I mean, it's the least you could do in return for stardom.'

'The least,' she said. 'We have an old sofa you could use.'

'Sounds divine.'

'My brother Davey sure won't think so,' she said.

* * * *

5

A Bowl of Cherries

They faced each other across the table, like silent combatants closely engaged in a high-stakes game of poker. Thin soup dribbled from a spoon, dripping noisily into a dish. Betsy could stand the enforced silence no longer and plonked a pitcher of water down hard between the two men.

'Thanks,' said Rick Mason, smiling awkwardly at her.
'How's your soup?' she asked, sitting down at the table.
'It's...' He paused to locate the right words.
'It's all we can afford,' said the man opposite him, dipping his spoon into the broth and stirring it around. 'What is he doing here?' he asked of Betsy, as if Mason wasn't in the room.

He was a handsome young man, he thought; had a woman's eyes, like his sister's. Dark hair in need of a cut, a sour face that hadn't altered since he came home from work and found a strange man in the house; a strange man who appeared to have taken up residence.

'I've told you, Davey,' she said, a little irritated. 'He's here for a couple of days, that's all, till he finds somewhere else.'

'I'm perfectly harmless,' Mason said, his smile failing to melt the young man's frosty expression. 'I've managed not to murder a single person this week, though I admit I have come close.' He saw the man's startled eyes widen. 'That's a joke,' he said.

'We can't afford him, Betsy,' he went on.

'He's not a dog, Davey!' Betsy sighed.

'But you picked him up off the streets like one.'

'Hardly...' said Mason uncomfortably. He rested his spoon on the table. 'Look, maybe this isn't such a good idea. I ought to be leaving.'

'No you won't,' Betsy insisted firmly. 'Davey will just have to get used to the idea.'

'I can't afford to keep the pair of you,' Davey said, pushing away his chair and leaving the table. He went over to the fireplace, took down a tobacco tin from the mantelpiece and began to fill a pipe.

'I'll pay my way whilst I'm here,' Mason said.

'You damn well will,' Davey returned, tamping tobacco into the bowl of his pipe. He stood stock-still, looking sullenly out of the window.

Betsy flashed Mason an apologetic glance. 'Davey is on edge,' she explained. 'He spends his entire life on edge. That's because he's a writer, and all writers are just so self-absorbed it makes them gloomy company.' Davey's eyes narrowed, but he refrained from being drawn in.

'Betsy tells me you're writing screenplays. What kind of things are you writing, Davey?' he asked.

He grunted. 'It's not real writing, but it's a way of earning a living whilst I'm here.' It strongly implied he wasn't intending to stay long. 'Motion pictures are facile, superficial amusements churned out for the masses. They won't last. It's a passing fad.' He looked across at Betsy, his gaze lingering on her meaningfully.

'Ignore him,' she said. 'He doesn't know the meaning of having fun. He's always been such a serious man. Mother said when he was born he didn't so much cry as complain. He's complained ever since.'

'You never knew our mother, so how come you know?' he sneered. 'There's no sin in being serious. Someone has to be serious for the both of us. So, Betsy, are we about to take in any more crippled little actors who can't fend for themselves, like you used to do with every injured dog, cat or bird you came across?'

'That's enough, Davey!' she said. 'You're becoming tiresome again. Tiresome and rude with it. You'll give Rick the wrong impression.'

'So where are you from, Mr Mason?' Davey asked unexpectedly. 'You have something of a foreign accent.'

'It's Slavonian,' he explained. 'My mother and I came over from Slavonia before the war. I can't seem to shake the accent off.'

'Slavonia? So where's that?'

'It's a part of Croatia, in the Balkans.'

'Ah, the Balkans – where the war started, huh? Planning on going back home?'

'This is my home,' he said, feeling himself getting hot under the collar. 'I'm an American citizen. I cut off ties with Europe when I passed through Ellis Island.'

'Don't mind him, Rick,' Betsy said, sensing the atmosphere in the room getting all charged up like the sky before a lightning storm. 'Aren't you going to ask how my audition went, Davey?'

'How did your audition go, Betsy?' he said in monotone.

'It went shit,' she said.

'Your language has sunk to levels I don't approve of since you started mixing with people round here,' he said.

'Tough. Rick here is going to ask his agent to help me out,' she said. 'That's good, isn't it?'

Davey looked across at Mason. 'Does your agent make a thing out of collecting the unemployed? Hardly seems to make good business sense. Still, you will have it your way,

Betsy,' he said. He plucked his coat from a hook and left the apartment. They heard his boots clumping in the corridor as he headed for the stairway down to the street below.

'He's not as bad as he paints himself,' Betsy said. 'He's trying to do his best to look after the two of us; to look after me whilst I find my feet in Hollywood.'

'I rather think we hit it off bad,' he said. 'He doesn't like me one little bit.'

'That's tough,' she said curtly. 'He doesn't own me and I can do just as I please, see who I please. So, you think your agent might be able to help me out?'

'Joking aside, if anyone can help you Victor Wallace can. He's a good man. He pretends to be a mean-hearted bastard, but he's as soft as melted butter inside. I've just had a run of bad luck, that's all. He'll get me something, I know he will.' He stared at her face. He couldn't make up his mind whether she looked like your average girl-next-door or a worldly-wise saloon woman. He couldn't fathom her at all, which made her seem all the more attractive. So unlike any woman he'd ever met. 'Why do you put up with Davey?' he asked. 'He's like a damp cloth over a fire.'

'Davey's all I've got. And I'm all he's got, too. End of story.'

'So I'm guessing you haven't got any sort of romantic attachment to anyone?' he asked tentatively.

'You mean have I got a fella somewhere? No, there's no one special that I'm seeing. Is there a Mrs Mason?'

He laughed. 'No Mrs Mason. When I got my contract at Prima there were a couple of attractive women wanting to become Mrs Mason, but strangely, since *Dust of the Sahara* did a nosedive, I haven't seen any of them since. Weird, eh?' He pushed away his dish of half-eaten soup. 'Tomorrow we'll take a trip to see Victor.' He took a silver cigarette case out of his jacket pocket. 'Never use this. It was a gift from one of my prospective wives. This should get us the fare there and back, but something had better come up soon because I'm running out of things to take to the pawnshop.'

She shook her head. 'Are you always so cheerful, even when you shouldn't be?'

'Life's a bowl of cherries, Betsy, and even cherries have pips you have to contend with. All you gotta do is spit the pip right on out and start on another cherry!'

'And what if you empty your bowl of cherries?'

He smiled. 'Then you have to fill it back up again with new ones,' he said, as if it were a foolish question she should have known the answer to.

'You really are weird, Rick Mason,' she said.

'And you really are the most beautiful woman I've ever met,' he said.

Her attention had already shifted to the window and she didn't quite catch his last comment. 'Do you think motion pictures are a fad? Do you think it's worth taking all this trouble to be a part of it?'

He shrugged. 'Who can tell? You have to take the ride whilst you can, see where it takes you. You can always jump off later down the line and hitch a ride on something else.'

'But you could be dumped miles from anywhere,' she said, 'with no means of ever getting back.'

'Maybe you shouldn't ever go back. What's the matter, are you getting cold feet?'

It was her turn to shrug. 'My ambition scares me at times. Davey says I'm too passionate, too focussed on what it is I want for myself, sometimes at the expense of others. And in truth I have few options; my cherry bowl's quite empty.'

'Davey doesn't like actors, or this entire acting game, for some reason. There's something deep down that's eating him.'

Her eyes flickered with concern. 'What do you mean?'

'You know, the eyes; the cold expression, the way he doesn't want to look at you when he's talking to you, like he's scared he might give something away if he did; or the way he resents strangers, openly distrusts me without even knowing me. What's eating him, Betsy? What's he scared of?'

She rose from the table, cleared away their dishes. 'That's enough about Davey,' she said quickly.

'Have I upset you?' he said. 'I'm sorry if I said something that...'

'It's fine,' she said. 'Just fine.'

But he knew she wasn't fine at all and the rest of the day he suspected she regretted agreeing to him entering their close-knit little world. Davey came back in later, went to his room and closed the door. Later that night, as Mason lay uncomfortably on the sofa in the dark, half-asleep, he heard someone talking. He listened intently. The sound came from Davey's room. He realised the man was rambling in his sleep. He appeared to be having an argument in his dreams, the words unintelligible. Then there was an almighty scream from him and it went deathly quiet.

Moments later, Betsy's door opened. Mason thought it best to pretend to be asleep, but through the corner of his eye he saw her go over to Davey's door, quietly open it and stand there looking for a while. She listened for a minute or two, then closed the door and went back to her room.

* * * *

6

A Man of Property

'Where the hell you been? I've been trying to contact you – your landlord said you'd left.'

Victor Wallace was sweating again, and getting himself all wound up, Rick Mason thought. 'Victor, this is Betsy Bellamy,' he introduced.

The tiny waiting room was stifling and Betsy's cheeks had flushed with the heat. Wallace swiped a handkerchief across his creased forehead and around his neck. 'Pleased to meet you,' he said dismissively. 'I got news for you. Come through, Rick,' he said, putting a meaty hand on his shoulder.

Mason told Betsy to wait a while, take a seat whilst he talked to his agent. The two men went through into Wallace's office. He had two fans working overtime, their blades noisy, their effect minimal.

'So who's the dame?' he asked.

'The next actor on your books,' Mason said.

'I've got enough goddamn actors on my books – take her somewhere else.'

'She's special, Victor. I tried her out. Got her to act out a scene. She really has got talent, not just a pretty face.'

'Well it takes more than breasts and legs to make someone special, Rick.' He looked at him from under his heavy eyebrows. 'We'll discuss the dame later. First, I've got some good news at last. I spoke to Conrad Jefferson yesterday.'

'*The* Conrad Jefferson? Metropolitan Studios-Jefferson?'

'The one and the same,' Wallace said, his face beaming at Mason's reaction. He made himself comfortable in his desk chair.

Metropolitan Studios were big, and growing. Conrad Jefferson had started out in partnership with the Dillon brothers when they set up Prima back in '15, but they had an almighty row and parted company acrimoniously to say the least, Jefferson insisting on getting his share of the fledgling Prima and nearly causing it to go under in the process. The Dillons never forgave him and there had been bitter rivalry between them ever since. Jefferson used his share to help set up Metropolitan Studios and had since done well for himself. Unlike Prima, Metropolitan concentrated on big-budget features as their primary output, with a small amount of adventure-based shorts that the public lapped up. They owned a fair amount of theatres through which they distributed and screened their films, and they planned to invest in more. Because of their growing success they attracted bigger names and bigger investment. Rick Mason had been turned down by the producers at Metropolitan, so to hear that Wallace had got a look-in with the head man himself was thrilling news.

'Well don't leave the damn thing hanging in the air, Victor. What did he have to say?'

'I put the feelers out, like I said I would, and next thing I know, out of the blue, Jefferson's contacting me,' said Wallace, reaching into his pocket for a cigar. He still couldn't find a light for it. 'Just like I said, seems he heard about your public spat with Luke Dillon at the Palm Club. He liked the idea you had balls enough to go up against the man and say what you did. He heard Prima dumped you, says the stuff they forced on you was shit, no fault of yours. Says you deserve another chance.'

Mason plonked himself down in the chair opposite Wallace. 'You kidding?'

He shook his head. 'Do I look like I'm kidding? He says he wants to meet with you personally.'

'When?'

'Tomorrow, at his place.'

'Jesus!' Mason gasped. 'Conrad Jefferson wants to meet me.'

Victor Wallace was grinning. 'Maybe now you'll start to pay your way and make all the trouble I've gone to with you worth the effort.'

'You're a genius, Victor!' he said. He rose, leant across the table and grabbed Wallace's head in both hands, planting a wet kiss on his forehead. Wallace batted him away, wiping the spot with his handkerchief. 'Did he give any details what it's all about?'

'The conversation was short and I didn't push it,' he admitted. He pointed hard. 'Don't you screw this up, Rick! There's a time for opening your big mouth, but this meeting ain't it. And don't agree to a thing without running it past me first, OK? He's a wily old devil.'

'Yeah, sure,' he agreed.

'Hal Bremner's going to be there, too.'

'The producer? Christ, Victor, this just gets better and better.' Hal Bremner was hot property; he'd produced some of Metropolitan's highest-grossing movies.

'I really could do with being there alongside you, but they insist on seeing you first. Maybe they're sizing you up. But whatever you do, don't you go loud-mouthing this to anyone yet. Remember, you're officially still on Prima's books until you accept their severance offer, and if the Dillons get wind of this they'll pull back from the deal and make you see out your contract, by which time Metropolitan's interest might have gone cold. Keep this one very much under your hat till you've met with Jefferson and Bremner.'

'So what about Betsy?' said Mason.

'So what about Betsy?'

'She needs a good agent. As a favour to me, Victor. I won't forget it.'

He gave an exaggerated sigh. 'I'll do a deal with you – clinch this with Metropolitan, up my percentage another four percent and maybe I'll consider it.'

'Three percent and no maybe about it,' he countered.

'OK, I'll give her six months, but if she bombs then I'll ditch her.'

'Deal,' said Mason, and shook his hand. 'You're an OK guy, Victor.'

'Don't let that get out. It won't do my reputation any good.' Then he remembered something. 'With all the excitement over Metropolitan, I almost forgot.' He opened a drawer and took out a calling-card. 'An old guy came into the office yesterday, looking for you. He was foreign. Said he was the Hungarian equivalent of a lawyer, or something.'

'Hungarian lawyer?' said Mason. 'What the hell does he want with me?'

Wallace shrugged. 'Search me. Turns out he's been trying to track you down for some time. Came all the way from some place I never heard of to meet with you. Said it was very important you meet up with him.'

'Did he say why?'

'Just that it was very important family business that needed to be taken care of.'

'I have no family,' he said. 'The only family I had was my mother and she's dead. Maybe it's someone having a joke.' He studied the name on the calling-card: Franz Horvat.

'This guy didn't have a sense of humour – he's a lawyer. He had all the warmth of a week-old corpse. He says he's staying at the Adelphi Hotel five blocks down – the address is on the back of the card. I told him you'd be in contact. He said someone had died, and in my book that generally means money, so if I were you I'd drop round and see him while you're here.' He leant across the desk, elbowing papers out of the way. 'If you take my advice, Rick, you'll ditch the broad. Now's not the time to get hung up on some dumb country hick. You need all your wits and concentration behind you. There'll be plenty of time for that kind of thing, and all the dames you'll every need if this deal with Metropolitan pans out.'

'Ever thought I might not need another woman?'

'You've fallen for her? How long have you known her?'

'All my life,' he replied. 'I'll let you know the results of my meeting with Jefferson as soon as I can. In the meantime I'll poke my head into the Adelphi hotel to find out what this lawyer-guy wants.' He flicked the calling-card with his index finger. He went to the door, stopped and turned. 'You know, Victor, I really mean it when I say I appreciate all you've done for me. I won't ever forget that. You're more than just my agent.'

'Get your ass out of my office before I start to weep,' he growled, his creased forehead creasing still further. He waved his hand as if he were slapping at a mosquito.

Mason smiled and went outside.

'What's he say?' Betsy asked.

'You're going to be just fine,' he said. 'I'll tell you on the way to the Adelphi hotel.'

'Why are we going there?'

'Someone died,' he said.

The Adelphi was the kind of place you stayed when you didn't have much money. The sort of place they often rented out rooms by the hour to guys with so-called wives they had to pay to spend time with. It wasn't seedy, thought Mason, as he and Beth sat in the hotel lobby, but it wasn't exactly grand either. It attracted a lot of hard-up hopefuls new to the area, who stayed long enough to get disillusioned and then packed their bags to head someplace else. It was the hotel equivalent of a railway station, he thought, some people headed on to Hollywood, others on their way back out, with many just passing through Los Angeles and hardly pausing for breath.

He saw an old man coming across the lobby towards him, a tired-looking leather briefcase in his hand. He wore black, from his black Homburg to his black suit and black shoes. Mason thought he looked like a funeral director. He was small, hunched slightly, wore round spectacles on his sharp nose, lenses sparkling in a dark tortoiseshell frame. His expression never altered from profoundly serious, almost near-grave, even when he came up to Mason and introduced himself.

'Good afternoon. You are Rick Mason?'

'That's right.' They shook hands. The old man's was cold and bony, the contact firm, brief and perfunctory.

'And who is this lady?' he asked crisply. His English was good, but his accent had a heavy Hungarian flavour.

'This is a friend,' Mason explained.

The old man shook his head. 'I'm sorry, but this is for your ears only, sir. Please leave us alone, miss.'

'She's fine where she is,' objected Mason.

'I insist,' he said bluntly.

Mason passed her an apologetic glance and Betsy nodded, leaving them alone together. The man sat down and bade Mason do the same. He snapped open his briefcase and removed a handful of papers wrapped in a cardboard file fastened with red ribbon.

Mason looked on, perplexed. 'What's all this about, and who are you?' he said.

The old man studied him intently from over the edge of his spectacles. 'I do see a strong resemblance,' he said quietly. 'It is quite uncanny. I could have easily picked you out as the man I was looking for in a crowd of people.'

'You see a resemblance to whom?'

'Sorry, it is rude of me not to introduce myself. My name is Franz Horvat. I represent the estate of the late Baron Jozsef Dragutin. He has died and his will leaves everything to his direct and sole-surviving relative. That relative, sir, is you. Baron Dragutin was your father and you are now a man of property.'

7

A Century and Five

'You've made a big mistake,' said Rick Mason. 'I think you have the wrong man. My father was no baron!'

The old man calmly removed his spectacles and cleaned the lenses in a most careful way on his handkerchief. 'There is no mistake, I can assure you.' He popped them back onto his nose and bent his head to business, taking a piece of paper out of the cardboard folder. 'Your real name is Stjepan Gjalski, which was duly changed to Steven Gallis on passing through Ellis Island. From there you and your mother inhabited various towns and cities on the east coast until she died. You came west to Los Angeles, where you adopted the stage name Rick Mason.' He looked up. 'I admit that this last change did cause some trouble. But, after twenty-five years of searching for you, here you are at last.'

Mason narrowed his eyes. 'Twenty-five years? How come you know all this about me?'

'My business is to know things, Mr Mason – by the way, is that the name you wish me to call you? There seems to be so many to choose from.' Mason nodded dumbly. 'Your mother kept up a regular correspondence with contacts back in Slavonia, and judging by the look on your face it was a correspondence you knew nothing about. Alas, it is also my duty to inform you that the woman you thought of as your mother wasn't in fact your real mother.'

Mason jumped from the chair. 'OK, you've said enough. It's time I was leaving. You've either got the wrong guy or this is some kind of hoax. Is that it – has someone like Luke Dillon set this up? It's the kind of sick thing he'd enjoy.'

'Please sit down, Mr Mason,' he said abruptly. 'I have travelled a very long way to see you on your late father's behalf and the least you can do is have the good grace to listen to what I say. I am not a man to waste both time and effort in pursuing the wrong man, nor do I make sport by telling you a pack of lies for the entertainment of your Luke Dillon, whoever he is. You may rest assured that what I tell you is the absolute truth. Who do you believe to be your father?'

'He was a Slavonian peasant, died of hunger when I was a baby. My mother blamed the Austro-Hungarian oppression for that. She blamed them for a lot. Can't say I blame her. One thing that makes my blood boil is man's ability to oppress their fellow man.'

'Very commendable of you, but a philosophical discussion for another day. Your real father was as far away from a peasant as you can imagine. Nor was he Slavonian. Your real father was Baron Jozsef Dragutin, and as such you are made heir to his considerable estate, investments and Castle Dragutin in Slavonia. Though it is true you were born in Slavonia, at Castle Dragutin, your mother and father were Hungarian, a fact I know may cause you initial discomfort and soul-searching, but you will adapt to the situation in time.' He waited, as if expecting some kind of response, but Mason's mind was reeling with what he was hearing and as yet struggled to have any words to hand. 'It is my duty to settle Baron Dragutin's estate, and to take you back to Slavonia with me to finalise all the details.' He removed his glasses again. His eyes looked smaller, more piercing. 'I know all this must come as a considerable shock to you, Mr Mason, but life has that ability.'

'Why should I believe a word you say?'

'I'm not here to influence your belief, Mr Mason, merely to relate the facts as they stand and to fully discharge my duty as your father's trusted representative.' He reached inside his coat pocket. Mason noticed how the lapels were a little worn. 'I have a trinket here that may help convince you.' His fingers peeled open like the petals on some grotesque flower. Sitting in the palm of his hand was a gold locket minus its chain. He pressed its catch to open it. 'See, here lays a lock of your mother's hair.' He held it up to Mason's head. 'And it is as close a match in colour to your own as you are likely to find. Rather elaborate measures to go to in order to perpetuate a hoax, wouldn't you say?'

Mason took the locket. In the other half was a tiny oval photograph of a dark-haired young woman. Her face was solemn. 'Am I supposed to believe this is my real mother?'

'You are correct.'

'What's her name?'

'Her maiden name was Dorottya Szendrey.'

'Is she dead? You referred to them both in the past tense.'

'You are correct. She is dead, Mr Mason.'

Rick Mason pinched the bridge of his nose between thumb and index finger. A headache was building, the pain cranking up behind his eyes. 'So you're saying I was adopted?'

'After a fashion. I'm afraid this is neither the time nor the place to go into fine detail. All will be explained when you come back to Slavonia with me.'

He held up his hands. 'Hang on there, buddy! Who said anything about me going to Slavonia? If there's anything to settle, we do it here, in America.'

'That is not possible, Mr Mason, for numerous technical and legal reasons. If you are to inherit all that is rightfully yours you must go to Slavonia. Once there it will take a week or so to sort things out.'

'Say I believe all this, I can't go running off to Europe, I've got a very important meeting tomorrow, the results of which could see me tied up here for a long while. If this inheritance really is mine, can't we settle things here, make an exception or something?'

The old man shook his head and released a tired sigh. 'You will be made a wealthy man, Mr Mason, trust me. But if it is not all sorted within an allotted period then everything will pass to the state. The time it has taken me to travel over here and track you down means that we only have a matter of months left to complete proceedings.'

'So I'm supposed to drop everything and sail to Europe on the say-so of an old man I've never met before, telling me a story that quite frankly stretches credulity?' He laughed, but it was a weak affair.

'What you eventually decide to do is naturally entirely up to you. My job is to lay out before you the situation as it stands.'

Mason stared hard at the photograph in the locket. He'd no idea who he was looking at. He had no emotional contact with the sad-looking young woman. A few minutes ago his life had seemed to have gotten a whole lot better, headed down the first positive track in years. And now it had lurched unexpectedly sideways into completely unknown and unsettling territory. Everything he'd ever know about himself, his entire life, appeared to be built upon a lie, from his cultural origins to his so-called mother. Yes, she'd always been distant, seemed to regard him with such fierce eyes at times that he wondered what he'd done wrong. She died disowning him, and he'd put it down to her illness. Many unexplained things in his life now made sense with Horvat's revelations. But it was all too much to take in at once.

'Look, Mr Horvat, I've got to think about this. I can't get my head around what you're saying.'

'I understand,' said Horvat. 'Ordinarily, to be the beneficiary in a will and the unexpected recipient of wealth would be most welcome; but of course, your news is tempered by facts about your origins that must cause considerable disquiet. I shall give you a day or so to think things through.' He looked about him. 'I am staying in this place in the meantime. I have kept costs to a minimum, as naturally my fees will be settled out of your late father's estate, but I would appreciate it if I could stay somewhere less...' He wrinkled his nose as if there was a bad smell. 'I think you understand what I mean.'

'Sure,' said Mason. 'This place is a dive. So you say I'll be wealthy?'

'Yes, very.'

'Can you put a number to that?'

'Not here, not now. All will be revealed to you in due course. But yes, I can confirm it will set you up for life, if managed appropriately.'

'Go ahead, find somewhere better for yourself,' he said.

'Very generous of you, Mr Mason.'

'I'll contact you the day after tomorrow. Leave a message at my agent's office as to where I'll find you – I'm sort of between houses at present.'

'Very well, Mr Mason.'

'Can I keep the locket?' he said, snapping it closed.

'Of course.'

He was about to leave when a thought came to him. 'Mr Horvat, you implied you could have picked me out in a crowd. So I look like my father?'

Horvat squinted at him. 'I have seen portraits of your father as a young man when he was about your age and I can say without doubt there is a powerful resemblance to him. Though your face is somewhat...' He chose his words carefully. 'Somewhat warmer than Baron Dragutin's.'

'How did he die?'

'Old age. He was a very old man.'

Mason frowned. 'Really? He can't have been that old, surely? I'm only twenty-five myself.'

Baron Dragutin lived for a full century and five. He fathered you at the age of eighty.'

* * * *

8

Here's to Horror

He was led quickly by a smartly-suited man through the building and outside to a swimming-pool. Rick Mason briefly caught a glimpse of the interior of the grand mansion as he was hurried through. He was reminded of an exotic Persian palace with its brightly coloured tiles, elaborate plasterwork on ceilings and walls, intricately carved woodwork everywhere; marble statues stood side by side with massive ceramic vases whose origins appeared to be middle-eastern; tables and chairs were constructed from polished mahogany standing on beautifully finished floors, with their ceramic tiles arranged in complex geometric patterns upon which their footsteps clicked. Conrad Jefferson, it appeared, rather fancied himself as some kind of Persian prince, thought Mason.

The pool was huge and inviting, fringed on three sides by lush greenery, with palms spiking into the blue Sun-drenched sky, their fronds swaying languidly in a thin breeze. The large space was empty save for two men sitting on wicker chairs on the opposite side of the pool to him. One of them raised a hand on seeing Mason and waved for the servant to walk him over. He was alarmed to see what he thought was a fur rug by the pool unfolding its limbs and shape itself into a full-grown leopard. It wore a diamond-encrusted collar and was fastened by a gold-coloured chain to a marble post.

'Don't worry about Sheba,' said the servant quietly. 'Mr Jefferson raised her from a cub; she's quite tame since we gave her the sedatives.'

'What if the sedatives wear off?' he asked uncertainly. The animal eyed him as if he were next on the menu. The servant didn't reply. He gave the leopard a wide berth.

'Rick!' said the man who'd waved them over. He was aged about fifty-five, he guessed, had a considerable paunch that pushed at his blue short-sleeved shirt and hung over his white shorts. His feet were inordinately large, thought Mason, long toes that didn't look good in sandals. But Conrad Jefferson could afford to not care about how he looked. He motioned for Rick to sit down in one of the wicker chairs near him, his eyes hidden behind sunglasses. He still had a head of thick blonde hair run through with silver, which was oiled back over his skull. 'Can I call you Rick?' he asked.

'Good afternoon, Mr Jefferson,' said Mason. 'Sure you can call me Rick.'

They shook hands. 'Would you like a drink?' He pointed to an array of spirits on a round mosaic-topped table. Mason had not seen that much alcohol on display since before prohibition, he thought.

'Thank you, Mr Jefferson, but I don't drink,' he admitted.

He raised a surprised brow. 'That's no bad thing,' he said. He held out his hand to the man at his side. 'This is Hal Bremner. Hal, say hello to the kid.'

Hal Bremner was younger, maybe nosing into his forties. He wore a light-tan suit, no tie, fancy brogues. He removed his sunglasses and reached across the shake Mason's hand. 'Hi, Rick, good to meet you.' His grip was firm.

'You've probably heard of Hal,' said Jefferson.

'Sure have. Who hasn't?'

Mason had seen photographs of both men in magazines; they looked far more formidable in real life, he thought. He'd expected Conrad Jefferson to be the serious, hardnosed business kind, but he was all smiles and laidback; Hal Bremner, on the other hand, didn't show his teeth in a smile once. His greeting had been mumbled through tight lips, and marbled through with a kind of distrust or suspicion. The only reason he took off his sunglasses, Mason reckoned, wasn't to be polite but to let him see his no-nonsense eyes of cold solid steel. His reputation as an intractable, humourless, hard-driving producer who got results appeared to be borne out, and they'd hardly exchanged more than a few words.

'So glad you could make it,' said Jefferson.

'My pleasure, Mr Jefferson,' said Mason. As if he'd refuse! Not many people got to see inside the man's inner sanctum and he wasn't sure yet why he'd been given such privileged access.

Conrad Jefferson leant back in his chair. Mason tried to make out the manufacturer of the gold watch that glinted on his wrist. 'I hear Prima gave you a raw deal,' he said. He wasn't expecting a reply. 'But that's the Dillons for you. And that bastard Luke is the worst of the pair. You'll be well shut of them and their two-bit outfit, eh, Hal?' Hal put his sunglasses back on and gave the shortest of nods. 'They tried a takeover of Metropolitan a year or two back, you know about that?' Mason admitted he didn't. 'I've got what many people want. I've got success. Metropolitan's got a big future in the motion picture industry. But it's like a feeding frenzy out there, Rick. Like there's some great big elephant been brought down and all the jackals and hyenas are stuffing their heads into the carcass trying to grab a chunk of the action. And if they can't grab a chunk of their own, well they turn and make a grab for someone else's. I've got jackals and hyenas all around me, all the time, making a grab for what I've got. And Prima is the biggest hyena of them all.'

Mason wasn't sure how he should respond, what was expected of him, but the venom with which Jefferson attacked Prima underlined what Victor had told him about Jefferson's relationship with the Dillons, and it was far from good. Mason suspected that he was little more than a pawn in their big game, but he guessed it wouldn't hurt to see where this particular move would take him.

'You're the envy of many, Mr Jefferson,' Mason said, which he thought did enough to acknowledge both the man's success and the dog-eat-dog consequences of that success.

Conrad Jefferson gave a grunt. 'The key is to stay ahead of the game. This business is changing year by year. What started out as an amusement, like it was a new but expensive toy that would have its day, is growing into something far bigger than anyone could have known. People want more, always more. They're already getting very particular about what they want, too. The old days of hammy stage actors bringing their old-fashioned acting methods to the screen are fast on their way out. People are looking for a new breed of actor. They're demanding a new breed of motion picture. That not so, Hal?'

Hal Bremner looked like he could hardly be bothered to bring himself to talk to Mason, but with a quiet sigh he flexed his fingers and looked out across the pool. 'Unlike on the stage, where the audience views you from a distance and actors need to exaggerate their movements and use various artifices to convey emotions, with the motion picture it's very different. The camera can get up real close. With a face blown up on screen the audience can read every tiny muscle movement, every flicker of the eyelid, every twist of the lips, the slightest tightening of the jaw. The motion picture is creating a new kind of actor that is unique to the industry, actors that are evolving alongside the medium. And one cannot exist without the other.'

'Emotional depth is the next big thing, Rick,' said Jefferson. 'Love, happiness, sorrow, and fear. These are the frontiers of the future which we must approach and cross. Movies are first and foremost about people, and those actors that can deliver not only slapstick and adventure but can connect with their audience on an emotional level, as real people, then for them the movie world is their oyster. We see that kind of talent in you, Rick.'

'You do?' he was taken aback somewhat.

'Sure, the films you were given at Prima were substandard affairs. Not even some of the biggest names could have salvaged anything from those. But we saw something special in the few decent scenes you were in, especially in the close-ups, and in the way you carried yourself. It was natural. It was believable. You had presence. Those morons at Prima don't know how to exploit what you've got, Rick. But at Metropolitan we are headed in a direction where we need people like you. And your foreign accent, that's going to serve you well, too!'

Mason frowned. 'My accent? What's that got to do with making movies? I don't understand.'

Hal Bremner took his cue from a sideways glance from Jefferson. 'Talkies, Mr Mason,' he said crisply.

'But sound is an experimental fad,' Mason pointed out. 'It's technically difficult and some critics say it will never catch on. Charlie Chaplin hates the concept and says he'll never use it in one of his movies, and if he's saying it...'

'You know nothing. You're an actor,' said Bremner. Jefferson gave a discreet cough and Bremner sighed. He was good at that, thought Mason. 'Sound is the future. Since last year, studios have been converting to the new Vitaphone system following Warner's success with their movie *Don Juan*. Theatres all over America are installing Western Electric amplifiers in response so they can screen movies with sound. We've been experimenting at Metropolitan. We tried out a number, including the Phonofilm system, but are investing in Vitaphone. We're looking to produce our first goat-glanded motion picture using the new sound system.'

'Goat-glanded – what's that?' Mason asked.

'Predominantly silent, but with a significant section included that has sound. Yes it's new, it might fail, but we feel it marks the next big stage in motion picture production, and Metropolitan wants to be at the head of things if it takes off, which we feel certain it will.'

Some pieces started to fall into place, Mason thought. If they were going ahead with an experimental film they couldn't afford to spend over the odds in case it flopped big time; they couldn't afford to risk going to their stable of big names and use them – that might be like killing the golden goose if the star went down with the movie – so they were opting for a safer bet by starring a relative unknown. Damage limitation. If the system took off they'd throw more money at it, and their bigger names, too. It could be the final nail in Rick Mason's movie career coffin, or it could be the break he desperately needed.

'OK, so how come my accent is so important?' he asked. 'What is it you're planning?'

'Horror, Mr Mason,' said Bremner. That's what we're planning. Have you seen Chaney's *The Phantom of the Opera*?'

'Yeah, I'm a big Chaney fan.'

'Audiences can't get enough of that kind of thing,' Bremner explained. 'They like to have the pants scared off them. Chaney's *Hunchback of Notre Dame* was the ninth biggest-grossing film of '23. There are big bucks in horror. It's a genre that's only just beginning to be explored to its full potential. That's the area Metropolitan wants to go into next. Metro Monsters! Got a certain ring to it, eh? More than that, we're going to have sound. You are going to be our first ever horror star, Mr Mason. And what's more, you'll speak!'

'Starring in what, exactly?' he asked, rather dumbfounded at what he was hearing.

'That has yet to be decided,' cut in Jefferson. 'We're toying with a few ideas around similar characters to the phantom, set the movie abroad, maybe, the main character will definitely be a foreigner – they make perfect horror material. We'd need to carry out sound tests on your voice, but your European accent would be perfect, and with your ability to act it should bring everything neatly together. We're still in the process of preparing for all this, nothing really coming together just yet, but what we propose is to work with you on creating the perfect monster to launch Metro Monsters. We've seen the way you breathe life into characters. We want to wrap this first one around you, so it fits like a glove. What's more we want to offer you a three-movie contract with Metropolitan. We'll double the pay they gave at Prima, with a pay review after the first movie. How does that sound?'

Rick Mason didn't have to think about it. 'Sounds good, Mr Jefferson.'

'A rather apt phrase, is it not?' said Jefferson, grinning broadly and revealing a gold tooth. 'And if all goes well, that would be a really big one in the eye for Prima, eh? Take their no-hoper and turn him into a star!'

Another piece fell into place with a loud bang. To get one over on the Dillons was irresistible to Jefferson. But what the hell, Mason thought, let them play their puerile politics all they want; if he could benefit off the back of it then he wasn't complaining any.

'I still need to sort things out at Prima,' Mason explained. 'But that shouldn't be a problem. When do you want me at Metropolitan?'

'Like I said, we're in the early stages of development yet,' said Jefferson, 'but we'd like you on the books as soon as possible. We can start getting together advance publicity, that kind of thing.'

'So I've another month or two before things get under way?'

'What's the problem?' said Bremner.

'I've got some unexpected family business to sort out in Europe.'

'You've got time, kid,' said Jefferson. 'Take a vacation. Once you're started at Metropolitan things won't let up much. We'll sort out some kind of advance in the meantime, but don't worry we'll work the details out with your agent.'

Mason let out a whistle. 'You know, Mr Jefferson, I think I'll take that drink now.'

Hal Bremner poured out spirits and all three raised their glasses. 'Here's to our new movie, whatever that's going to be!' said Jefferson.

'In with sound, out with silent,' said Bremner, his voice low and meaningful.

'Here's to horror!' said Mason, downing the fiery liquid and gasping.

* * * *

9

Dump the Past

'I can't go with you to Europe, Rick – that's a ludicrous idea!' she said.

'Betsy...' he pleaded, going to her and taking a light hold of her arm. He noticed Davey didn't take too kindly to the contact. 'I'd like you to come along.'

'She doesn't want to,' Davey said, standing up from his chair and advancing on Mason. 'And get your hands off her.'

Mason lifted his hand. 'No problem,' he said. 'What's with you, Davey, you got a razor stuck up your ass?'

Betsy rolled her eyes at them both. 'For goodness sake, boys, give it a rest. Davey, sit down; I'll decide what's best for me. Rick, I simply can't go with you to Slavonia, or whatever other goddamn country nobody's ever heard of.'

'Why? Give me one good reason.'

'I hardly know you, for one thing.'

'She don't know you,' echoed Davey, slumping down on to the chair. He stared daggers at Mason.

'Yeah, I think I heard that much, thank you, Davey.' He paced the small room. 'OK, Davey can come too. That way he'll be happy and you'll be happy. Please, Betsy, think of it as a vacation. When was the last time you took a trip to Europe, huh? It would be the trip of a lifetime.'

'I haven't got the money, Rick,' she said. 'Even if I did want to go with you.'

'I've got money. There's the severance from Prima, then an advance from Metropolitan coming through, and this guy Horvat tells me I'm going to be a very wealthy man. See, from nowhere I get all the money I need. What do you say, Betsy?' He turned to Davey. 'Come on, man, lighten up!'

'Why us?' he returned. 'I ain't your friend.'

'Because you're the nearest thing to friends I've got right now. I don't want to go alone. Hell, the last time I made a trip across the Atlantic I was a kid coming over here, and that wasn't exactly a picnic in steerage. It would be good to have company. Even yours, Davey.'

Davey glowered at him. 'I dunno. I've got to stay here. I've got jobs to hold down.'

'Those sorts of jobs are ten-a-penny, Davey. Look, I'll even pay you what you'd have earned.'

'I don't take charity,' he growled.

'And I've got my career to think about,' said Betsy.

'Career? There isn't any career yet. And didn't I get Victor Wallace to take you on?'

'So now there's a price to pay?' Her expression went frosty. 'You think you can buy me that way? You think I'll do anything you want out of gratitude?'

'I didn't mean that. Hell, it came out all wrong. Look, Betsy, I'm asking you to come because I want to be with you. There, I've said it. I want to be with you. Even if that means having your watchdog around all the time.' He put his hat on. 'Suit yourself,' he said to her. 'But you can't always do what Davey says you've got to do. You've got to think for yourself once in a while.' He went to the door. 'I'm meeting Horvat again to make travel arrangements. There's still time to change your mind.' He hesitated, perhaps hoping Betsy would say something, but she remained silent so he shouldered his disappointment and went out.

Davey watched him from behind the curtain at the window. 'I don't like him,' he mumbled.

'You don't like any man who likes me,' she said.

'And why is that?' he said, his voice low and filled with many things left unsaid. 'You know we have to keep low. Why do you insist on drawing attention to yourself? All this motion picture business, it's not safe…'

'Correction; you have to keep low. I'm not going to be a recluse because of some idiot thing that happened.'

His cheeks flushed red. 'Idiot thing? You've only got a life because of me – don't ever forget that!' He stormed away into his bedroom and slammed the door.

She stifled a squeal of exasperation, closed her eyes and tried to calm down. She went to the door and tapped quietly on it. 'You know, maybe Europe's not such a bad idea. I mean, I ran into a couple of strange guys down at the drug store yesterday…'

There was silence, then the sounds of shuffling from his room. The door opened. 'What guys?'

She shrugged. 'Maybe I was imagining things.'

'What guys? Why didn't you tell me before?'

'I didn't want to worry you.'

'Jesus, you don't think they've found us, do you? What did they look like?'

'Hard to say, regular guys, but they kinda spooked me.' She sighed. 'It's this constantly having to look over my shoulder, that's what gets to me. Maybe it was nothing. One of them made small-talk, but he started asking questions.'

'What kind of questions?'

'Whether I was from around these parts, where I'd come from, that kind of thing.'

'We've got to leave,' he said, his eyes terrified.

She placed a calming hand on his arm. 'No we don't. All we need do is disappear for a while. I played hard-to-get when Rick was asking us, but I was thinking this trip with him might not be a bad thing. No one's ever going to find us in Slavonia, are they? If it was them then they'll sniff around, find nothing and leave. It might be wise to go, just to be on the safe side.'

'Do you trust him; trust Rick?'

'I like him. He's an OK guy.' She put her arms around his waist. 'It's not as if I don't appreciate everything you've done for me. You've done more than any brother has a right to. But I'm tired. We have to stop running at some time, make a new life for ourselves. We can do that if you'll let us. We can be different people, start all over again. Dump the past. Rick might be just the ticket we need to do that. Please, let this be the place where we finally stop running.'

'And Mexico? That was always the plan. This place was only a stop-off.'

'But I could be an actress!'

'You have to stop that. It's not real. Can't you see that's what got us into this mess in the first place?'

'You're blaming me?' she shrieked. 'Blaming me for what he did to me?'

'No...' he said, hanging his head. 'I wish it had never happened.' He stared hard at his fingers. 'I had his blood all over my hands. I can't stop thinking about it. It's with me every day...' His lower lip started trembling. 'It haunts my dreams. I see his face. I see the blood. There was blood everywhere...'

She shook him by the shoulders. 'But it did happen and there's nothing we can do about it now. You have to forget all about it. Do you hear me? Behaving like you do only draws attention to you. To us. They'll still be looking for you and we don't need that attention, do we? Do you want to go to the chair? Is that what you want?' He shook his head. 'Then we have to act normally, and that means you have to try to forget everything that happened. We're different people now. We can have a new life.'

'A man was murdered,' he said quietly. 'I can't simply forget that.'

'He was an animal,' she said coldly. 'He deserved to die.'

'No one deserves to die like that.'

'I'm not listening to this again.' She left him and went to the door.

'Where are you going?'

'I'm going to see if I can catch Rick up, tell him we're going with him. Rick's right, we can't go on living in each other's pockets, it causes even more suspicion and we don't need that.' She put her felt hat on, stared at him straight in the face. 'And you've got to watch that temper, keep it in check for both our sakes. You know where losing your temper can lead…'

'Please be careful, sis,' he said. He went back into his room and closed the door on her.

* * * *

Part Two

Dragutin

10

A Friendly, Generous People

The village of Krndija was small, the mean cottages constructed of wood and stone spread along a single dirt-track road occupied only by a pig and two goats chewing at weeds. The air was crisp and clean and Rick Mason sensed snow in the air. The village sat at the foot of the Krndija Mountain, which loomed dark and oppressive before them, its base swathed in bleak-looking forest. The cloud hung low, sweeping the mountain top and streaming down its craggy side like a slow-moving river of steam. The cry of strange unseen birds fell from a still white sky and echoed around the steep mountain sides.

'See that?' said Franz Horvat pointing out the mountain. 'It is at present being swallowed by the cloud, but that peak there, the highest, is called Kapovac.' He hardly seemed breathless, the old man enduring the walk up the track to the village better than Rick, Betsy or Davey. Each of them was pausing to catch their breath. Mason could see now why they had to abandon their car about a mile away; the place wasn't meant for automobiles and there was no way their old thing would have been able to make it. It looked like most of the road – such as it was, a collection of hard-packed rocks and small boulders – had been recently washed into deep criss-crossing channels by heavy rain.

Rick Mason placed his suitcase on the ground and sat on it, waiting for Betsy and Davey to catch up.

'Vacation of a lifetime?' Betsy panted, dropping her case by his and sitting on it.

'You should have let me help you carry that,' he said.

She looked exhausted. They all were. Everyone except old man Horvat, who was standing looking at them impatiently. It had been a long haul to Slavonia and they hadn't finished yet.

The first week or so of travel had been the easiest and most pleasurable. A long haul to the east coast, then a seven-day crossing of the Atlantic on the White Star Line's RMS Majestic – or the Magic Stick as someone had nicknamed her. They docked at Southampton, England, then crossed over the channel to France and took to the train on a gruelling journey across Europe, heading south and eventually reaching Zagreb, the capital of Croatia. They rested up a day before heading out by train again to the city of Slavonska Pozega. The city sat in the Pozega Valley, surrounded by the Slavonian Mountains.

'You are close to home,' Horvat had said as Mason stared out of the train's window to the miles of rolling countryside beyond.

'This is no longer home,' he said quietly. 'America is now my home.'

'You were born in Slavonia,' he returned. 'The place of our birth burns in the heart always. It is a flame that never goes out.'

Franz Horvat had his offices in Slavonska Pozega, and he suggested the small party rest up for a day or so in the city whilst he sorted out and picked up a number of legal papers. The city was small by Californian standards, thought Mason, and the buildings far older. There were fewer automobiles, a great deal of the traffic still being pulled by horses. There were signs that it was a city on the cusp of change, but reminders of its more primitive beginnings and its mix of cultures were never very far away. Mason felt he was on the verge of a different, very alien world.

Horvat had explained that it was a stipulation of the will that its full contents had to be disclosed within the walls of Castle Dragutin itself, which they'd reach the following day, so he would see at first hand what he had inherited. There were some restrictions as to what he might do with the property, but he refused to say what those were till the proper time.

The next day, reasonably refreshed, they hired a car and driver to take them as far as they could to the village of Krndija, which, they discovered, couldn't get as close as they would have preferred. They had to abandon the car and make the rest of the way on foot. Mason looked around him at the village and wondered if it had all been worth the effort. The further away from Slavonska Pozega they travelled the more remote and inaccessible it felt; almost as if the countryside itself tried to deny them access. Which was an idiotic thought, of course, and brought on by tiredness. What had initially started out as a jolly adventure had turned into something of an endurance test. And Franz Horvat's irritatingly healthy constitution didn't make him feel any better.

The one enduring benefit of the lengthy travelling was his time spent with Betsy and how they'd grown closer with every day that passed. And with every day that passed Davey grew more protective of her. He remained sullen and aloof throughout, sitting alone and occupied by his writing, the subject of which remained a mystery to Mason. He went to great lengths to prevent even the most tentative of intimate contact between him and Betsy. Mason tried sneaking down the corridor to her cabin, but as if Davey possessed some kind of sixth sense he would spring from his own cabin to confront him and Mason found himself constructing ever more elaborate and unbelievable excuses why he should happen to be there.

On one particular evening, when he raised his hand to knock on Betsy's cabin door, having arranged to be with her at a certain time, Davey's cabin door across the corridor opened. He was in his dressing gown. He didn't say anything, simply leant in the doorway passing one of his trademark sultry looks at Mason.

'Got some kind of alarm rigged up, Davey?' he asked, irritated by the man's continued claustrophobic presence. He didn't reply. 'Always silent, eh, Davey? Why is that? Is it because there's some danger of revealing too much if you talk? What have you got to keep quiet about, Davey?'

'You'd do well to keep away from her,' he said quietly.

'Or what? That a threat?'

'It's a warning.'

'Should I be scared?'

'It's up to you if you don't want to listen. Leave her alone.'

Betsy's cabin door swung open at the sound of voices. She saw Davey. Also saw the bottle of champagne and two glasses in Mason's hands. 'For me, Rick?' she said. 'Come on in.'

Mason nodded uncomfortably in Davey's direction. 'Maybe not tonight; the searchlight is on.'

'Davey, go back to bed,' she said. He hesitated, squinted at her, but an abbreviated flick of her hand saw him duck reluctantly inside his cabin and close the door.

'What is it with him?' said Mason

'Forget Davey. Are you coming in or what?'

'If looks could kill…' he said, his eyes fixed on Davey's cabin door. 'Here,' he said, handing her the bottle and a glass, 'have this on me. Maybe some other time.'

'Welcome to Krndija, 'Horvat said. He eyed the gasping threesome through his spectacles. 'You're not tired, are you?'

Which was the nearest he'd come to expressing humour the entire journey, albeit heavily laced with sarcasm. 'We have a horse and carriage waiting for us here and we must get a move on if we are to reach Castle Dragutin before nightfall. There are no streetlamps here, you may have noticed.'

'There's nothing here,' said Betsy light-heartedly. In spite of her tiredness she was quite excited by all she was experiencing. She responded to Horvat's little dig and got to her feet. Davey came to her side and she picked up her suitcase.

'Can I carry that for you?' said Davey.

'I can manage,' she said curtly. She'd resented Davey's repeated attempts to prevent her from seeing Rick, and the most they'd been allowed to share were occasional lengthy conversations. Mason suspected they'd exchanged heated words over it on more than one occasion, but they never let even a glimmer of that private unrest show publicly. Davey still looked at Mason as if he was a rattlesnake and was thinking about getting the first blow in.

'Hang on – you said horse and carriage?' Mason said, turning to face Horvat who had started up the hill on his own and making his way further into the village. A number of people – two old men and a woman of similar vintage – had come out of their cottages to observe the strangers.

'Of course,' said Horvat. 'When these tracks were originally laid in the 13th Century they didn't have automobiles in mind. A horse and carriage is still the only way of reaching Castle Dragutin, and only then if the rains have been kind to us and not washed away the track too much. You can ride by donkey or mule, if you wish, but I suspect that would not be to your liking.'

'You suspect right. How far have we to go?' He picked up his case and joined Betsy and Davey as they followed Horvat.

'Perhaps another eight miles, that way,' he pointed. 'Through the mountain pass.'

'Perhaps?'

'It could extend to ten or more if we are forced to take a detour.' He halted and waved in exasperation. 'Please do hurry. If we are not there soon the coachman will refuse to take us and there is nowhere we can stay in this village overnight.'

'I'm not sure I'd like the idea anyway,' said Mason, a little unnerved by the old woman whose gimlet eyes were fixed on him. She wore a long ankle-length black dress, a rough white blouse over this, a matching headscarf on her head with a curious knot at the top. He noticed she wore woollen stockings in black and curious, pointed leather sandals that looked like they came from ancient Rome or Greece. He guessed the style of dress hadn't changed in decades, maybe even centuries. In fact it felt like he'd been transported back a hundred years or more in time. But somehow it all seemed vaguely familiar, like the echo of a distant memory, a picture in his head that was always on the verge of forming but never coming into focus.

Then, to his complete surprise, the old woman spat at his feet. An old man wearing a tatty waistcoat over a woollen shirt, short breeches and long stockings, dashed forward and took her by the shoulder. He avoided looking directly at Mason, instead pulling down the rim of his straw hat to hide his face further, and he led the woman away.

'The weirdest thing!' said Mason, puzzled and alarmed at the same time. 'She spat at me! Don't they take kindly to strangers in these parts, Mr Horvat?'

'Generally their reaction to strangers is quite the opposite,' he said. 'They are a friendly, generous people.'

'So friendly they spit at me?'

'It is possibly because you bear a resemblance to your father.'

'They hated my father?' said Mason.

'Yes, they hated him, Mr Mason. But more than that, they feared him.'

* * * *

11

Castle Dragutin

The man reached down from the roof of the coach, his face shaded by a broad-rimmed hat, and he hauled up the suitcases one by one, stacking them carefully and then securing them with leather straps. The two black horses stood motionless and obedient as Betsy stroked each of them in turn.

'How beautiful they are,' she said, leaning her head close against one of the horses and whispering something to it.

'You're good around horses, for a city girl,' Rick Mason observed. 'I don't trust them myself. Is this thing safe?' he asked Franz Horvat, pointing at the battered, scarred and mud-splashed wooden coach. 'It's ancient. You sure this will get us to where we want to be?'

'Quite sure, Mr Mason,' Horvat reassured, beckoning them to climb inside. He held the door open and took Betsy's hand as she put a foot on the step. The coach springs gave under her weight.

'How gallant!' she said, grinning at Mason. She made herself comfortable on the padded leather seat. 'Makes me feel like some kind of Victorian countess or something.' She peered out of the small glass window. Beyond the low-roofed cottages she saw a dark wall of plum-purple mountains. Snow sat thinly on the highest points, almost aglow in the dull light.

Davey followed her, silently taking his place at her side. Horvat waited for Mason to clamber aboard before joining them and closing the coach door. The driver climbed down from the roof, showed his face at the window. Horvat nodded that all was well and the coach rocked gently as the driver climbed to his seat and took the reins.

'It's not as comfortable as a motor car,' Horvat explained,' but it is a tried and trusted method used for centuries to get around these parts. The horse can take us where your spluttering little motor cannot.'

'How long will this take us,' asked Mason.

'It will take as long as it takes,' Horvat returned. 'Put away your watch for now. Such things have less of a meaning in the mountains.'

The coach gave a lurch and Betsy expelled a little whoop of delight, holding onto leather straps by the door to steady herself. Within minutes the small village was left behind, the coach negotiating a twisting rutted track that rose steeply. Soon they entered a dense forest of closely-packed firs, the light at once reduced to that of dusk, with some parts of the forest in almost total darkness. The light inside the coach was such that it was almost as black as night, and their voices gradually became hushed and eventually fell silent, all eyes watching the passage of the tree trunks through the windows.

The forest seemed to go on forever, and there was palpable relief when the coach emerged from its melancholic embrace into the light again. They were clearly in a mountain pass, walls of steep-sided, jagged rock pressing in on both sides, which came closer together the further the coach trundled into the pass. Then the narrow pass gave way to yet another stretch of forest, which in turn widened out into a lush meadow-like valley threaded through with rocky mountain streams, till once again the mountains came together into yet another mountain pass.

The air became thinner, colder, the track ever more snake-like in its twists and bends, the ruts and potholes deeper, the large wheels seemingly finding every rock there was to find, the jerking of the coach causing every occupant some discomfort. Betsy's initial whoop of delight at the prospects of a thrilling coach ride had long dissipated and had been replaced instead by groans every time they struck something. The hard leather seats were not as comfortable or accommodating as they first appeared.

'This is a veritable wilderness!' Mason exclaimed. But yet again he felt the same bubble of recognition and familiarity beginning to form. How curious, he thought, given that, as far as he was aware, he'd never been here. His life had been a series of cities and small towns. He knew nothing of the mountains.

'It is deceptive,' said Horvat. 'It is not quite a wilderness. People live hereabouts, spread out thinly, but live here all the same. Yet it pays to show the land due respect. It has claimed the life of many lost or careless travellers.'

'Not sure I like it,' Mason admitted. 'It's gloomy.'

Horvat studied him. 'Perhaps you had better grow to like it, Mr Mason. After all, what you see, as far as you can see, now belongs to you.'

'No kidding!'

'No kidding, Mr Mason. We are now within the boundary of the Dragutin estate.'

Betsy laughed and all eyes turned to her. 'He's pulling your leg, Rick, can't you see? I mean, no one owns a mountain, for God's sake!'

Horvat shook his head slowly. 'There is an owner for everything. Even a mountain.' He turned his attention to the countryside flashing by outside the window, ignoring Betsy's stifled giggle.

'So why did they fear my father?' Mason asked. It had been bothering him for all this time, but Horvat had managed to evade the issue.

'This is not the time to enter into such things, Mr Mason. All in due course, as promised.' Horvat made it clear there would be no further conversation and closed his eyes, blotting them out and pretending to be asleep.

'It's like one of those creepy Victorian novels,' Betsy observed, her arms folded, her body tightening against the growing cold of the evening. 'A coach ride, dark forest, a castle…' She laughed. 'I bet there are wolves and bears in the forest. Are there, Mr Horvat, wolves and bears?' His eyes remained resolutely closed. 'Mr Horvat?'

'Leave him be, Betsy,' said Davey, who had been uncomfortable at the way the old man looked at him; almost as if he could see right into his soul. He preferred him with his eyes closed.

'Soon there'll be a thunderstorm,' said Mason dramatically. He leant across to Betsy, his voice playfully deep. 'The thunder will roll out loud across the mountains as if the gods are angry, and the rain will come dashing against the coach window. The driver will get lost and we will end up stuck fast in the mud. We leave the coach, step out into the night, spy lights from a lonely old house, and there we will seek shelter…'

'The driver has never got lost,' said Horvat, his eyes still closed. 'You actors are too melodramatic.'

'I am not an actor,' Davey murmured indignantly.

Horvat opened his eyes, fixed them on the young man. 'No?' He closed them again. 'You are the best actor of them all,' he said.

Davey scowled. 'What's that supposed to mean?'

'Look!' interrupted Betsy, leaning close to the window and pointing. 'Isn't that just the most beautiful sight?'

The countryside opened up, on one side a forest clinging to a steep mountainside reaching up as far as the eye could see; and on the other a vast lake, the silvery-grey waters made choppy by a stiff breeze, reflecting the heavy grey sky. More mountains and hills rose from the far banks of the lake, blurred by the mist of distance. The coach now took a road that skirted close to the edge of the lake, at times rising on a ledge so narrow that Mason feared one wrong move by the horses, or hitting a rock that might overbalance them, would tip them all into the bleak-looking waters below.

'Let me guess,' said Mason. 'I own the lake, too.'

'You own the lake, too,' Horvat said, opening his eyes. 'In a moment you will see Castle Dragutin. It is a most impressive sight. It sits on a narrow isthmus of rock that juts out into the lake.'

And true to his word the castle hove into view. It was not constructed of dark blocks of stone, like a Norman castle, as Mason had pictured in his head; it was instead reminiscent of a French château, largely painted white so that it stood out from the dark forest behind it, as if some mighty god had dipped a thumb in white paint and smeared it across the forest.

It did indeed stand on a low-lying spit of land that wasn't visible on first approach, so that the high rock on which the castle stood appeared to float in the water like a giant ship. As they drew closer they could make out three cylindrical towers, each capped with a conical roof, the plain walls of the castle studded with many square windows. They were impressed by the sheer size of the building, which they hadn't fully appreciated on seeing it from a distance. But as they came closer it towered above them, made to appear even taller by its construction on the sheer-faced island of natural stone. Mason was in awe of it, but was undecided whether he found it beautiful or disturbing.

'There has been a building on this spot since the thirteenth century,' Horvat explained. 'First for religious purposes, then defensive, and finally as a means of...' He hesitated. '...a means of governance.'

'It's not like a real castle,' noticed Betsy.

'As I told Mr Mason some time ago, it is really a manor house – or rather a very grand manor house. But it has always been referred to as a castle, even before Baron Dragutin came to live here. I'm sorry you're disappointed.'

'I'm not disappointed at all. This is marvellous!' Betsy chimed. 'Is there a drawbridge?'

'No drawbridge, miss. Nor knights in shining armour. There are only two people now living in Castle Dragutin. They have been sole caretakers there following Baron Dragutin's death. They have been in Baron Dragutin's employment since they were children. They have not left the castle once in all that time.'

'Not once?' said Mason in disbelief.

'Not once. They have seen it as their solemn duty.'

'Or done it out of fear,' said Mason half-jokingly.

Horvat's face remained as expressionless as ever. 'Fear and duty are not so far removed from one another. We are almost there.'

* * * *

12

The Hanged Man

They were glad to step out of the coach, and as if to rush to greet them an icy wind blew over from the lake and caused them to fold their arms and shrink back from the sudden gust. They were in a large paved yard, spacious, laid with monstrous stone flags in bleak grey, the whole enclosed by a low wall beyond which the lake was clearly visible stretching into the distance. Mason noticed steps leading steeply down from the yard, hugging the rock on which the castle had been built, and he presumed these led all the way down to the shore of the lake. He could just make out a wooden jetty, the posts of which were being snapped at by foam-flecked waves. But save for the sound of the lapping water and the wind ruffling the trees in the distance, all was strangely quiet and still.

He turned to look up at Castle Dragutin. Its walls didn't appear half as pristine as they had from a distance; they were in need of fresh paint and repair, but solidly impressive all the same. The light was fast sinking into dusk but the building stood out ghostly-pale, as if it refused to acknowledge the coming night and resisted it. It was not an ornate affair by any stretch of the imagination, Mason thought as the coach driver handed down cases from the coach roof. It was austere and angular, utilitarian almost, and reminded him of pictures he'd seen of Alcatraz prison.

Horvat thanked the driver, paid him and said goodbye. The driver mounted the coach and they watched as the horses drew the coach in a large circle to turn it around. He didn't acknowledge his former passengers as he made sure the twin oil lamps fixed to the coach burned brightly before flapping the reins lightly to urge the beasts into motion. The coach trundled noisily over the stone flags. They all watched in silence as it disappeared from view. All except Horvat who was striding, case in hand, to the main door of Castle Dragutin.

'Bit late for travelling back, I'd have thought,' said Mason. 'I wouldn't have liked to ride in that thing in the dark.'

'He preferred not to stay,' Horvat said. He motioned to them with his gloved hand. 'Come; let us not stand out here in the cold.' He yanked hard on a bell-pull by the towering oak door.

Mason noticed how weeds had taken hold in whatever crack in the stone they could find. Great clumps were dotted all over the castle walls, grew out of fissures in the stone flags, sprouted at the base of the low wall. Two large flower urns, one on either side of the door, were also choked with weeds. Horvat became aware of him staring at the urns.

'Sobering thought, Mr Mason, that man need only stay his hand for a brief while and nature begins its assault.. A sign that all things give way to weeds, Mr Mason.'

'Very sobering,' he replied. 'A little weed killer is all that's needed.'

'Baron Dragutin was not one for prettiness,' he said and yanked the bell-pull again, trying the heavy brass circular door handle to no avail.

'I wish they'd hurry,' said Betsy. 'It's getting cold out here.'

'So is it locked to keep people out, or keep people in?' Mason joked.

Just then the door opened and a frail-looking old man in a dark crumpled suit looked apologetically at them. He was panting and wiped a bony hand over his bald head. He said something in Hungarian to Horvat, then in broken English he said to the rest of them that he was sorry for the delay; he had been at the far end of the castle making final preparations for the guests, lighting fires in all the bedrooms. He glanced briefly at Mason then quickly averted his gaze. He swung the door wide, standing aside to let the travellers enter.

It took a little while for their eyes to adjust to the gloom inside, in spite of the fact that a number of oil lamps burned fiercely. The floor was of plain marble in a mottled-brown colour, a fine layer of dust clouding its sheen. Above them hung a spidery chandelier with empty candle sconces and dusty crystal evidence that it hadn't been lit in a long time. Ahead of them was a wide staircase, flopped out onto the tiles like a grotesque brown tongue; its dark wooden steps swept upwards to an upper balcony. The treads were part-carpeted, but it looked faded and worn. Dark paper from a bygone age lined the walls, here and there the dull flash of gold picture frames; empty vases that once must have held lush broad-leaved plants, stood on rosewood furniture pressed tight against the walls, alongside marble busts of what appeared to be Roman emperors.

But the piece that immediately caught the eye was a life-size bust in white marble of a handsome young man, his head a mass of writing curls, his face angled downwards, his languid eyes pointing curiously to the floor. It was in such a prominent position, high on its black marble plinth that it obviously must have been of some significance to its owner. The name engraved into the marble was *Antinous*.

'This is Uncle Zsigmund,' Horvat introduced the old man, who immediately offered a half-bow to each of them. 'As I said, he has been in the service of Baron Dragutin since he was a child. He met his wife, Margit, in the castle, and was married in this very room. They have been tending to the castle ever since and are the last of Baron Dragutin's servants. They have been waiting for you, Mr Mason.'

Mason shook the man's hand, but the contact was brief on the servant's part. Once again he refused to look directly into Mason's face. Now he could understand why this place was gradually going to seed with only a couple of old people to look after it. It was a massive undertaking.

The old man took their hats and coats and told them he'd prepared a fire in the drawing room. His wife would be cooking something for them soon, now that they were finally here, and he asked if they'd like refreshments in the meantime. Horvat took him to one side to engage him in hushed conversation and the old man hung up the coats and wandered away.

'Come through to the drawing room,' he said. 'Let's not stand on ceremony.'

'Uncle Zsigmund?' said Betsy leaning close to Mason as they followed Horvat deeper into Castle Dragutin.

He smiled. 'It's a polite Hungarian term for addressing older people. Uncle for the men, aunts for the ladies. It doesn't mean there's a family connection in the way you're used to back home.'

'Talking of home, how is all this making you feel? What's it like being in Slavonia, is it strange?'

'Yeah, very strange,' he admitted. 'But I'm surprised how much is still inside me that I'd pushed away in order to feel more American.' He laughed. 'Even my accent, I notice, has become more pronounced since we came here. Isn't that bizarre?'

'Perhaps you are turning into Baron Dragutin,' she said, chuckling. She linked her arm through his, aware that Davey was behind them staring hard.

Mason could feel the cold of her hand through the sleeve of his jacket. 'And you will become my baroness!' he said.

There was a log fire blazing in the maw of a huge stone fireplace, yet the warmth did not penetrate all corners of the immense room. They sat on a variety of chairs and sofas pulled up close to the fire. Mason counted five oil lamps burning in strategic places around the room, their flickering causing the deep shadows to dance on the monstrous pieces of highly carved wooden furniture that, in this subdued light, took on the appearance of rocky outcrops.

Zsigmund came in, offered and poured warming spirits into glasses that caught the firelight. He went over to the heavy drapes that hung long and thick at two tall windows and drew them against the encroaching night.

'He tells me snow is on its way,' said Horvat, raising his glass and studying the amber liquid inside. He sipped at it carefully, as if it were hot.

'Is that a problem?' asked Mason.

Horvat shrugged. 'The driver will be back for us in three days, time for us to conclude business, for you to take a look around the castle and its grounds, and time to rest in preparation for your long journey back home. Snow is a frequent visitor here, even at this time of year, but as with everything we can only go with the flow of nature.' He set the glass down on a small table. 'Your rooms have been prepared. There is a fire laid in each and Margit has warmed all the beds with pans of coal. It is cold and much of the place has been little lived in, but your rooms will soon feel comfortable enough. The castle's walls are very thick and will keep the cold winds at bay. It isn't for nothing that the wind that rushes down from the cold mountains and across the lake to the castle is called Wolf's Teeth. California it isn't, I'm afraid.'

Presently they caught their first sight of Zsigmund's wife, Margit. Though she looked as old as him she seemed in a far more robust condition; she was a rounded woman, large, cheeks weathered red, eyes but tiny black slits when she smiled. She wore the same style dress as the woman in the village, ankle-length black dress and pale blouse over the top; she also sported a grey-white apron around her considerable middle. She came into the drawing room and told Horvat that food was ready to be served.

'Thank heaven!' said Betsy. 'I'm famished!'

They filed into the dining room, Horvat at their head showing the way. Again a fire crackled in the cavernous grate of a huge fireplace. A long mahogany table sat in the centre of the oppressively dark room. The table had been laid for five, silver candelabras set with guttering candles in the middle, the silver cutlery reflecting back the candle flames like sparks. They sat down and Mason commented on the extra place that had been set.

'Who is that for?' he asked. 'Is someone joining us?'

Horvat arranged his napkin and didn't look at Mason. 'It is set for Baron Dragutin. It was a stipulation of his that a place at the table should always be set for him, even after he is dead.'

'How peculiar!' said Betsy, eyeing the empty chair. 'It's almost as if he might walk in at any moment.'

But in spite of the faded grandeur of the room and the majestic table settings, the food when it came was a bland and plain affair. A thin vegetable soup to start, some kind of flavourless chicken dish for the main course, the whole concluding with a traditional Slavonian dish of layered pastry filled with raisins, nuts, cottage cheese and apple.

'I'd kill for a coffee,' Mason said when the last of the empty dishes had been removed. Horvat told him they had no coffee, but tea aplenty. It was at this point, as Mason was glancing around the room, his eyes having grown accustomed to the limited light, that he caught sight of the large black and white print held by a broad ebony frame.

'That is a curious picture to have in a dining room,' he observed.

At first he simply thought it depicted a smiling woman in some kind of bucolic wooded glade, but he saw the shape on the left of the picture was not a tree as he had imagined, but the body of a man hanging from a tree's bough. On his right shoulder a crow was perched, pecking at his dead eye. Mason rose from his seat out of curiosity, went closer to the picture. The hanged man was barefoot, had his hands tied behind his back, two more crows on the limb from which he hung awaiting their turn to feast on the corpse. The woman, it turned out, was pregnant, a basket over one arm, a pitcher of wine in the other hand. There was a lake in the background not unlike the lake outside Castle Dragutin, on which two boats sailed serenely past. On the whole the entire picture was quietly disturbing.

'It was originally a pen and ink drawing created in 1525.' Horvat came to his side. 'This was one of the Baron's favourite pieces. It is a very old print. He greatly admired this Swiss artist, Urs Graf. Not for his work particularly, though it has some artistic merits; he admired him for his personal attributes. Graf was a cruel man, a foul-mouthed, vulgar mercenary who relished the bloody violence and the rape and the pillage that accompanied war. He had no need to resort to becoming a landsknecht – the name of the feared Swiss mercenaries – he did not need the money. Slaughter, you see, was his abiding pleasure. And violence of any kind. He once attacked a crippled man in the city of Basle, a man with whom he hadn't exchanged a single word. Sport? Drink? Who can say? He was, by all accounts, a repulsive man. This print is of a camp follower who has come across a hanged soldier, but if you are looking for some kind of treatise on the abiding injustice of a cruel military system or some wider social comment you would be sadly mistaken. Graf drew this because it gave him a thrill to do so.'

'And you say my father actually admired the man?'

'Very much so. You see, in Urs Graf he saw a distinct similarity to himself. Your father was also a mercenary in his younger days, seeking out any war he could find. But he had no need to do so, and he was never one for fighting the cause of larger political or social ideals. He was, like Graf, a self-centred man whose aim was to live life to the full, live it for all the base pleasures it offered, and suffice to say he drank his fill of every vice available.' Horvat smiled thinly. 'But it is of no business of mine to pass judgement on a man's desires or carnal drives. Only God has the authority to do that, and any earthly sins that must one day be accounted for will be dealt with by Him and Him alone.'

'Sins?'

'It is growing late,' Horvat said,' 'and we are all tired after our long journey.' Strangely, his expression as he looked upon Mason was one of sorrow. 'Tomorrow I shall tell you more about your father.'

Mason studied the picture again. The woman's moonlike face seemed to be focused on him, her leering smile almost mocking.

* * * *

13

A Living Soul

He awoke shivering. At first he didn't know where he was and was seized by a blind panic as his eyes scanned the strange room. Then realisation seeped in and he sat there in bed feeling slightly foolish.

The fire had gone out and was but a mound of cold grey ash in the grate. The room had seemed cheerful enough as he clambered under the heavy sheets the night before, the fire casting a warm comforting glow on the joyless walls. He'd fallen instantly asleep. But the morning stood in sharp contrast. The air was cold and damp and the weighty top blanket felt clammy and uncomfortable to the touch. It forced him from his bed. Rick Mason went immediately to the long window and threw back the drapes.

The light was leaden, the sky filled with a crawling sludge of dour cloud; a faintly luminous mist hung over the lake, languidly tearing off into feathery strips beneath the light-fingered ministrations of a cruising breeze. There appeared to be no colour. The world was monochrome. It did not lift the spirits; it chilled the soul.

The mood at breakfast was rather tepid. Mason put it down to them all suffering the last dregs of tiredness, yet he thought there was more to it than that. It was as if the castle were exerting some kind of subliminal influence over them. Or perhaps it was just him, he thought, allowing his imagination to run away with itself. After all, he was the only one returning to the place of his birth and that had to have some kind of effect on you. It hadn't been an easy time for him. So many new things for his mind to assimilate. The discovery of his true mother and father, the inheritance, the fact he was largely Hungarian by blood, which didn't sit well with him. He'd gone from being one of a people oppressed, to the oppressor. This explained a great deal about why his mother – *he really must stop thinking that* – became so hostile towards him. She knew the truth about his birth; the truth about his father. And why had she adopted him in the first place? What on earth had gone on?

What he did find a little disconcerting was the behaviour of Zsigmund and Margit towards him. Neither of them would look him directly in the eye, at least not for more than a second or two. Initially he wondered whether it was some kind of cultural deference, a hangover from the days of Baron Dragutin, but the more he studied them the more he was convinced he detected a little fear in them. Yet only with him. With any of the others, even cold old Horvat, they were as warm and as affable as if they'd truly been their aunt and uncle. When the time was right, he told himself, he would ask Horvat about it. It was probable it was all in his imagination again.

What wasn't in his imagination, though, was the custom of setting out his father's place at the table. That was decidedly strange. Almost as if he were still there in spirit; that they were afraid not to set it lest something terrible befall them. Stranger still was that Horvat didn't think anything of it.

Afterwards, when a weak Sun came out to burn away the last of the mist, Mason persuaded Betsy to take a walk with him outside whist Davey was up in his room. He told her he had something important to ask her.

They wandered into a sprawling courtyard, a rectangle of overgrown lawn at its centre on which stood a beautifully carved fountain consisting of a tangle of naked water nymphs with limbs so entwined it was difficult to separate out one from the other. No water flowed, only green streaks where it had once run many years ago. A row of empty, forlorn-looking stables lined one wall, but it was an ivy-wreathed arched doorway that they were drawn to at the far end of the courtyard.

On pushing the stiff-hinged door open they found it took them into what remained of an overgrown garden constructed in tiers on the steep hillside, a stone path snaking downwards. Beyond was a fine uninterrupted view of the solemn lake, the smudged blue shapes of mountains in the hazy distance.

'This is weird, huh?' he said as they paused by a stone balustrade encrusted with plates of lichen and miniature meadows of moss. 'All this…'

'It's hard to believe it even exists,' she admitted. 'It's like something from a strange dream.'

'Or a strange nightmare,' he said thoughtfully. 'It should be beautiful, but everything is in a state of decay.' His fingers pulled away a piece of crumbling masonry, which broke easily under his fingers and fell as dust to the ground.

'It needs a few improvements carrying out, that's for sure.' she quipped.

She turned to face him. He found he could hardly take his eyes off her; drank in every tiny inch of her beautiful features; the down on her cheeks; the puffed red pillows of her lips; the gem-like quality of her eyes.

'Why are you staring?' she asked. 'Is something wrong?'

'No, everything is just perfect. You are just perfect.'

She laughed. 'Rick, you try to be a charmer but you are not very skilled at it.'

'I'm hurt,' he said with a smile and put a hand to his heart. 'I'm trying to be genuine.'

'And I always find I'm wondering whether it is you that speaks, or whether it's the actor pretending to be someone else.'

'Never think that!' he said. 'I could never be like that with you. I care too much for you.'

'Really?' she said, raising a brow.

'Really.' His hands gripped the stone balustrade and he surveyed the wilderness before him. 'The thing is, Betsy, I really do care for you. I love you.'

Her face fell serious. 'Love me? Careful, Rick, I don't take too kindly to those sorts of slide-off-the-tongue sentiments. I've heard them before.'

'But you haven't heard it from me. I love you, Betsy Bellamy. I knew it from the moment I first met you. Call me a romantic fool, but I can't help the way you make me feel. I don't ever want to be apart from you. I want to be with you always.'

'You don't know me, Rick…'

'I know enough, and we can spend time getting to know one another.'

'Are you trying to tell me something here, Rick?'

'Will you marry me?'

'Are you serious?' she laughed. 'We've hardly known each other.'

'I know more than enough to know I want you to be my wife, to have children with you, to grow old and plant roses together.'

'Roses? You're rambling.'

He took her hand. It was deathly cold. 'Will you marry me?'

She slipped it from his grasp. 'I'm very flattered, Rick…'

'Flattered? You don't care for me, is that it?' His face clouded. 'Hell, I'm sorry, Betsy, I've made a goddamn fool of myself. It's all this, what's happening to me, I guess…'

'It's not that!' she exclaimed. 'I care for you too. You have made me so happy. You've changed my life in so many ways. But I simply don't want to be someone's wife and mother. I want a career for myself. I want to be an actress so desperately, and the two things are not easy to reconcile.'

'That's no problem,' he said, his eyes lighting up. 'You can have anything you please. You can be an actress – you *will* be an actress. I will support you every step of the way.'

'You promise?'

'Cross my heart, hope to die!' he said. 'I will not take that away from you. Just say you'll become my wife, say you'll marry me.'

'And suppose I say yes, will you think it's because I'm a title-grabbing woman after your inheritance?'

He looked momentarily confused. 'What? God no! I never once gave it a thought, and anyhow, I'm not certain what all this means yet. However, now we're onto it, every baron needs his baroness. And what a stage name, eh? Baroness Betsy Mason! I can see it in lights now.'

'Baroness Betsy Bellamy,' she corrected.

'Whatever, I don't care. Is that a yes, then?'

'Not until you have gone down on one knee and proposed properly, like any self-respecting baron would.'

He bent down to the stone flags, reached up and took hold of her hand again. 'Betsy Bellamy, will you become my wife?'

'Why, Baron Rick Mason, a lady would find it hard to resist such a romantic proposition, and the prospects of inheriting your mouldy old castle. Yes, I'll marry you.'

He jumped up, hugged and kissed her, clasping her tight to him. 'God, you've made me so happy!' he said. Then he pulled away. 'What about Davey? He's going to hate the idea.'

She sighed, her lips a thoughtful dash of red. 'Can we not say anything about it till we get back to America? I will have to think how best to break the news to him.' She turned from him, went over to stand at the balustrade and look at the lake. 'And there's something else you should know about him. About us. About me. It's not as straightforward as it seems.'

'Is there something you want to tell me? What's wrong?'

'Something that happened. An awful thing. If I tell you then you have to promise me you'll never tell a living soul.'

'I promise.'

She chewed at her lower lip. An eerie silence fell. Not even the sound of a bird broke it. 'I can't, Rick, I'm sorry. And you will not want to marry me because of it. Perhaps it was a foolish idea after all…'

She made as if to walk away but he grabbed her wrist. 'You can tell me. I love you. I don't care about anything that happened in your past. I only care about the woman I know now, and she's the most beautiful, gifted woman I know. I'll do anything for you, I promise. Whatever it takes for you to become my wife. Don't do this to me, Betsy.'

Her wide eyes were sorrowful, edged with tears. She appeared to be wrestling with something inside. 'Do you mean it, Rick?'

'I mean every word. I don't give a damn about anything that's happened in the past. Look, whatever it is, you can tell me if you like, but if you can't well that's fine too. Just say you'll marry me.'

'I'll marry you.'

But as she held him close her smile faded and she glanced out across the lake to the forlorn forests in the murky distance, to the snow-topped peaks of mountains, and tried not to dwell on the horrors of the past.

* * * *

14

The Mask of Antinous

'You appear pleased with yourself,' Franz Horvat observed as he beckoned Rick Mason to take a seat at the desk opposite him. It was a fair-sized room, lined with bookshelves containing dusty-looking tomes, and an array of furniture whose sole purpose was the storage of files and paperwork. 'This used to be the office from which the estate business was run. It has not been used properly in a long time.'

'So who runs the business?' Mason asked, in truth his mind still ringing from his conversation with Betsy.

'It has all fallen into disarray,' he answered, putting on his spectacles and separating out a number of thick cardboard files. 'Many things changed since the Austro-Hungarian Empire was dismantled following the end of the Great War a decade ago. People lost positions, lost wealth, lost land, lost power. It had its effects on Baron Dragutin, naturally, but he weathered the storm better than most. The estate is not what it once was, but it is still, as you see, far from trifling.'

'I need some answers, Mr Horvat...'

'I am sure you must have many questions to ask, but first you must hear me out.' His fingertips tapped on the desk, perhaps betraying some inner irritation. 'I have had the privilege of tending to your father's legal affairs since I myself was a young man. I first came to Castle Dragutin as a junior, but for reasons known only to Baron Dragutin he insisted his dealings with the firm I then worked for was done entirely through me. Perhaps it was my youth. He had a certain fondness, one might say fascination, with the young. You may come to hear many things about your father whilst you are here, but I urge you not to treat them all seriously. Myth, legend and superstition have conspired to create...' He paused. The drumming of his fingertips increased in tempo. '...to create a situation where it has become difficult to separate out truth from falsehood.'

'And has that anything to do with why the village woman spat at me yesterday, or why Zsigmund and Margit refuse to look me directly in the face?'

The old man studied Mason closely. 'Alas, those things are symptomatic of what I say. Needless to say, you must remember that this is not California, Mr Mason; this is a remote community whose traditions and customs have little altered in many hundreds of years. It might be 1927, and we live in a so-called modern era with automobiles, ships, aeroplanes and trains that appear to be shrinking the world, but for people who live hereabouts the outside world is a rare intrusion, and in the villages it has made little or no impact. They hold true to their superstitious natures, as did their forebears. You will have to make allowances for their apparent backwardness. Not least because of his private nature, your father has become enmeshed into that superstitious fabric, so much so it is doubtful it will ever become untangled.'

'You say they feared him. Why is that? And why has that fear passed to me?'

'We move ahead of ourselves,' Horvat said, holding up a hand as if to stem the flow of the conversation. 'We shall return to the business of the will.'

'Before we get into details,' Mason interrupted firmly, 'what I really need to know is how I came to be separated from my real mother and father, how I never even knew all this existed and was led to believe that another woman was my real mother. As you can understand, my life has been turned completely upside down and part of me is as angry as hell. I want some answers.'

'Yes,' he returned, adjusting his spectacles. 'I can appreciate that, Mr Mason.'

'I want you to tell me more about my father,' he insisted. 'Who was Baron Jozsef Dragutin? You've avoided telling me much about him, and I want to know why.'

Horvat stroked his chin. 'Very well. The truth, Mr Mason, is that not a lot is known about your father's early life. Even his exact age at his death is under dispute. He was born around the year 1821 or '22 in Budapest, apparently into a family boasting a noble lineage, perhaps even having links to the Boyars, the indigenous Hungarian aristocracy. Yet before his death he burned many of his papers which might have confirmed this.

'As I say, his younger life is shrouded in mystery, but it was Baron Dragutin himself who told me about his time as a mercenary, joining whatever war was to hand. It is true he appeared to revel in his tales of the bloodletting of his youth, and I confess he became greatly excited and animated whenever he related these stories. But as to which European wars he was involved in, he was careful never to reveal, and it was none of my business to pursue it. He once told me the war itself and the reason why it was being fought was unimportant; it was the opportunity of taking part which drew him like a moth to a flame. He spoke freely of the cruelty committed in the name of war, as if it were a sport, hounds setting about a cornered stag or fox.

'Castle Dragutin had long been in his family's possession, and he had resided here many years as an older man, but around 1880, when Hungary gained unrestrained rule over the Slavs, Baron Dragutin acquired more land by ousting its Slavonian owners, and even more power and control over the people. He was already aged about sixty. German and Hungarian landowners, your father amongst them, brought in labour from outside, forcing Slavs into greater poverty, and with no employment, their lands reduced, this persecution and oppression, as Slavs call it, left them little choice and caused a mass exodus to America to seek better lives.

'Your father relished this addition to his already considerable power and influence. Exactly what his role was for the Budapest authorities we shall never know for certain; but he was hated by the Slavs as a sadistic symbol of Hungarian Imperialism.'

'Sadistic?' Mason said.

'There are many tales told about your father, Mr Mason, as I said earlier. They tend to filter down like water through rock, and as such sometimes it takes many years for them to come to light. Rumour started to circulate that during his time as a mercenary he had taken much pleasure in the torturing of his prisoners. He would devise ever more cruel methods to inflict pain, for no other reason than to inflict pain itself, and he would calmly observe its results. One such tale told how a favourite method of his was to strip the skin off his victims using pliers.'

'Christ!' Mason said. 'That's inhuman!'

'The victim could take days to die. But of course, you must understand they are only tales told by old men who said they knew your father, and their details become richer and ever more gruesome with every telling. Hate amplifies even the tiniest rumour. Yet what little your father told me about his time at war, or the reasons he included himself in it, did nothing to water down those rumours.'

'Are you saying you think he was actually capable of such terrible acts? Even relished them?'

'I am saying it is not without the bounds of possibility.'

'But for that hatred to pass down to me there has to be more. I mean, hatred has become fear, hasn't it? They had a reason to fear him, even fear me. What's driving that?'

Horvat sighed. His lips looked thin and pale, his eyes were troubled pools. 'The devil is driving that fear, Mr Mason, as the devil drives much that is still to be feared in Slavonia – or so the locals will have you believe.'

'That's crazy,' Mason said dismissively. 'Who believes so strongly in the devil these days?'

Horvat shook his head. 'Good and evil, Mr Mason. Two forces perpetually waging war against each other. That's what people here believe. As they believe your father, on the side of evil, made a pact with the devil to further his own earthly aims.'

Mason laughed out loud. 'He did a deal with the devil? You can't be serious.'

'I am never anything but. I relate the facts as I know them. This story was told by a man who knew you father personally, a fellow mercenary, who was also responsible for relating many of the so-called truths circulated about your father, about his sadistic pleasures, about his unbridled lust for great wealth, great power.

'The story goes that Baron Dragutin openly confessed he would willingly sell his soul to the devil to have eternal youth, to indulge his perverse passions without regret or ramifications. He was heard to brag – whether to strike fear and awe into people, as was his way – that he had found a means of conjuring up Satan, that he'd relinquished his soul to the beast in return for all he desired. But as is the way with such things, there would be a price to pay. That price, he said, was to forfeit the soul of every Dragutin heir. His entire line, he confessed was cursed to do the work of the devil for all eternity. The last clause, he said, was that he must produce an heir before he died so that the devil's curse might continue.

'And so it is said that Baron Dragutin did indulge every vice he wished, no matter how vile or inhuman. Tales abound. Tales, even, of him torturing people in ways so brutal they were said to be the acts of the devil himself; and a habit of bathing in tubs full of the hot blood of freshly murdered young women, which he believed helped keep him young and handsome.'

'But that's absurd, surely?' said Mason. 'Even if any of these violent acts had been true he'd have been found out, put on trial at some point. It's a case of drunken tongues wagging in order to get another beer, that's what I think.'

'Ah, but think on, Mr Mason. What if the pact with the devil were true? He might commit any crime without consequence.'

'Which of course is total baloney. As a logical man in the legal profession you know it to be nothing more than foolish superstition.'

'I know of three men who came forward independent of each other, relating details of such crimes it caused the blood to freezer, so logic would then ask me to consider such stories as having a basis in reality. Then there are more recent local tales – admittedly tales that might be the product of the resentment of so-called Hungarian Imperialism – but still in circulation nonetheless. Young women going missing, and fingers pointing in Castle Dragutin's direction…'

'He was old, in heaven's name! He wasn't young enough to gallop around the countryside abducting Slavonian peasant girls. Pure nonsense! The stuff of old gothic novels.'

'Old, you say?' He smiled a knowing smile. 'You asked and I am telling, Mr Mason. Do you wish me to go on?'

He waved a hand. 'Sure, let's hear it; there's nothing showing at the Roxy.'

Horvat raised his brow. 'Quite. Well, whatever version of the truth you prefer one truth is without question and that is the fact of his disfigurement.'

'Disfigured? In what way?'

'One day Baron Dragutin was confronted by a prostitute he once knew. She was a woman who had been turned from vice because she said she had been called by God to do his work. One day she meets Baron Dragutin, swore the man looked as young as the day she met him thirty years before, and, in carrying out God's work, sought him out again and threw acid in his face in an effort to purge him of the devil. It is said his flesh melted away almost to the bone, that he was blinded in one eye and lost a great deal of his hair that would never grow back. You see, perhaps the devil has a twisted sense of humour. Baron Dragutin never expected to lose his looks so young; he expected them to vanish with age. Anyhow, from that day forward he took to wearing a specially crafted porcelain mask and never left the house. No one ever saw his real disfigured face.'

'That's a mighty fine story, Mr Horvat,' said Mason. 'But it's just that.'

Horvat rose from his seat and went across to a large cupboard. Taking out a set of keys he unlocked one of the drawers and took out a box covered in black velvet. He laid it carefully on the desk, opened the lid. Inside was a mask in pristine white porcelain, ribbon threaded through holes so that it could be fastened to the face.

'Do you recognise the face?' he asked Mason.

He screwed his eyes up in thought. 'Yeah, it looks vaguely familiar.'

'That's because the face belongs to Antinous. It is the same as the statue downstairs. Antinous was born to a Greek family in the Roman province of Bithynia. He was Emperor Hadrian's lover. Antinous drowned in the Nile. Hadrian was so grief stricken at his untimely death that he proclaimed him a god, out of which a cult of Antinous grew. Cities have been named in his honour, coins minted bearing his likeness, and many, many statues erected to the handsome young man. Your father said the face of Antinous was the most beautiful face he'd ever seen, and so had this mask cast in his likeness. It became the face he wore until his death. A god's face. I knew your father from being a young man, and I never once saw him without this mask, or one of its copies. All I saw were glimpses of his one good eye...' He pointed; one of the mask's eyes was blocked in, the other a blank hole. 'Here,' he said, offering Mason the mask. 'Careful, it is eggshell-thin, light as a feather. There are two others, in the drawer, which your father kept as spares. Take a look inside...'

Mason gingerly held it before him, looking deep into the sightless eye. He turned it around to inspect the interior of the mask. He frowned and then flinched involuntarily. 'Is this...?'

'Yes. He made a plaster cast of his face to ensure the inside of the mask fitted the contours of his disfigured face exactly. On the one side there is beauty; on the other side there is ugliness. If you were to make a cast of the inside of the mask you would get an impression as to what your father looked like in real life, but the little I can make out makes me shudder as it is.'

Staring into the inside of the mask it gave the optical illusion that he was staring straight at an image of the man himself and he almost dropped the mask in repulsion. He handed it quickly back to Horvat. 'That's plain grotesque,' he said.

'Yes, it is. Perhaps it is wise not to make pacts with the devil, eh, Mr Mason?' he said with a touch of cold humour, putting the macabre mask into its velvet-lined coffin and closing the lid.

15

The Breath of the Dead

Franz Horvat led Rick Mason outside. The sky was white, the land ash-grey.

'Snow,' said Horvat flatly. 'It'll be upon us before the day is done.'

Mason shivered, but it was more than the frigid air that brought it on. They were standing before a huge building, squarely constructed in austere grey stone, a metal-studded oak door flanked on either side by thick Corinthian-style pillars. Above the door was a crest carved in stone – the Dragutin crest, Horvat said – a sinuous dragon swallowing a lamb against a shield background; a variety of swords and spears forming an intricate lattice-work behind the shield. There was a magnificent bronze dome topping off the building, now turned green.

Doleful yew trees, their gnarled trunks twisted as if in agony and testament to their great age, stood on either side of the mausoleum, their shaggy branches reaching over the dome to touch in the middle, as if embracing it protectively. Horvat lit an oil lamp and inserted a finger-thick key into the iron lock of the door. The branches of the yew trees shuddered in a breeze as he turned the key, the noise of the mechanism sounding like some great machine part. A mound of dead leaves had accumulated near the entrance and his boots disturbed them as he opened the door, some of them scuttling inside the mausoleum like so many mice. Holding the lamp high, he bade Mason follow him inside.

It took a moment or two for his eyes to grow accustomed to the almost pitch-black interior, the feeble light from the lamp failing to penetrate the darkest recesses. A strong odour of damp and decay pervaded the room. In the room's centre was a large stone sarcophagus, the stone intricately carved with curling representations of ivy wrapped around a number of open-mouthed skulls. As with the crest outside, there were also representations of a number of weapons, from rifles to spears and swords, banners and military sashes, and a repetition of the Dragutin crest. Atop the sarcophagus was the marble figure of a dead man lying in state, covered by richly ornamented, flowing marble robes. Horvat brought the lamp closer to the statue to reveal the face of Baron Jozsef Dragutin.

'It is a face that is still young,' said Horvat. 'Forever so. A face that is uncorrupted, vibrant and healthy, at least on the outside.'

Mason went closer. The eyes were depicted as being open, not closed as in death, as if he stared upwards mockingly to heaven. Was he imagining it or was the expression one of defiance?

'You see, there is a strong resemblance to you,' Horvat observed.

Mason could see it but he didn't like it. 'In appearance only,' he qualified. 'So where is my mother's tomb?'

'It is not here,' he said. 'This place is for the Baron and the Baron only. Your mother is buried elsewhere.'

'I don't get it. What was so special about my father that would attract a young woman like Dorottya? A man you say was a deformed sadistic. Something doesn't hang right.'

Horvat stood still and silent for a moment, studying Baron Dragutin's marble face. 'Baron Dragutin, at the age of around eighty-one, a man who had never married, had never fathered a child, decided to remedy the situation. He was desperate to produce an heir. Perhaps it was his growing old, getting closer to death, which stirred these singular thoughts. Death is the great organiser, Mr Mason. Putting your life into order before it is extinguished – it affects us all.'

'Or maybe he believed his own stories about his pact with the devil,' said Mason mockingly.

'Or simply to produce an heir to whom he might pass on his estate. It is a natural urge for a man in Baron Dragutin's position. Whatever the case, I remember the time well. He became like a man possessed. I was sent out to find a suitable young companion. She had to be a woman of Hungarian birth, attractive, with proven child-bearing qualifications.'

'It's as if he was choosing a cow,' he said, sneering in disgust.

'I was a man given a task to perform. It is no business of mine to contemplate the motivations behind that request. Choosing a wife along such lines is not a new thing, Mr Mason.'

'So you say,' he mumbled.

'A number of suitable ladies were put before Baron Dragutin. From them the Baron chose Dorottya, a widow who had lost her husband and two children to cholera whilst abroad. She had no real family left living, and no great wealth to speak of. But Baron Dragutin singled her out for reasons only he knew. She was invited to Castle Dragutin, and there my responsibilities in the matter came to an end.' He fell thoughtful, staring down at the dead leaves that scuttled around his boots. 'But it is easy to wash your hands, as you say. The next occasion I had to visit Castle Dragutin I learned that there had been a wedding which no one outside knew about. Dorottya Szendrey had become the bride of Baron Dragutin.'

'So let me guess, she was some kind of money-grabber, after his title or something. It certainly wasn't for his good looks and sense of humour.'

'Dorottya was never that shallow, Mr Mason. A kinder, more honest and down-to-earth woman you would be hard-pressed to find. I assumed the marriage to have been the result of mutual agreement. I soon came to have my doubts. Dorottya, the new bride, was rarely to be seen. I asked after her when my business took me to the castle, but on each occasion I was informed she was ill or tired, or had suffered some other calamity that kept her confined to her rooms and shut away from view.

'Then one day she happened to find me in Baron Dragutin's office where I was waiting for him. She was in quite a wild state, her hair previously as neat as a pin was now deliriously unkempt, her dress equally so, and I noticed she wore neither shoes nor stockings. I asked her if she were feeling unwell, and she begged me to take her away from Castle Dragutin, that she was being kept a prisoner, that she had never intended or wanted to be the wife of Baron Dragutin; that she had never wanted to be the wife of the devil's advocate. She maintained she had been forced against her will into the entire thing.

'She was raving so, when Baron Dragutin came into the room and called immediately for a servant to take her from the room. He apologised profusely and said she was ill and not in her proper mind. I was concerned, naturally so, but he assured me everything was perfectly well. In fact, he said, they had something to celebrate, for Dorottya was going to have a baby, and he said the stress of this mental excitement, knowing that she had already lost two children to disease, was perhaps affecting her mind. She would recover in good time with the proper care and attention. I convinced myself this was the case.'

'And did she? Ever get better?'

Horvat seemed reluctant to go on, again staring hard at Dragutin's likeness as if it exerted some kind of hold over him. 'She found peace, yes,' he said cryptically.

'Where is she buried? I'd like to see her tomb.'

'She has no tomb, Mr Mason. A simple headstone.'

'Show me,' he demanded.

'We should be getting back to the house. I have much to show you and much to discuss.'

'Show me,' he said more forcefully.

He was glad to get out. Mason felt as if the cold breath of the dead blew on him. Being so close to the body of his father had somehow unsettled him, and no amount of reasoning on his part would make that feeling go away. Horvat locked up the mausoleum and led Mason down a stone path and into an overgrown section tucked behind the mausoleum, both men having to push back encroaching shrubbery and clawing brambles that had been allowed to get out of hand. Finally they came to a headstone, small, inconsequential, choked by weeds, sitting under the dank shade of another yew tree. The grave hadn't been cared for in the least, as if the dead woman had been dumped here and forgotten.

Mason bent to his haunches, swept back the tangle of weeds and dead grass. 'Why is she buried here, of all places?'

The name on the headstone was Dragutin Jozsefne – the official title she would have been referred to in written form. The suffix *ne* was the equivalent of *wife-of* or *Mrs*. Informally she would have been known by her first name.

'Dorottya Szendrey,' said Horvat, as if reading his thoughts. 'She was a pretty woman, aged thirty-three when she died.'

Mason cleared away leaves. The date on the headstone read 1869 – 1902.

'She died the same year I was born.' He looked up quizzically at the old man. 'So young...'

'Yes,' he said evenly, a curious faraway look in his eye. 'So young.'

'How did she die, and why has she been buried here, as if she had to be forgotten?'

He gave a shiver, which might have been a shrug. 'Twenty-five years ago I was invited to Castle Dragutin, both to celebrate the birth of a son – you, Mr Mason – delivered by Margit, and to take immediate charge of legal matters pertaining to your inheritance. Baron Dragutin appeared overjoyed, as much as I could glean from his voice, as his face was always behind his mask. It was almost as if a weight had been removed from his shoulders. He told me one evening, perhaps the spirits he'd imbibed relaxing his tongue, that life had made him a tired man, that the many years of the pain of disfigurement had been an extra burden he now could no longer bear, and that death would be a welcome relief. But that it wasn't possible for him to let go until he had a son. Until you came along, Mr Mason. However, his happiness quickly passed, for you were only a matter of a few weeks old when you disappeared.'

'What do you mean, disappeared?'

'You were kidnapped.'

Mason frowned. 'Run that by me again.'

'Mountain bandits after ransom money, or angry Slavs out to get vengeance – the Baron had made many enemies over the years. The oppression had created many dispossessed people, and a few took to living in the mountains, there to live the lives of thieves and bandits. A band of them broke into the castle, and clearly knew what they were after and where to go. There was evidence in Dorottya's room that there had been a struggle of some kind. Her jewellery boxes empty, her rings and necklaces gone. Apparently she fought hard. But unfortunately, during the kidnapping they dragged your mother to the balcony, the one in her room that overlooks the cliffs, and threw her over the edge. She died instantly on the rocks far below. Such a terrible night. A frantic search was instigated immediately to try and find you, but you had vanished without trace. We waited, but no ransom note ever arrived. No news came of where you were. The Baron never gave up searching for you. Not once in twenty-five years.'

'Dorottya was murdered? Jesus,' he said. 'Poor woman.'

'Then, many years later, certain unexpected correspondence came to light following the death of a village woman who lived but six miles from here. It transpired she had been in regular and frequent contact with a woman who had been raising you all this time – the woman you believed to be your mother. They also discovered clear instructions from this woman to burn every letter, which, fortunately for the Baron, hadn't been heeded. They provided details of your travels, how you had lived in Zagreb for a time, how you moved around Europe and, finally, when the money gave out, you went over to America. But the Baron was never to experience the joy of seeing you, for the day after I informed Baron Dragutin about your exact whereabouts, he died.'

'Why was I taken? Why did this woman keep me for so long if I wasn't her son? None of that makes sense. If it were purely for ransom they'd have made their move, and if nothing was paid they'd have abandoned me, or killed me. But she looked after me till the end. OK, so she acted like she resented me sometimes, but nothing beyond that.'

'Some things we will never know,' he said guardedly. 'It is believed you were sold like so much booty by the bandits, passed from hand to hand, eventually falling into the woman's hands. But enough of events we cannot fathom, Mr Mason. We must contend with the here and now.' He averted his eyes.

'The old guy wanted me here in person, didn't he? It wasn't really a stipulation of some Slavonian legal ruling.'

'Partly, yes, but not entirely. As for my part, I am merely carrying out the request he made. And now you are here. But that is no bad thing, Mr Mason. It is best you see this estate for yourself.'

'Is this about the curse, Mr Horvat? My father's sick request is so that I inherit more than his castle, huh?' he said mockingly. 'The man was crazy.'

'I do not believe in such things as pacts with the devil or curses, Mr Mason. I am a logical man, as you have pointed out.'

'But you followed his instructions to the letter, every step of the way, no deviation, whatever he asked of you, even though he is dead. Why is that, Mr Horvat?'

'It is my job.'

'Or is there something more?'

'I don't follow you, Mr Mason.'

'I think you do, Mr Horvat. You fear him, too, don't you? Even though the man is stone-cold under his marble statue, you still fear him like you did in life. You struggle, don't you, Mr Horvat, to separate out truth from superstition. I can see it in your eyes. You were afraid of him then and you're afraid of him now. He's still got some kind of hold over you.'

'I have my duties to perform, that is all. You read far more into things than is necessary.'

'OK, let me ask you; do you think I'm cursed now? Is that why everyone looks at me in that strange way? Am I now to become my evil father, take over from where he left off, doing the devil's work?' He said it half-mockingly. 'A curse? It was a load of baloney before, and it's still a load of baloney, Mr Horvat.'

'Quite,' he said shortly. 'And yes, you do inherit more than a castle, Mr Mason. You are also bequeathed the equivalent of nearly two-million dollars in investments and in bank deposits. You are a rich man. That is the reason I came to fetch you. Would I deny any man such an inheritance?'

Mason stopped short. 'Are you joking?'

'Please stop saying that, Mr Mason; it is getting tiresome.' He continued walking.

"Hell, you could have told me that before all the curse-crap! That puts a very different gloss on things!'

Horvat's watery eyes were solemn. 'As you say, Mr Mason. But a curse can take many different forms.'

* * * *

16

An Inescapable Truth

Mason stood up, looked up from his mother's grave and in the distance he saw a shadowy mound close to the ground. The shadow rose and became the familiar form of Margit. On seeing Mason and Horvat she turned and hurried away.

'What is she doing here?' Mason quizzed.

'It is nothing,' he replied. 'We must go inside now, I think. The snow must come soon.'

Ignoring Horvat, Mason went over to where Margit had been standing, amidst a tangle of weeds and feathery grass stems, dead and dried. A small patch of earth had been cleared and at its head was a headstone. It was new, the pale stone looking like a white bone sticking from the earth. He read the name carved into it. Lengyel Imre, 1883 – 1902. He looked at Horvat for an explanation.

'Imre was Margit and Zsigmund's only son,' he said.

'He died the same year as my mother, the year I was born.'

'Yes,' he said. 'He was so young, too, about nineteen-years old. When Baron Dragutin died the few servants who worked here all left. All except Margit and Zsigmund. They refused to leave their son. If it were not for them, the castle would have been left completely empty.'

'How did he die?'

'He was found murdered,' he said shortly, 'a few days after the murder of your mother. At first the talk was that he'd been involved in the kidnapping, working with the bandits; that's how they gained entry to the castle. But his body was found in the forest not far away. It was then said rather than working with the bandits he had stumbled upon them trying to break into the castle, and tried to prevent the kidnapping. They took him, maybe as a hostage, who knows? His body had been brutally tortured and his head staved in with a rock or some other blunt instrument. Margit and Zsigmund were understandably distraught.'

'But the headstone is new, recently erected as far as I can see.'

'The Baron prevented a monument from being put up when Imre died.'

'I don't get it,' said Mason. 'Why, if he tried to save Dorottya?'

'The workings of your father's mind have never been easy to understand.'

Then the snow came, as Horvat predicted. Fine, powdery, swirling almost mist-like around them. Soon the far mountains melted into the corpse-white sky and disappeared from view. Presently the snow tumbled down in large fat globs and forced Mason and Horvat to abandon their tour of the grounds and seek shelter inside. Mason did not need an excuse; the land was bleak, colourless and cheerless, like dead flesh, upon which stood Castle Dragutin like a crusty white scab. The atmosphere affected him deeply, seeped like the cold into his bones, his very being, and filled him with an uncharacteristic melancholy in spite of the heartening news of the fortune he was to inherit.

As Horvat continued his tour inside, leading Mason through empty corridors and silent rooms filled with sheeted furniture that had all the appearance of lurking spectres, the more his mood sank. Of course, he didn't believe any of the tales. It was mere suspicion born of hatred and even jealousy. But here, in the castle's full grip on the imagination, anything seemed possible. Even a logical man like Horvat wasn't immune to its inveterate, invidious influence. And yet so much remained unanswered, which disturbed him further. He knew Horvat was holding something back, but he wasn't easy to open up. And no matter that the tale of a Dragutin curse was nonsense, there was no disputing his father's undoubted unsavoury character. That wasn't an ingredient he found in the least comforting to have as part of his makeup.

Eventually he said 'I've seen enough for one day, Mr Horvat.' He felt drained to the point of exhaustion. He needed to get back to where there were people, light and warmth. 'And you still haven't told me how my father made his fortune.'

'Ah, yes,' said Horvat. 'It may sit uneasy with you, Mr Mason.'

'I'm getting used to sitting uneasy.'

'Baron Dragutin had long invested in armaments factories. He made his fortune manufacturing the weapons that killed so many during the Great War. What's more, his investments took little heed of national boundaries or interests. It is sobering to think that he made money from the shells that rained down on the allied armies, as well as the bullets that brought down many a German. Some people, Mr Mason, get rich off the back of making war. Your father was one of them. And rather fitting, don't you think, for such a martial man?'

'The bastard,' he said. 'Profiting from death.'

'You can always give away the money if it offends your sensibilities, Mr Mason,' he said. Mason remained tight-lipped. 'What we have not yet discussed are other stipulations of his will,' Horvat said.

'Discuss away,' Mason replied as they headed back. 'What else is Baron Dragutin insisting from beyond the grave?'

'The will and its legal provisions make it very clear that you cannot sell Castle Dragutin or its land until you have lived in the castle for a period of twenty years.'

Mason stopped and looked at Horvat incredulously. 'Jesus, I couldn't live here twenty days! I've never been in a more depressing place in all my life. If it's mine I intend to put the entire lot up for sale and be shut of it. There's too much bad feeling attached to it; I'd have the thing demolished if I could.'

'You are prevented from doing that,' Horvat said calmly.

'Then I'll contest the will.'

'It will do you no good, Mr Mason. You will have to trust me on this, as your father's representative. The rulings are legally watertight. I saw to it myself at his request.'

'So I inherit something I can't do a thing with. Unless I pack up and live here for twenty years – sure, like that's ever going to happen! I've heard of white elephants but as a white elephant this castle takes some beating. And what happened to what you said about everything falling into the hands of the state if I didn't get over here? Will it get the castle if I don't do anything; sign no papers, that kind of thing? It's one way of ridding me of it.'

'You must sign papers to get your two-million dollars, Mr Mason. And with the money comes the castle. You cannot have one without the other. They are legally bound together.'

'That's what we call a done deal in the States, Mr Horvat.'

'I did not make the rules, Mr Mason, I merely follow instructions.'

'So you keep saying. It's easy to keep telling yourself that isn't it, Mr Horvat?'

It appeared to strike home, for he flinched as if stung on the cheek by a bee. Then he recomposed himself immediately. 'Perhaps you will reconsider, in time. The castle exerts a strange hold on people. It has a habit of being able to pull you back time after time.'

'Well not this guy. I'll find some way of disposing of this place, one way or another. You'll have to help me, Mr Horvat.'

'I cannot do that. I am sorry.'

'My father is dead. You may work for me now.'

'Alas, this will be my final act for Castle Dragutin. Once the business of the will is concluded I shall be retiring. I will be free of having to work for anyone.'

'Help me out here, Mr Horvat.'

He shook his head firmly. 'I wish to leave Castle Dragutin and never return. It has sapped much of my life, Mr Mason. But I wish you the very best for the future, whosoever you deal with. But my final word; Castle Dragutin is with you now, even if you do not wish it. It is destined forever to be a part of you. It is an inescapable truth.'

At the end of the second day at Castle Dragutin the mood of the travellers had plummeted. The evening meal was subdued, though they had brought in extra lamps to brighten the room, and stacked the fire high with logs. They could hear the snow rattling against the window panes like rice being tossed onto an open umbrella. Mason didn't mention the fact he was now a millionaire, or the curious bindings of the will. For now he thought he'd keep that to himself.

Everyone appeared to be occupied with their own thoughts. Davey and Betsy were unusually quiet. Horvat explained that the snow might delay their departure by a day or so, but that it wouldn't interfere greatly with their travel arrangements and the various tickets booked for trains and ships, provided the weather didn't take a drastic turn for the worse. He made it clear to Mason once again that after he'd said goodbye to them all at Slavonska Pozega that would be the end of his dealings with the party and with the Dragutin estate. He finished his meal in unassailable silence and retired to his room. Davey excused himself and went to his room also, leaving Betsy reading a sheaf of papers by the fire and Mason staring at the dancing flames through a brandy glass. She appeared quite absorbed by what she was reading.

'What have you got there, Betsy?' he asked.

'Something Davey has written. He wants me to read it through, tell him what I think.'

It was the first evidence he'd seen of Davey's writing. 'Can I take a look?' he asked.

She seemed a little reluctant, but handed him a few sheets of paper. 'It's a novel he's working on,' she explained.

'Are you OK?' he said. 'You look a tad down. I would have expected, you know, in light of me asking you to…you know.'

'Down? So do you,' she noticed. 'I'm fine,' she added. 'Just the cold, I think, and this place.'

He read the hand-written story. Finally he laid the papers on his lap. 'This is great, Betsy. I had no idea he was this good.'

'He has a talent,' she said.

'Thing is, where did he learn to write like this? I mean, he's a mechanic, handyman, that kind of thing.'

She held her hand out for the papers. 'Natural gift, I suppose.'

'Come on, Betsy, this is professional stuff…'

'I don't want to discuss it, Rick,' she said smartly, placing the papers down on a table.

Davey entered the room. He glanced at his writing, picked it up and folded it. 'Just been saying, that's good writing, Davey,' complimented Mason.

'Thanks,' said Davey, sitting down and pouring out a drink. He put his pipe into his mouth, but had no tobacco to fill it with. He sat quietly, joining them in looking into the fire.

'Hell, this is so gloomy!' Mason said. He went over to a line of bottles and brought a couple back. He cracked them open. 'Let's let our hair down!'

The mood shifted perceptibly as the alcohol started to flow freely. Even Davey laughed a little, relaxing for the very first time.

'This castle, this entire country, it's very strange,' Davey observed.

'It gets stranger,' said Mason as the wind howled around the walls. He went on to explain what Horvat had told him about his father, his murdered mother, the curse, the kidnapping by bandits and finally the condition in the will barring him from selling the castle. Discussing it with Betsy and Davey had made him see the absurdity, even humorous side, to the entire thing.

'You don't really believe in that curse-thing, do you?' Betsy said with a mischievous gleam in her eyes.

He laughed. 'Not at all. A pact with the devil? It shows how backward this place is. It would make a great story though, eh, Davey? All the makings of a gothic novel.'

As if in approval the wind rushed down the chimney and caused the logs to spark and spit.

'This room – this castle – it reminds me of a huge set from a Hollywood movie,' Betsy observed dreamily, a glass of wine held to her lips. 'A creepy movie, all cobwebs, dust and death. It gives me the chills.'

Mason placed his glass down on a table, his brows furrowing thoughtfully. 'Yes, you can imagine the movie, can't you? A snowstorm ravaging the dark mountain forests. A coach is travelling a lonely road, through a narrow mountain pass overlooked by towering mountains. It's bringing with it a young woman to Castle Dragutin. The castle is perched on its lofty rock, white against a boiling, snow-flecked sky…'

'Yeah, and there's an old man, like Horvat,' Davey suggested. 'He's the guy who's brought the young woman here. Her name is Dorottya, and she's going to be the bride of Baron Dragutin.' He set his glass down alongside Mason's and leant forward in his chair. Betsy eyed him uncertainly. 'But we don't see the Baron at first. He's kept back. We get hints of him, hints of what he's done in the past, what he continues to do. Women going missing in the villages. That kind of thing. Then we get glimpses of him in his uniform, lurking in the shadows as the young woman waits to meet her suitor. She's seen portraits of the handsome young man, but she is not aware of his true age. She's been tricked. She doesn't know what's in store for her, because she's to be forced into marriage, forced to bear Baron Dragutin's son to satisfy the pact he made with the devil.'

'You've had far too much to drink,' said Betsy, the two men now so close together that their heads were almost touching.

Mason ignored her and continued. 'Then the chilling moment when she meets Baron Dragutin in the mask of Antinous...'

'And then, when his true face is eventually unveiled...' Davey said.

'Yes,' said Mason. 'The tension builds, the sense of horror grows. The woman has unlocked the secrets of Dragutin, and one last secret remains; what does he look like? She both fears and needs to see what lies behind the pretty-faced mask.'

'A close-up,' said Davey. 'Head and shoulders of Dragutin.'

'No, cut in close, almost to his face,' suggested Mason. 'Increase the horror. Dragutin's hands go up to the mask...'

'Dorottya puts her hand to her mouth in terror, but she can't turn away. She is transfixed,' Davey said excitedly.'

Suddenly Mason jumped to his feet. 'Do you know what we have here? Do you know what the hell we have?'

'A scary story,' Betsy said, downing her drink. 'A scary story for scary nights in a scary old castle in scary Slavonia.'

'It's a movie!' he said. 'It's our movie! Just the movie Metropolitan Studios are looking for. It's perfect. It has all the ingredients they're after, and what's more it's made for you and me, Betsy.'

'You and me?'

'That's what I said.' He sat back down, his hands working excitedly together. 'Davey, I've seen your writing, you're great. Betsy told me you had started to work on screenplays. How about you working on a screenplay for our movie?'

'Our movie?'

Dragutin's Bride?'

'I dunno...'

'Think about it; if we can drop something almost fully formed in front of Conrad Jefferson and Hal Bremner at a time they're looking for ideas they'll most likely jump at the chance. Davey, it could make you as a writer.' He looked up at Betsy. 'And this could be the start of your career. I mean, you could be cast as Dorottya. Why not? Like me you're cheap and an unknown.'

'Cheap? Thanks for that, Rick. I think Metropolitan will have its own thoughts on the subject of casting, you know.'

Undaunted, he turned to Davey. 'Could you do it, work on an outline for a screenplay?'

'Yeah, I suppose so...' He said, frowning.

Mason drained his glass, refilled it. 'How soon can you begin?'

Davey glanced at Betsy then turned back to Mason. 'First thing tomorrow,' he said, his lips breaking out into a smile that transformed his entire face. 'We'll go through the skeleton of a story first, then leave me to get together a first draft.'

'Great!' Mason said, sitting back. He raised a glass to the ceiling. 'Thanks, pops; you might just come in useful!'

The logs in the grate shifted and fiery devils of flame shot into the air.

'I think he heard you,' said Betsy.

* * * *

17

A Step Too Far

By the next day the land had turned white, and true to what Franz Horvat had said the road to and from Castle Dragutin was temporarily impassable. But that hadn't dampened the enthusiasm of the night before. Even in the sober light of day, Rick Mason remained excited with his newfound storyline and talked animatedly over breakfast about all aspects of it. Betsy looked on bemused as Davey and Mason sat in the drawing room before the window, sketching out ideas on sheets of yellowed paper borrowed from Baron Dragutin's office. She had not seen her brother so engrossed in something like this for so long. She thought she had lost the brother of old, but he was gradually coming back to her. Perhaps he was finally pushing what happened to him to the back of his mind. Perhaps he would forget that horrible, sick, corrupt man once and for all. Forget how he died.

    She grew bored and left the two men alone, deciding to wander the castle. She met Margit in one of the many corridors, but the old woman spoke very little English and Betsy no Hungarian, so they spent a good while grinning inanely at each other before parting company.

As she walked she could not help but remember that fateful day, how her brother came running to her, dishevelled and distraught, his words barely comprehensible, his hands soaped with blood. She comforted him, washed the blood from his hands as he sobbed uncontrollably. All would be well, she told him. He was her brother and she would take care of him as he had always taken care of her. They had to get away, she said, because if he were caught they would send him to the electric chair. And so they ran. They had been running ever since.

Most doors were locked or filled with sheet-covered furniture. She made her way up spiralling staircases and wandered floor upon floor of similar rooms, quiet and empty, as if the entire place were sleeping. Or patiently waiting.

The higher she went the chillier and more oppressive it appeared to become, and at one point she was so enveloped by the cold that she was on the verge of abandoning her aimless ramble and going back downstairs to the warmth below. But the sight of massive double doors at the end of a carpeted corridor on the uppermost floor made her stop and want to investigate. There were bulbous circular handles in the centre of each door, one of which she grasped, her small hand dwarfed by it, and turned it expecting the door to be locked. She pushed at it and the door opened.

The room was in darkness, as she'd come to expect. But she could immediately tell that this room was different from all the rest. It was very spacious, filled with lavish decoration, from the high painted ceiling dripping with plaster details, to the many paintings hanging from walls papered with richly patterned wallpaper. She noticed the room held a number of doors that beckoned her enticingly with the promise of further discoveries.

Betsy drew open the drapes at a window. They hid a pair of long, many-paned double doors that led out onto a stone balcony. Beyond this she could see the lake and mountains. She guessed the balcony overlooked the cliffs of the neck of land on which Castle Dragutin stood. The one from which Dorottya had been pushed by the bandits? Could this be Dorottya's room?

She tried the door knob, but it was locked, so she went to every window and yanked back the drapes, the snow-white light flooding in and momentarily blinding her. It revealed long gilded sofas, cabinets, tables, Turkish-style rugs at her feet and a pair of matching chandeliers above her dripping beads of crystal, like frozen tears.

It had a distinctly feminine feel to it all, she thought. Not half as austere or functional as the rest of the castle. She went around the room, opening cupboard doors and drawers and came across neatly folded clothes made from the finest silk, some edged with flourishes of beautiful lacework. The wardrobes contained lines of dresses and blouses on hangers, hat boxes stacked like so many bricks on shelves above them. There were rows of beautiful shoes, old-fashioned now but at one time the height of fashion. But the thing she noticed was how everything appeared to be unused, as pristine as the day they had been bought.

Betsy took out a pair of shoes, took off her own and tried them on. They fitted perfectly. How strange, she thought. Lifting out a long coat she slipped her arms into the sleeves and was surprised to find that this fitted also. As if it had been made for her.

'They belonged to Dorottya,' said Mason from behind her.

She started and put a hand to her chest. 'Rick! You startled me!' Then she laughed and began to take off the coat.

'It suits you,' he said. 'It makes you look elegant. Margit told me I'd find you up here. Decided to go exploring?'

'It's all very beautiful, but it's hardly been worn,' she observed of the clothes. 'Is this Dorottya's room?'

'That's because she died before she could ever wear any of it. Yes, it is her room, or rooms, as there are a number that lead off from this. Horvat showed me this yesterday, that's why it's unlocked. I told him I didn't like it being locked. Not after knowing what happened to her, poor woman."

'Do you think she was forced into having a baby?'

'What do you mean?'

'I don't know. There's something freaky about all this. About her being forced into marriage, being kept up here, in her room.'

'Raped? That's strong stuff, Betsy.' He shrugged. 'I don't like to think that I came into the world forced on my mother.'

She shuddered. 'I hate the thought, too...'

'Hell, it's a story, Betsy. This entire place is filled with them. The reality is probably so boring that's why they had to invent things. Never mind all that. Come with me...'

He led her through one of the doors into what had been Dorottya's bedroom. The bed was a huge affair, the headboard padded with green silk and heavy with carved wooden details edged in gold paint. She was drawn immediately to an iron ring fastened hard into the wall beside the bed. She lifted it, studying the two-inch-diameter ring. 'Whatever do you think this is?' she asked.

Mason wasn't listening. He went instead to a white sheet that was covering something angular and he lifted it off. Under it was a painted portrait of a pretty woman.

'That's Dorottya?' she asked.

'Yes, that's my mother,' he returned unemotionally.

'She's so beautiful,' she said, moving closer to the oil painting. 'Yet she looks so tragic.'

'Maybe that's just hindsight, or the romantic in you.'

'Your father was a monster. He took joy in killing, he tortured people and I reckon he made your mother a virtual prisoner and even possibly raped her.'

He shrugged. 'Not your average guy, I'll grant you that. Who knows what's true.' He draped the cover back over the painting.

'I'm so glad you're not like him,' Betsy said, linking her arm through his. 'You must obviously take after your mother.' Unexpectedly she sighed and said, 'You know, you mustn't lead Davey on so.'

'What do you mean, lead him on? I wasn't aware that I was.'

'All this screenplay business. It might all come to nothing. I'm glad to see him smiling again, coming out of his shell a little, but please don't make false promises. That could do more harm than good. The same with me, Rick. Metropolitan aren't going to give me a second glance in any movie you're doing for them. I'm a nobody. At least you've had a bite at the cherry and they can see the potential you've got. And you know as well as I do that even though the Baron Dragutin story is a good one they aren't bound to take it on board.'

He smiled at her. 'Do you still love me?' he asked.

'Since yesterday? Sure I do. I'm not so fickle, you know.'

'Even though I may not be the baron you thought I was, and penniless save for a dump of a castle I can't do anything with?'

'I don't care about any of that. It's you I love, not the phoney title. As for money, if things don't work out at Metropolitan then I guess we'll get by. People always do.'

'And what if I told you that I wasn't penniless and that I'd actually inherited a fortune?'

'Then I'd either think you were pulling my leg or out of your head.'

'I'm neither, Betsy. Straight up, I've inherited around two-million dollars. So to hell with this miserable old castle, it can rot for all I care. When we get back to the States it's a taste of the high life for us!'

She stared at him, open-mouthed. 'Have you been at that foreign hooch again, Rick?'

He grinned broadly. 'I'm far from drunk, Betsy; I'm a bona fide millionaire. So you know what? If Metropolitan Studios aren't interested in the movie I'll bankroll the thing myself.'

She couldn't quite take it all in. 'You're a millionaire? You're not having me on?'

'Cross my Dragutin heart,' he said. 'My father made a fortune out of manufacturing munitions during the war.'

Her eyes hardened. 'So he made money on the back of death and destruction. That figures.'

'Sure, but it's here now and it's what you do with it that matters,' he said.

'It's money made from other people's blood, Rick. It's profiteering. Nothing you can do with it will ever make it clean.'

'Does that matter?'

Her brows furrowed. 'It would have mattered to you greatly at one time,' she said.

'Well things have changed.' He laughed at her serious face. 'Don't worry, I'm not about to change into my father, am I?' He grabbed her hand. 'Come with me, I want to show you something.'

Her foot caught the cloth that covered Dorottya's portrait and it slipped away. Betsy found herself looking back at it. Dorottya's face appeared even more grave, as if her frozen eyes were trying to tell her something. It sent a shiver through her as Mason half-dragged her from the room.

They went back downstairs to Baron Dragutin's office and Mason opened the cupboard where his father's masks were kept. He took one of the black velvet-covered boxes out.

'I've smeared the inside of one of the masks with butter,' he explained.

Her face crumpled into confusion. 'Whatever for, Rick?'

'Then I melted a few candles and poured the wax into the mask. You see, he had the inside of each mask made to fit the contours of his disfigured face. By pouring wax into it I can hopefully make a cast of his real face.' He reached inside the box and carefully lifted the mask out.

'Are you sure you want to do this?' she asked tentatively, a little apprehensive.

'I wanted to see if it was as horrific as they say, or just a tall tale. You can almost make it out by looking into the mask, but this will let me know for sure.'

'I'd leave it be, Rick,' she urged, the troubled image of Dorottya floating in her mind. 'It's enough you want to bring him to life for the benefit of the movie, but isn't this a step too far? Let him be.'

He ignored her, his fingers prising away at the yellow candle wax. It came away from the porcelain mask quite easily, finally separating the wax impression from that of its mould. He slowly tilted it towards Betsy.

She gave a tiny scream of disgust. The flesh on the right side of the face had melted away, revealing skull-like teeth, an almost fleshless cheekbone. The eye socket was empty, the nose all but eaten away, the ear missing completely.

'Put it away, Rick!' she said. 'It's too horrible!'

He stared at the wax face, fascinated. 'You were one ugly son-of-a-bitch,' he said. 'And this is just perfect!'

* * * *

18

The Curse Lives On

Franz Horvat was staring out of the window. Dusk was folding over the land. The snow glowed as if illuminated by its own light, unreal, as if in a dream, he thought. The snow would keep them locked inside the castle for another day or so longer than expected. He shivered, his eyes watering with his intense gaze. How he wished this could all be done and finished with, that he might finally wash himself clean of this castle's dark hold on his soul.

Though he was careful never to let it show, he was glad Baron Dragutin had died. Immensely relieved. But he remembered he could not believe it when he stepped into the bedroom and looked down upon Baron Dragutin's dead, marble-like face. That horribly deformed, sordid, blasphemous face. They could not close his one good eye, though they had tried. In the end the doctor had placed a neckerchief over his face so his frozen skull-like glower would not upset people. The mortician will stitch down the eyelid, the doctor assured Horvat.

'Strange,' observed Horvat, 'that he insisted the likeness he commissioned for his tomb that sits in the mausoleum has its eyes open, and here he is defying anyone to close his eye.'

'Strange indeed,' said the doctor, but did not believe what he said. 'He was a strange man, was he not, Mr Horvat? But rest assured, even strange men die.'

'Are you certain he is dead?'

The doctor smiled at such a peculiarly naive question. Then he gave an insubstantial laugh. 'Of course the man is dead. There is no beating heart, no blood pumping through his veins.'

'The same as could be said of him in life,' Horvat murmured.

'He is dead,' said the doctor with clinical finality. 'No matter what a man did or did not do in life, he cannot come back from the dead. His sins, whatever they may be, will be answered for in a far higher court than we possess.'

'A curse lives forever.'

The doctor laughed, this time laced through with derision at the foolish old man. 'Mr Horvat, I had expected better of you than to believe in something so absurd. You had better tread carefully; you are starting to sound like those illiterate, clod-hacking Slavonian peasants outside.'

'I myself am Slavonian, doctor, though through necessity I had to change my name, as so many Slavs did under the Austro-Hungarian occupation.'

'That was no bad thing, and you have done well out of it.'

'You Hungarians treated our country like servants' quarters and our people like dirt beneath your boots. I for one am glad the war helped unravel Austro-Hungarian imperialism and limit the power of people like Baron Dragutin.'

'I didn't take you for a political man, Mr Horvat.' He took papers out of his bag. 'I will sign a death certificate presently.' He smoothed his wax-tipped moustache with an index finger, studied the corpse lying in the bed, candles burning on either side of it, and guttering so that it gave the impression the neckerchief twitched with movement from under it. 'The Austro-Hungarian Empire had been a civilising force in this backward country, Mr Horvat. Without it I see evidence that it will be plunged into the backwardness we rescued it from. We were never in collusion with the devil, though many would like to believe it was so. If reliance on superstition is you and your people's means of expressing yourselves then it is a sad affair.'

But Horvat knew what the doctor did not. The man had never met Baron Dragutin, had never had to gaze into that soulless eye that blinked from behind its forever-young, forever-beautiful mask of Antinous. He had never heard Baron Dragutin's chilling voice and the menace every word carried. He knew nothing of his corrupt life, his unhealthy, demonic urges that had to be satisfied. What's more, he had never been haunted by a dead man.

Franz Horvat had been plagued by nightmares ever since the Baron had died. He had visited him every night without fail. Dreams so real he woke awash with sweat, his heart crashing wildly in terror. And always the same message: carry out the task, or your soul will be taken.

Unreasonable fear? Perhaps. For dreams are not real, they are created in the head and they say they are reflections of deep, subconscious scars that need to be healed. They are not the place for dead people to make demands. That's what Horvat, as a logical man, had tried to tell himself. But he was tired, worn out with the nightly experiences, which were not getting better or fading with time, but becoming clearer, assuming the guise of hard reality with every nightmare. The Baron refused to die.

The snow outside had tried its best to hide the cheerless roll of the landscape, to obscure the mountains in the distance, like a virginal white sheet. But it was a thin, insubstantial disguise. It was there always. The poison could not be covered.

In this very room where he now stood, the Baron's private quarters, thinking about the past, thinking about the man he'd persuaded to come back to Castle Dragutin, he had been shown something by the Baron that he was determined no one else should ever see.

One evening – whether for sport or as a barely-disguised threat designed to keep the lawyer in his place – Baron Dragutin had invited Horvat to take a look at a few items in his personal collection. They had been discussing the terms of a will, at the time his young wife Dorottya being heavily pregnant. He'd suggested that the Baron might like to deal with another lawyer. The business with Dorottya had upset Horvat and he was more than ever determined to sever all links with Castle Dragutin. Dragutin did not take too kindly to the suggestion, and it was then that Horvat realised the full extent of Baron Dragutin's hold over him, over his very soul.

Dragutin lifted down a wooden box, the kind so often used by collectors to house their collections of coins or butterflies. Horvat shrank back in repugnance when a drawer was slid open by the Baron to reveal about ten slender bones, some bearing evidence of flesh, each about three inches long, and each bearing a ring – plain gold, signet, diamond, a wide variety.

'They are the ring fingers of some of the people I have personally killed,' said the Baron. 'See, each is carefully labelled so that I will never forget where, when or during which war their lives were taken. The rings are a beautiful touch, don't you think?'

Horvat's face paled in horror. 'You murdered them?'

'There is no such thing as murder in war, Mr Horvat,' he said, his voice calm, deep, unwavering, even for an old man. The mask remained expressionless. 'But I have one more thing to show you.' He went to a bookshelf and eased out a large black leather-bound volume. He handed it over to Horvat.

'It is a copy of the Bible,' said Horvat, puzzled.

'There was a man,' said Dragutin. 'A man who tried to kill me. He was sent by another, an enemy of mine, a fellow mercenary. It was a long time ago now, a campaign I scarce remember, and an argument over some spoil or other – gold, silver, a woman, I cannot recall the trinket. Mercenaries are such a vile lot, Mr Horvat; they will kill each other as easily as they kill their chosen enemy of the moment. But the plot to kill me failed, I had the would-be assassin apprehended and I had him taken to a forest where I ordered him stripped naked and tied to a wooden cross. I skinned him alive, Mr Horvat, peeling back his flesh an inch at a time. He lasted three days before dying. He confessed everything, of course; no man can resist the pain that being skinned alive brings. But I did not kill the man who sent the assassin. I terrified him. I used my would-be assassin's tanned skin to bind two Bibles, making a present of one to my enemy, whilst the other I saved for myself.'

Horvat looked at the Bible. He tossed it back at the Baron. 'That is monstrous and sacrilegious!' he said, wiping his hand on his trouser leg as if the human leather had transferred dirt to it.

Baron Dragutin's eye burned fierce behind his mask. 'No more nonsense about leaving me, Mr Horvat,' he said. 'I value your discretion too highly. When I am dead and you have completed what I ask of you, then your soul will be free to leave.'

His soul. Yes, he had heard clearly. And yes, Rick Mason was correct. He had been afraid of Baron Dragutin, and he still was afraid. He was sad that he'd been instrumental in bringing Mason back to the castle. It would never end, he thought, the Baron's all-consuming evil; it was like a poisonous barb, the castle's black venom already circulating in Mason's innocent system, already infecting his poor, unsuspecting soul…

He shook his head. Foolish, foolish old man, he thought. Superstitious nonsense. There was no devil's curse. There was only the evil made real by the living, breathing man that was Baron Dragutin, a man who had died and taken that evil to the grave with him. This young man was different. He was kinder, he had a warm heart. Baron Dragutin was dead and would remain forever so. As for his own part in things it had been his duty, that is all, the execution to the letter of a will's legal stipulations, no more. He was glad to hear Mason was heading back home, allowing the castle to crumble, fall into ruin. It would be a loss to no man. He would be free of it for good, and free of Baron Dragutin.

Franz Horvat looked down at the collection of finger bones, tipped the drawers of their macabre contents one by one into a paper bag. He would destroy these things, crush them to powder, and bury them in the castle grounds.

Next he put on his gloves and pulled the flesh-covered Bible from off the shelf. He thought he felt it shiver under his fingers and with a flick of the hand tossed it onto the log fire that burned brightly in the grate of a fireplace that bore the Dragutin crest. He watched intently but it appeared to defy the flames so he shoved a poker into the red-hot centre of the fire and caused the logs to crackle and spark. Eventually, the pages began to catch light, the leather to bubble as if it were erupting into black sores.

To burn a Bible tore at his heart, but he convinced himself it had been corrupted by its hideous binding, as Baron Dragutin intended it should. Then blooms of blue flame spread across the Bible's surface like sprays of otherworldly flowers, and Horvat sat in a chair and did not take his eyes off the fire until he was certain the unholy book would be fully consumed and transformed to ash.

'I want to leave this place,' Betsy said. 'I really do not like it.'

Rick Mason laughed. 'We will, as soon as we can. Look at these things,' he said, trying to distract her.

The old trunk was filled with military uniforms, medals, an ornamental sword in its scabbard, black leather boots wrapped in paper. He lifted out a blue jacket, resplendent with gold buttons, epaulettes, white piping and sleeves edged in red. He held it up in front of him.

'Put it away, Rick. I don't like it.'

'But it belonged to my father. Horvat says he preferred to wear uniforms to anything else.'

'Put it back in the trunk,' she urged.

'It might fit me,' he said, starting to unbutton the tunic.

'No!' she cried, taking it off him. 'Do not put that thing on.'

He looked at her, bemused, but saw she was quite upset. He laid it back in the trunk. 'You're getting jumpy. What's with you?'

'Nothing, Rick. Maybe making this movie isn't such a good idea. Maybe you just ought to let the man and his memory rest. What good can it do bringing him back to life?'

'It's a great story!' he protested. 'And it will make a great movie!'

'But that's just it, Rick; it's not a story, is it? It's based on truth, so let it be. Let's go back home, forget this place, and forget all about Baron Dragutin. Some things are best left alone.'

'No way, Betsy. This is gold dust.'

'You don't need gold dust, Rick, you're a rich man.'

'It's not about the money, Betsy. I'm not giving up on becoming a successful actor just because I happened to inherit some guy's fortune. I've still got dreams, and plans for you and me. None of that has changed. When I get back to New York I'll telegraph Victor in Los Angeles with our proposal, which should be in good shape by then. It'll be perfect, you'll see. When I show them the wax effigy of Baron Dragutin that'll clinch the deal.'

'You're not seriously going to use that, are you?'

'Sure I am! Audiences thought Chaney's Phantom was frightening. Well if we can replicate the Baron's face through makeup then we'll have them wetting themselves with fright.'

'He's dead, Rick. Leave it that way.'

'No, Betsy. I'm going to bring Baron Dragutin back to life. That's the magic of the motion picture. He'll live, he'll breathe, and he'll frighten and torture people all over again! The curse lives on! Hell, Betsy, think of the publicity! On movie posters six-feet tall; up there in lights above theatres – *The Curse Lives On!*'

* * * *

19

The Edge of Reason

The day came for their departure from Slavonia, and not a day too soon, thought Betsy Bellamy. She was more than happy to leave Castle Dragutin behind.

She stood in the yard before the brooding building, flapping her arms to fend off the cold, watching as the coach driver climbed down from his seat and silently began to load the cases onto the roof of the coach.

'What is that?' she said, pointing to a wooden trunk wrapped tight with metal bands. She knew what it was, of course, and it filled her with a chill equal to that which blew off the cold lake.

'A few things I need to take back with me,' Rick Mason said, avoiding her eyes.

'What can you want with your father's old uniforms and things? Leave them here.'

'I thought they'd be useful.'

'Please leave them behind, Rick,' she said.

He went to her, patting her arm lightly. 'Don't get yourself all hot under the collar, Betsy. It's only a few old clothes.' He turned around in time to see the driver bending down to the trunk. 'Here, let me give you a hand with that,' he said, darting to the trunk and taking hold of the leather strap at one end. Between them they heaved it up onto the roof. 'Make sure it's fastened securely,' he ordered. 'I don't want any damage doing to it.' He glanced at Betsy. 'It also has the masks in it,' he admitted.

Betsy sighed. 'You're not taking those as well, are you? They're horrible.'

'I need to take them and that's final,' he said, a look in his eyes she'd never seen before.

Franz Horvat trudged through the snow to her side, and the pair of them watched as Mason fussed over the strapping of the trunk to the roof.

'He's becoming obsessed,' she said to Horvat. 'If it was up to me I'd destroy the lot. Everything.' She looked hard at the castle. 'I don't know why, but I hate this place, Mr Horvat.'

'I cannot blame you,' he replied evenly. 'It might be best if you step inside the coach, Miss Bellamy, out of the snow and the wind. Look, your brother is already doing so.'

'He never once liked the cold,' she said absently.

'He is a quiet man,' Horvat noticed. 'We have scarce exchanged but a handful of words the entire time. Perhaps he is afraid to talk.'

'Afraid?'

'Lest he says something he should not. Is that the case, Miss Bellamy?'

'You're not so talkative yourself,' she countered. 'What are you afraid of talking about?'

He smiled. 'I have nothing to hide.'

'I used to know this guy, played poker professionally. He told me there are all sorts of ways you can read a man, when they're bluffing, when their eyes lie. He'd have taken one look at you and said you were bluffing, Mr Horvat.'

'I don't know about such things. I am not a gambling man,' he said, tipping his hat and walking over to the coach. He paused, held the door open for her.

Rick Mason stood and looked up at Castle Dragutin one last time. Part of him was also glad to be making tracks home. Yet something else clutched at his emotions, as if he were being drawn back against his will towards the crumbling old building. He tore himself away, shaking his head at the thought, knocked snow from his boots and stepped aboard the coach.

They drove back the way they had come, through dense, claustrophobic forests and mountain passes to the village of Krndija, which didn't seem to take half as long as the outward journey. A trick of the mind, Mason thought. Betsy was quiet the entire way, though he tried to engage her in idle conversation. At Krndija they struggled to find anyone who would help carry the extra trunk all the way to where the car would be waiting for them. In the end, Mason had to pay well over the odds for two young men from the village to carry the thing, but he said such a price was meaningless to a millionaire.

'I'm surprised you managed to engage anyone, even at that price, Mr Mason,' said Horvat. 'The feeling is such that I half-expected us to have to leave it behind. Had you not covered over the Dragutin crest with a pasted label, as I suggested, you might have found it thrown over the nearest precipice.'

They were taken by car to the city of Slavonska Pozega, where Horvat said he must part company with them.

'It will take a little while to sort out the final details, the transfer of funds from the bank here to one in California, but once that is done I expect my work with you to be finished,' he told Mason.

It sounded like a firm but unnecessary reminder, thought Mason, just in case he had other ideas. Mason thanked the old man, shook his hand, but Horvat seemed on edge, reluctant to let go of Mason's hand.

Mason said, 'Is everything OK, Mr Horvat? You look pale.'

The small city was busy, mainly horse-drawn vehicles crowding the cobbled roads, interspersed with the odd-motor car. They were standing outside the hotel in which Mason, Betsy and Davey would spend the night before setting off on their long train journey across Europe. The cases and Dragutin's trunk were being piled from the car onto the sidewalk where a hotel porter was bending to help carry them inside.

'Please, will you walk with me a while?' said Horvat. 'Just a little way.' His expression was grim.

'Are you going to tell me I'm not really a millionaire?' Mason joked.

Horvat took Mason by the arm and led him away from the hotel, down the street, across the road and towards a tiny park studded with bare trees. He bade Mason sit beside him on a bench.

'I have not been entirely honest with you, Mr Mason,' he began. Then he smiled nervously. 'Not to worry, you are still a millionaire. My people in the office down the way are working on your inheritance as we speak. No, it is not that which troubles me. It is about your father...' He stopped talking as if an icy-cold wind had taken the breath from him.

'What about him?'

Horvat's breathing seemed unduly laboured, as if the very air had grown desperately thin. 'I attempted to gloss over what your father was really like. I have tried to be a professional man, leave all my feelings at home, that kind of thing. But it is never that simple, is it? Yes, you were right; I admit I was – I *am* – afraid of your father, for I know what kind of man he was. The things he had been capable of...'

Mason tried to laugh, to make light of things, but he saw how serious the old man was and thought better of such a tactic. 'I'm all ears. More about Satan, is it?'

'Don't mock these things, Mr Mason,' he said suddenly, his eyes wide and fierce. 'Do not mock what you do not understand.' He shuffled uneasily in his seat. His hand was trembling. 'I have not told you the entire truth about your mother's murder, or your disappearance.'

'Go on.'

'I am more than certain the entire story about kidnappers was a fabrication to hide the true events of that tragic night.'

'Fabricated by whom? My father?'

He nodded. 'Margit's son Imre developed a soft spot for Dorottya. Perhaps he even loved her, in the way young people launch themselves headlong into love. She was a beautiful woman, Mr Mason, and I expect turned many heads in her time. And young heads turn far more easily. With hindsight, perhaps Dorottya even loved Imre in return. Or she may have been using him, who knows at this distance? It was obvious they had been in close contact, because Imre came to me secretly telling me that Dorottya was asking me for my help. But I refused…' Horvat lifted his chin so that he looked to the sky beyond the old city buildings; it was cold, white and unblemished. He turned to Mason. 'She and Imre had made plans for them all to be taken to a place of safety. To escape Castle Dragutin. Her garbled message was that she wanted to escape Satan and his curse and she depended upon me to help. I was the only person the Baron had ever allowed into his locked private chambers. That's where he kept the keys they desperately needed…'

'The keys to what, Mr Horvat?'

At this point he had to look away. 'The key to her shackles, Mr Mason. She was chained by the ankle, you see, to keep her in her room. A good length so that she might have the freedom of her rooms but little else. It was very brave of Imre to allow Dorottya to involve me, for if the Baron ever found out about their plans then the consequences would have been dire for them.'

'A chain? You're telling me my mother had been kept in chains?' Mason said. He thought about it. 'The ring in the bedroom, by the bed…'

'I assume the chain was fastened to that,' he said, 'for I never once saw evidence for myself of this chain.'

'Why didn't you tell me any of this before?'

'I admit I was ashamed to do so. I admit I first heard rumours of this chain from Imre some time before the murders. Not believing him, I went to his mother. Margit avoided telling me one way or the other, which piqued my unease. So I plucked up the courage to ask the Baron whether this story had any basis in truth, as I had not seen Dorottya in a long time. He denied such a thing, and being very annoyed he sent upstairs for Dorottya to prove it.

'She eventually came down, but her quiet demeanour, the way she avoided eye contact with myself or the Baron, caused me some concern. There was fear in her face, Mr Mason. Like a child afraid of a spider crawling over the carpet towards it. She stayed long enough to elicit but a few words that she was in good health and spirits and then was escorted back to her room. But before she left she turned quickly towards me and I caught such a pitiable look of despair that it tugged at my heart.

'But I behaved as a coward. I told myself it was none of my business. I convinced myself she was a little highly strung and that Imre's story was just that, the imaginings of youth and yet another example of how stories about the Baron's inhumanity were even now being fabricated. I chastised him for it and told him quite severely that if he ever uttered such foolishness again I would inform Baron Dragutin at once. I thought this had put a lid the affair, but when he came to me with details of their plan to steal Dorottya and her baby out of the castle I told Imre that I would have nothing to do with such an absurd plot. In the first instance, I told him, I did not believe in the existence of the chain, or that she was being kept prisoner but that she was obviously desperately ill to be talking thus and confined to her rooms because of this and nothing more. However, I told him I would not reveal the details of our discussion to the Baron if he agreed to abandon such ridiculous ideas and refrain from seeing Dorottya. I also told him that I felt he could no longer expect to stay employed at the castle and I would suggest to the Baron that he be removed. His presence was only aggravating a sensitive situation.

'But in the end it made no difference. You disappeared, Dorottya and Imre were murdered. And I stood by and let it happen. I could have saved her if I hadn't been so afraid. My crime of denial was as great as any crime the Baron committed. Dorottya's jewellery boxes were found open and empty, stolen by the bandits they said. But there were no bandits; Dorottya had cleared out her jewellery in order to finance looking after her child. To pay someone to take care of you, Mr Mason. It appears they had made secret plans for you to be taken from the castle and placed in safe hands, perhaps in the hope that eventually Dorottya would join you when she could find her own means of escape. At least that's what she must have told Imre. In his naïve way he might have believed they would make a new life together free from Baron Dragutin. But I fear she knew in her heart she would never leave the castle alive. She sacrificed herself for your sake.'

'So if there were no bandits, who killed Dorottya and Imre?'

'The answer lies in the chain that bound her. Following Imre's funeral, I pressed Margit for the truth about the chain, and she collapsed in tears telling me she had been afraid to confirm its existence to me when I first pressed her. It was true, Dorottya had indeed been chained, and she also told me the chain was never unfastened from her leg. Even through childbirth, and afterwards when she was briefly allowed to nurse the baby, the chain remained in place. Which means Dorottya could not have been thrown out of the window to the rocks below, not unless the chain was unfastened by Baron Dragutin's own keys.'

'You're saying he murdered my mother? He was an old man!' Mason protested.

'A man possessed of a terrible rage and with the strength of the devil!' Horvat retorted. 'Remember, she was weak. She maintained he kept her drugged. I now see that to be true.'

'And Imre – what happened to him? If the kidnapping was a lie, then that means… Are you saying Imre was murdered by my father, too?'

'Yes. There can be no other explanation. It was obvious someone inside the castle had been working with Dorottya to get the baby out, and it was relatively easy for the Baron to find out who had access to her rooms. It is my belief the Baron had Imre taken, tortured to find out where you had been taken, and when he refused to speak, he had him killed. The boy's death helped assuage his fury, no doubt. And he was the only other witness to the true events of that night. The Baron could not let him live.

'Poor Margit and Zsigmund. They suspected, of course. But they had no choice but to keep quiet and go along with the story of the bandits. They even confessed to seeing a glimpse of them, confirming the Baron's version of events. But they were frightened, Mr Mason. You see, the Baron insisted Imre's body stay at the castle as punishment for what their son did. He told them that whilst Imre's body lay within the walls of the castle, his soul was earthbound, and at any moment, should he command it, the devil would come and take their son's soul for his own and carry it to hell and damnation. He taunted and terrified them with this, Mr Mason, for they have strong religious beliefs. And so they are scared of you because you are his son and strongly believe you are cursed and share his association with Satan.'

'That explains why they looked damned afraid of me all the time. But Imre wasn't the only person who knew about the murders, was he? Someone else had knowledge. You knew, Mr Horvat. So why did you keep quiet?'

Horvat paused whilst someone walked by. He watched them out of the corner of his eye. 'There was no clear proof that bandits hadn't entered the castle, Mr Mason. I never once saw a chain. All I had were my suspicions. It might have been coincidence that Imre's and Dorottya's plans coincided with a kidnap attempt. There had been past attempts on the Baron's life.'

Mason sneered. 'Coincidence, my ass! You had more than enough information to go to the authorities.'

'You must understand, Mr Mason, your father *was* the authorities.' He lowered his head. 'He would have brought all his influence to bear down on me. And what was I but a Slavonian nobody? Up against the full weight of Hungarian autocracy I would have been discredited, ruined, driven from my home. I had worked so hard to build up my career. I was born of a poor, starving family, Mr Mason. I would not give it all up so easily. And Margit and Zsigmund would not have stood up against the Baron to give evidence in a court of law.

'However, I suspect the Baron knew about Imre coming to me with a request to help Dorottya and her child. After all, I confronted him with knowledge about Dorottya's shackles. And he was aware Dorottya had tried to speak to me privately about her situation at the castle. He could not prove it, of course, but he alluded to certain things that made me realise my own life might be in danger, too, and the lives of my wife and children. Looking back, perhaps it is easy to say I should have confessed all at the time, faced the consequences, but to put my own family at risk because of it? I could not do that. And you must understand this; he had a curious hold over people, and not just because of his political cronies in the authorities. We were all afraid of him. I confess I was afraid of his dark powers…'

'He had no dark powers! He was a murdering bastard! You should have said something, anything, not kept quiet about it.'

'It is easy for you to preach, Mr Mason, and it is a sermon I am more than familiar with, as I have been preaching it to myself for over twenty-five years. But I cannot undo what is done. In the end, I took some solace in the fact you were free of Baron Dragutin. But he never once rested in his efforts to locate you. He used everything in his power to find you, detectives, researchers...'

'Maybe I could forgive you failing to come clean about your suspicions about my father's part in Dorottya's and Imre's murders, but you still carried out his bidding, right to the very end; once they located me you came to bring me here to the castle even after the man was dead. You needn't have done that.' There was a sharp splinter of resentment in his voice. 'You could have told them to find someone else to do the work.'

'Fear, Mr Mason. You have yet to feel real fear and know what it can do to a man. He had the devil on his side. My soul was in peril. As it is now, sitting here telling you all this.'

'He's dead, Horvat. He can't hurt you now. Your pathetic cowardly soul is safe,' he added scathingly.

'I cannot make good anything I failed to do, but I can at least help prevent Baron Dragutin's evil influence claiming more lives in the future. I have seen you with Miss Bellamy. You have something special together. Forget about this film you are planning. Destroy all that you have in your father's trunk. Leave him in the past. Let him keep his sordid millions. Do not let any part of him touch and poison your life. Do all that I say and I feel you will be safe, though I cannot promise anything. Break the curse, Mr Mason. Here and now, otherwise your father will creep into your heart and blacken it.'

Rick Mason rose quickly from the seat. 'I can't do that, Mr Horvat. I don't believe in curses. I'm not going to abandon this story, my movie, or pass up my rightful millions to help make you feel better about something you should have done twenty-five years ago. And you know what, having that money will help compensate me for all the crap I've had to endure over the years. Thanks but no thanks, Mr Horvat. You've done your job again. Stick to it; it's what you do best. I'm not going to give up a future because you feel bad about the past. And don't fret – Baron Dragutin isn't going to punish you for what you've told me today, because, buddy, I've got good news for you; the old fucker is dead and once you're dead there isn't much you can do about it. All done with, finished, end of story. The best you can do is get a life and leave me to get on with mine.'

Horvat got to his feet, sighed heavily. 'Then we must part company,' he said, his old self taking over again. The timid, frightened old man had disappeared. 'Forgive my ramblings. Perhaps I am overly tired.' He smiled thinly. 'Goodbye and good luck with your future, Mr Mason.'

They shook hands, the contact brief, and Mason left Horvat in the park, walking towards the hotel across the road. He was deep in thought, and had almost reached the hotel doors when he heard a commotion behind him. A small crowd of people had gathered in the middle of the road, someone trying to steady a black horse that was neighing loudly and jerking the coal cart to which it was attached. Mason had a strange feeling come over him and went over to the crowd. He eased his way through.

Lying on the floor, blood foaming at his lips, was Franz Horvat, stone dead, his chest crushed flat.

'I don't know what happened,' said the coal cart's distraught driver in Hungarian. 'The horse went crazy, just took it into its head to bolt for no reason. This man went under the horse's hooves as he was crossing the road; the wheel, I felt it go over his chest.' He shook his head, dazed. 'It was almost as if the horse went for him,' he said.

Mason looked up at the wide, wild eyes of the huge black horse. It appeared to stare right into him. Its yellowed teeth, locked around the bit, took on a slobbering, malevolent grin.

* * * *

20

Our Davey

He saw the two guys hanging about the yard through his office window. He swung his feet off the desk, leant forward to sneak a better look, crushing his cigarette out into a metal ashtray. Frank Macey had seen such guys before. They were either cops or hoods working for some big shot somewhere looking to muscle-in on someone else's territory. He thought he'd seen the back of protection rackets but these guys looked similar to those who'd been running them back in Illinois.

He squinted. Nah, they had to be cops. They wore casuals, good quality, but that didn't fool Frank Macey, no sir. They were asking one of the two mechanics he employed a few questions. The mechanic was stooped under the hood of a car. He stood up and wiped his hands on a rag whilst he talked to them. Then he pointed over in his direction and the two men sauntered across to Frank's office.

Shit, what kind of trouble was heading in his direction now, he thought? He'd come to California to escape trouble, set up Frank Macey's Auto Repair Yard and thought he'd found a sunshine-lit corner of the country where he could live an easier life. But he discovered Los Angeles was as bad a place as anywhere else.

The glass-panelled door to his office swung open and the two men stepped inside.

'Hi,' one of them said, whipping his hat off and wiping a sleeve over his forehead. 'You Frank Macey?'

'Depends who's asking.'

The man grinned. His face was red, like he'd been caught out in the Sun too long.

'We just wanna ask you a few questions.'

'You the law?'

'Maybe.'

'Maybe I want to see some ID,' said Frank.

He flashed ID, stuffed it back into his pocket. 'Do you know anyone by the name of Peter Harvey?' said the other guy. He was younger, hard-faced, had all his sense of humour surgically removed, thought Frank.

'Don't know anyone called Peter Harvey,' he said truthfully.

The man took a photograph out of his pocket, showed it to Frank.

It was a police mugshot. A young kid captured in the glare of the flash, like a scared rabbit in headlights. He looked over the photo.

'Have you seen him?' said the first man, slapping his hat back on. 'This is the only photo we've got of him, when he was a kid arrested for petty larceny. He's a lot older now. Take a close look; does it jog your memory?'

Frank Macey looked hard at the crumpled photo, shook his scraggy head. 'Sorry, guys, I've never seen this kid before.'

'He's older now...'

'Whatever, never seen him. What's he done?'

'You ever heard of the Louisiana playwright John Saunders?'

Frank's eyes remained glazed. 'Do I look like I ever heard of any playwright?' he said. 'Hell, I don't even know what a playwright does.'

'He writes plays,' said Mr Hard Face scratching at his balls. 'He's a dead writer of plays, to be more exact,' he added. He took the photo from Frank. 'This guy Peter Harvey shot him dead. Three bullets to the chest, another to his head at close range when he was already stiff on the floor. Harvey sometimes used to get work as a grease monkey. We got wind he was in this area and we're checking out all the repair yards he might try to find work.'

'Well I'm sorry I can't help you there, fellas; I ain't ever seen this guy Harvey before. There's just me an' Billy an' Jo-Jo there.' He nodded towards the yard. The mechanic was back under the hood again.

'You see him you let us know, OK?' said the first man, handing him a card with a pencil-written number on it. 'He's a dangerous son-of-a-bitch.'

'Sure will,' he said. The two men left the yard, getting into an automobile and driving away. He waited five minutes or so and then went out to the mechanic. 'Billy, what did you say to those fellas?'

'Nothing, boss,' said Billy. 'They just asked for the owner and I pointed you out. What they want?'

'They showed me a picture. A man they're after.' He paused. 'It was Davey.'

'Davey? What they want Davey for?'

'They say he murdered some fancy writer in Louisiana.'

'Jeez! Davey?' He shook his head. 'Our Davey?'

'You heard from him at all?'

'Not for weeks, boss. He just disappeared.'

'Well make sure he stays disappeared. I don't want anyone finding out I take on people who don't pay their taxes, let alone people who also take to murdering fancy writers, you understand? You get into big trouble avoiding tax and things, Billy. If anyone else comes sniffing around asking for Davey, or anyone called Peter Harvey, you never heard of any of them.'

'Peter Harvey? They looking for him, too?'

'Davey and Peter Harvey, they're the same, you moron. You never heard of him, got that?'

'Yeah, boss, I never heard of either of them.'

'We don't want to get mixed up with the law; I need to avoid that kind of nosing around. You get the picture?'

'Yeah, boss, my mouth's all buttoned-up. Davey shot a man, you say?'

'Sure did. Then shot him some more for good measure.'

'Jeez! Our Davey?'

'He ain't our Davey no more, OK, Billy?'

'OK, boss.'

* * * *

Part Three

The Devil Rises

21

Long-Time Friends

Pale, watery moonlight filtered through the slender arched window, casting its spectral shape upon the steps of the spiral staircase. Almost total darkness lay around this single pool of unearthly-looking light. A man's foot stepped into it, the light bouncing off polished knee-high boots of black leather. Slowly he descended the stairs, the patch of light travelling up his thighs to his midriff, rising to his chest, and then he stopped, his face immersed in shadow.

'You cannot leave,' he said, his voice deep, his Hungarian accent as heavy as the cloying air. 'You know you can never leave.'

The woman turned around, her eyes circles of fear, her spidery dark lashes unblinking, lips painted with thick lipstick parting as if to form words, or release a scream. She raised a crooked arm in terror, to try to shield herself from him. Then she desperately tried the door again; it was locked, would not budge.

He glided slowly down the stairs, padded purposefully and unrushed across the tiled floor towards her. She struggled with the door, scratched at it with her long nails as if trying to claw her way through the wood, her head flicking back to look at him. He loomed closer, his shadow falling over her like a chilling black blanket of death. She turned to face him, her back rigid against the unyielding door, her features contorted by abject fear and yet so mesmerised she could not tear her eyes from him.

The eye behind the porcelain mask widened, showing a large part of the eyeball and she had to put her hand to her mouth, cowering before the man as he folded gloved fingers around her slender white throat. She screamed and lashed out with her hand, knocking the statuesque mask from his face. It fell and shattered into a hundred tiny pieces on the unyielding tiled floor.

She looked up slowly, into the face – that monstrous, vile face of corruption and evil, and she screamed like she'd never screamed before, as if her very soul depended upon it…

A number of women in the audience screamed with her. One woman fainted outright and had to be carried from the theatre on a stretcher.

That's when Rick Mason knew they were onto a winner. That's when Conrad Jefferson leant across to his seat and shook his hand.

'We've cracked it, Rick!' he said, puffing on a huge cigar, grinning so broadly Mason thought he'd cut his face clean in two with it.

When the end credits rolled and the theatre lights went up, the entire auditorium was deathly quiet, then erupted spontaneously into a firestorm of applause. Mason and Betsy stood up, took a bow. A spotlight found them and the applause grew to deafening, thunderous proportions. Newspaper reporters, invited along to the premiere and not really expecting that much from the latest Metropolitan

Studios movie, swarmed around them like wasps around jam.

'Who devised your makeup, Mr Mason?'

'I did. I invented it. I'm a fan of Lon Chaney...'

'They tried to ban this movie, that right?'

'Sure they tried,' said Jefferson. 'We beat the censors.'

'Is it true that *Dragutin's Bride* is a movie based on the life of your own father, Rick?'

'Never knew my father,' he said evasively.

'Listen, guys,' said Jefferson, wafting them away, 'another time, huh? You'll all get your shot.'

'Miss Bellamy! Betsy!' someone hollered. 'Did he frighten you in that makeup?'

She smiled. 'I wasn't frightened at all,' she said. 'I'm hardly going to be frightened of a man I've just married!' She laughed, clutching Mason's arm tightly as the crowd of people pressed closer.

Jefferson bent close to Mason's ear and spoke quietly into it. 'Enjoy it, Rick, you've earned it. I know box-office gold when I see it, and I'm seeing it good and strong now. Trust me, life ain't going to be the same for you and Betsy from now on.' He slapped Mason firmly on the back.

Someone from Jefferson's large entourage was fending off hungry reporters, who complained they had more questions to ask. A few bulbs flashed on cameras, as if lightning burst into the auditorium. Jefferson took Mason by the arm, tried to lead him away.

'We've got to speak to them...' Mason complained.

'First rule of publicity, leave them gagging for more. Don't worry, there's a press conference been arranged. For now let's get you both out of here, crack open a few bottles of champagne to celebrate at my place. Leave this to our press agent.'

'Did you see that?' Mason enthused breathlessly as Betsy and he tumbled into a waiting car. 'They loved it! They loved us! Betsy, you were brilliant up there. The screen was made for you! I'll bet Jefferson's thanking his lucky stars he listened to me.'

She was waving to disappointed reporters who were hammering on the car's windows as it drove away. She blew them a kiss. 'He was right, though, that reporter,' she said.

'About what?'

He asked me if you'd frightened me during filming. You did frighten me, remember? Keeping the makeup secret till we filmed the scene.'

He waved it away. 'But it was all worth it, Betsy. This is beyond my wildest dreams. Hell, they loved us, Betsy! We're going to be famous!'

'Now that's scary,' she said.

'You know what, it couldn't get any better,' he said, relaxing into the car's plush leather seat and placing his hands behind his head. What a swell day!'

'That depends. Maybe it can get better.' She opened her handbag and checked her makeup in a compact.

'Yeah? In what way?' He was smiling like a kid who's got the keys to a candy store.

'Well that depends if you ever saw yourself as a father…'

His eyes narrowed, then realisation seeped in. 'Are you trying to tell me what I think you're trying to tell me, Betsy?'

'I'm pregnant, Rick,' she said guardedly.

'With a baby?' he burst.

'What else, a horse? Of course it's a baby, you fool! You're going to be a father.'

He threw himself against her, smothering her face with kisses. 'Jeez, Betsy, we're having a baby!' He shouted to the driver up front. 'You hear that? We're going to have a baby!' The driver waved back at him in acknowledgement. Mason wound down the car's window and put his head out and shouted at the top of his voice: 'We're having a baby!'

She dragged him back inside. 'I take it you're pleased, then?' she said, smiling nervously at him. 'I was a little concerned about telling you. Now might not be the right time to have kids...'

'You bet I'm pleased! This has to be one of the most amazing, beautiful nights I've ever had!' They held each other close, their heads touching. 'I reckon it's a boy, or a girl,' he said.

'You don't say.'

'Baron Dragutin is going to be a father!' he said theatrically.

She pulled away from him, her expression suddenly very stony. 'No, Rick, Baron Dragutin is not going to be a father; Rick Mason, husband of Betsy Bellamy is going to be a father.'

'Sure, honey, I know that. I was just joking, is all.'

'Some things are not that funny, Rick,' she said.

'Come here,' he said, taking hold of her again. 'Don't spoil it. It's marvellous. The best news ever.'

'Don't you go letting Conrad Jefferson know about this, or anyone else for that matter,' she warned. 'At least, not until Victor Wallace manoeuvres a better deal on my contract with Metropolitan. You're OK, they gave you three years; me, I've got this one movie so far. The news that I have a kid on the way won't go down well. I know that guy.'

'You don't have to worry on that score, Betsy. Things are going to work out just dandy. I heard him telling Hal Bremner about a follow-up movie. They want to speak to me about it in a few days. It's just as much yours as mine.' He saw how glum she looked. 'You're the heroine, remember? You defeated Baron Dragutin. Any movie has to have you back in there.' She avoided looking at him. 'Are you OK, about the baby, I mean?'

She shrugged. 'I don't know, Rick. Things are just starting to take off for me and now I'm going to start growing a bump. You know as well as I do that the studios don't like their actresses growing bumps and becoming mothers. If they really do push ahead with another movie I might not be in a position to…'

He put a finger to her lips. 'You'll be fine. Don't look so down. It's supposed to be a happy time for us.'

'Sure, for you maybe. But things aren't that simple for a woman in Hollywood. If being pregnant screws up my big break…'

'It won't!' he said, clasping her hand.

'It's what I've always wanted, Rick. My dream. I don't want this to ruin things.' She frowned. 'Maybe this just isn't the right time for me to be having a baby…'

'Hold on there – what are you saying here?'

'We can have kids any time. We're young…'

He shook his head emphatically. 'No, absolutely not; whatever you have in that head of yours you can scrub it out once and for all. We're having a baby – our baby, Betsy. I promise you that you'll have your career, too.'

'You promise me that?'

'Absolutely! I love you, Betsy.' He placed a hand softly on her stomach. 'I love you both, you and the horse.' He laughed, put a finger under her chin and raised it. 'Smile, in heaven's name. Things can't be going any better for us. I inherit a fortune, we get married, we made a hit movie…'

'Let's not count our chickens, eh, Rick?' she warned. 'One premier doesn't a hit movie make.'

'We made a hit movie,' he emphasised, 'and we're going to be parents. Life is on the up, Betsy, and you and me deserve a piece of that. Lord knows, we've struggled hard enough in the past. Don't knock good luck when it comes knocking.' He fell thoughtful for a moment. 'Shame Davey couldn't have been there to see it tonight. If anyone deserves plaudits it's him and that screenplay he came up with. It bowled over Metropolitan's executives like they were ninepins. Why the hell does he want to keep such a low profile? I thought as a writer he'd be up for it.'

'He's got his reasons,' she said, glancing in the direction of the driver.

'But to refuse to even be credited on the movie…'

'Like I say,' she said stiffly. 'Look, can we discuss this some other time?'

'We're here,' said the driver, pulling up outside the front of Conrad Jefferson's mansion. Lights were burning brightly, people were standing on the lawn outside, dressed in fancy tuxedos and dresses. A party was already in full swing. A number of other limos were spilling guests. The driver went round to the passenger door, opened it for Mason and Betsy and the pair stepped out into the fine Californian evening. A knot of guests started to applaud, their cufflinks and tie studs, bracelets and rings glinting in the lights. 'Congratulations,' sir, said the driver as Mason passed him.

'Thank you,' said Mason, momentarily lost for words at the attention they were receiving.

The pair was sucked into the glitzy maelstrom, and suddenly it was as if everyone had been long-time friends and wanted to get up close to touch them.

* * * *

22

You Can Never Escape

Such a turnaround of fortune like this can only happen in Hollywood.

Movie aficionados might remember it wasn't so long ago that Rick Mason's star seemed to be going out following, quite frankly, a couple of stinkers he starred in for Prima Motion Picture Company. The now infamous "timber" quote about his so-called (and undeserving) wooden acting appeared to be the final nail in his acting coffin. But as many a movie-goer knows, all that is far behind the new 'King of Terror'.

And not a moment too soon for ailing studio Metropolitan. Shares in the company had sunk to an all-time low, with internal wrangling threatening to tear the organisation apart and Conrad Jefferson fighting to keep the creaking ship afloat. Many argued it was a risk investing in a new genre for the studio, a cast of relative unknowns for the leads and by producing a talkie. But it looks like they knew something we didn't, because it all paid off for them. Mason was a revelation as Baron Dragutin, and Betsy Bellamy as Dorottya, a newcomer with star potential. Nice move, boys!

The distributors have been busy, too, milking the cash-cow while they can. Since the premier, **Dragutin's Bride** *opened simultaneously in hundreds of theatres across the country, and we've been reliably informed that the motion picture has grossed ten-times its original production costs and it's still climbing.*

So what is it about this picture that's driving people nuts? Terror, sheer terror. You've got to give Rick Mason and the entire production team credit here. Against a lavish backdrop (reports have it that it's based on a real European castle) Rick Mason has given us one of the most chilling, nightmarish creations in Baron Dragutin since Chaney's Phantom. Some say it's more frightening. I can't argue with that. Chaney, though, true to his generous character, was seen exchanging a few makeup tips with Mason, so no bad feeling there (Metropolitan's press agent would have you believe). But makeup aside, Mason's heavy European accent pays dividends in the sound sequences, sending shivers up the male spine and weakening feminine ones.

Talking of feminine, we must not forget the new darling of the screen, on-screen and off-screen wife Betsy Bellamy. Pretty, looking gorgeous in Edwardian dresses, she's the perfect beauty to Mason's beast. We predict great things for this gal once she's had time to hone her obvious talents. Whenever the couple turn up as some event or other – and they've been kept busy on that score by Metropolitan's publicity team – she attracts as much attention as her husband. Some stores are even displaying a Dorottya-range of clothing, which are selling like hotcakes to those wanting to indulge themselves in a little piece of doomed elegance.

You've got to wonder exactly how far Mason can take this – there are rumours of a sequel to capitalise on the success of Bride *– or more to the point, how far will Metropolitan push Mason? He won't want to be typecast, you can bet – he sees himself as a character actor with a broad range – but for now I guess he's enjoying being the centre of attention. Get it while you can, Rick; we all know the centre of attention moves like the centre of a hurricane, never stopping long in one place.*

So there you have it folks. There's money to be made in blood!

Rick Mason folded the newspaper, a self-satisfied smile on his lips. 'Even the *New York Times* love us, Betsy,' he said, leaning to look out of the car's window. It was late evening, but New York being New York, the streets were bathed in artificial light from shops and stores, from apartments, from hundreds of car headlights; and the sidewalks never seemed to empty of swarming people. Mason had the feeling he was being taken like a leaf down a fast-moving stream. He only knew it was New York because it was Wednesday. They'd be on an overnight sleeper someplace else later that night.

He turned to Betsy. She was quiet, huddled into a tight corner of the limo, almost as if she were trying to put a little distance between them. 'What's wrong?' he asked. 'You're edgy. Something spooking you?'

'You're spooking me,' she said. 'Why are you wearing those things? You know I don't like them.'

'My clothes? This is Baron Dragutin's uniform…'

'I know what it is, Rick. And they're not your clothes; they belonged to that horrible man. You don't need to wear them.'

'It's expected of me.'

'No it's not.'

'They've come to see Dragutin,' he defended. 'I'm giving them what they want.'

'They're coming to see Rick Mason and Betsy Bellamy, not Baron Dragutin.'

'It's called promoting the movie, Betsy,' he said shortly.

'It's called a growing obsession with the man, Rick. You've not been the same since we came back from Slavonia. Since Mr Horvat was killed. You've changed.'

He said, 'Don't talk nonsense!' He saw lines of people standing in a snaking queue on the sidewalk. A number of them started to wave when they realised who was in the fancy limo cruising past them. He waved back. 'It's this pregnancy,' he said. 'They say having a baby sometimes screws up a woman's emotions.'

'I'm tired, Rick; I want to go home. We've been on the road for weeks now, plugging this picture.' She stroked her midriff. 'The baby is due in three months and we never seem to have time to rest up, to have time for one another. Metropolitan is pushing you too hard. You're pushing yourself too hard.'

Mason clutched her hand. It felt cold. 'I'm doing this for the both of us. You know what Hollywood can be like. Like it says in the *New York Times* article, one minute you're the main course, the next you're leftovers being scraped into the trashcan. We've got to grab this while we can. You wanted to be an actress, babe, remember?'

Her face had a grey sheen to it. Her eyes distant. 'Seems lately you're more interested in your career at the expense of mine.'

'What's that supposed to mean, Betsy?'

'My role in the next movie has been so thinned out of the screenplay that I'm being reduced to nothing more than a simpering bit-part.'

'I fought to have the production delayed in order for you to have time to have the baby, Betsy, you're forgetting that. And it's not up to me how the movie shapes up, you know that.'

'That's rubbish and you know it. Metropolitan wouldn't have been able to finance Dragutin's Bride without you bankrolling a lot of it, and without Davey's brilliant screenplay. You helped steer the last movie, so what's different about this one? And anyhow, they've managed to do a great hatchet-job on Davey's new screenplay and I notice you've not said one word against it. You were given a sizable amount of shares in Metropolitan in return for your investment in the movie, which gives you a voice at Metropolitan, but you choose not to exercise it.'

'Let me tell you something about the screenplay – Davey's never around to discuss changes with him. He keeps his goddamn head so low we never know where he is these days, and people get edgy dealing with the invisible man. This is big business, Betsy; they can't afford to screw it up. Maybe if he showed his face once in a while he'd have a say, but it sure ain't going to work with his head shoved in the sand somewhere. What's eating him? Why play the recluse?' He let go of her hand, folded his arms and ignored the cheering line of people. 'Whatever it is you're not telling me, I think it's about time you considered spilling the beans.'

'You said what's past didn't matter, remember?' she returned.

'Yeah, sure I do. But the past is impacting on our future, Betsy. The guy is becoming a crazy recluse.'

She thumped him on the arm. 'Don't you ever say those kinds of things about him! Davey, he's all I had for a long time. At least I know where I am with Davey. I can trust him.'

Mason was stung by her words. 'You can trust me,' he said.

'I'm not so sure anymore…'

'We've got each other, Betsy, and soon we'll have a kid of our own. We'll be a family…'

The car pulled up outside the cinema. It was lit up like a fairground, the title of *Dragutin's Bride* in large red letters lit up by a circle of bulbs. He noticed thoughtfully how his name was printed bigger than Betsy's on the six-foot-high posters, and it was his masked face that loomed out at them. There was a dense, swaying crowd being held back by a thin blue line of NYPD officers, their buttons and badges gleaming beneath the lights. The people grew ever more frenzied on seeing the car. Mostly young women, he observed. It had been the case wherever they went. What was their slightly unhealthy fascination with a repulsive, cruel, deformed creature that used women as mere objects upon which to enact his evil appetites? What was it about him they found so appealing, so magnetic? What sick part of the mind had he unwittingly tapped into?

Without waiting for the chauffeur to open the door for them, without waiting for her husband to take the lead, Betsy got out of the car and strode out over the red carpet that had been laid in their honour for this special screening. Mason watched as she worked the crowd, smiled, waved, her fur stole draped in such a manner that it hid the mound of her pregnancy. Not for long, though, he thought. Camera flashbulbs popped and fans screamed out 'Dorottya! Dorottya!' Eventually she stopped half-way to the theatre entrance and turned to her husband.

He emerged from the car, slowly, deliberately; his dark-blue uniform resplendent under the gleam of the bright lights, and the crowd erupted into the loudest screams he'd ever heard. The women were pushing against the officers who struggled to hold them back. Like a pack of baying she-wolves, Mason mused, their eyes wild and hungry, almost maniacal. It was almost frightening, he thought as he stepped over to his wife and she linked her arm through his. Almost.

'You can never escape!' he said above the din, and it was like putting a flame to a keg of gunpowder. The crowd roared its approval. It had become a kind of catchphrase for him, so much so that it had started to appear on the billboards and promotional materials.

He went to where the officers held back the crowd, reached out his white-gloved hand through them to stroke the outstretched fingers of the young women.

'Take me to your castle, Dragutin!' one of them shouted. 'Do whatever you want to me!'

He waved at the woman, who gasped and put a hand to her breast. He looked at Betsy, but her eyes had gone cold again. She appeared strangely alone, standing there in the centre of the red carpet, surrounded by pandemonium and yet somehow separate in a bubble all of her own. He went back to her, held her close and kissed her on the cheek. 'I'm sorry,' he whispered into her ear. 'I forgot myself.'

'When's the baby due, Betsy?' a reporter asked. A small clutch of them had been allowed beyond the flimsy rope barrier and the line of hard-pressed police officers.

'Three months,' she said, her face at once beaming.

'What do you want, a boy or a girl?'

'We don't care as long as it's healthy. That's all that matters to us.'

'Does that mean you're going to be more of a mother than an actress, Betsy?'

'We women can be both, you know,' she returned crisply. 'Having a baby isn't an illness, and being a mother isn't debilitating. I'm going to continue making movies.'

'What are you going to call it? Jozsef? Dorottya?'

'Certainly not!' she said. 'Look, aren't you tired of all this baby talk? What about asking me about my role in the next Dragutin movie?'

Attention suddenly flicked to Mason, as if they'd grown bored with Betsy. 'Hey, Rick, is the Baron going to be even more of a monster in the next movie?'

'Guess you'll have to wait and see. We're still working on it. We've got a bigger budget this time round. We may even go to Slavonia to film on location in Castle Dragutin.'

'On location? Nobody shoots on location, Rick. Can we quote you on that?'

'Sure, go ahead,' he said.

'No one said anything about going back to Slavonia,' Betsy confronted Mason.

'Ah, just talk for now,' he assured, patting her hand. 'Stories designed to keep the press happy, something new to write and gossip about.'

'Why didn't you tell me?' she said coldly.

'Like I say, just talk. Later, eh, honey?' He faced the crowd again and waved. They went up to the grand doors of the theatre, where he turned once again to face the people, like a royal prince at the gates of a palace.

'You can never escape!' he cried from the top step.

The crowd loved that.

* * *

23

Bunny Foster

The next time he stepped out of a limo at the Palm Club he didn't have to pretend to be someone big just to get in. This time they all knew who Rick Mason was. They fell over themselves in their efforts to welcome him into the club. No trouble either in getting a table for Betsy and him.

Outwardly he was calm, assured, even faintly dismissive of all the attention, but inwardly he was grinning like a fool, lapping it all up. He even felt disdain for the way they fawned all over them. How curious, he thought; he was the same person inside, but now elevated to the status of a king, to sit alongside the other kings of Hollywood royalty on their false thrones made of fresh air and cardboard. And yet why, he thought, did he feel above them, not of them, as if he peered down at them all from some lofty vantage point and they were nothing but insects scurrying around at his feet?

Conrad Jefferson joined them. He was smoking his trademark cheroot, his face already flushed red with the wine he'd consumed privately in a plush backroom reserved for special clients; the prohibition didn't seem to have any effect on Jefferson's enjoyment.

He'd brought along with him a young woman, extremely attractive, chestnut-haired, swan neck rising from a low-cut evening dress in shimmering red silk. Diamonds – the real deal – flashed at her throat, on her ears, on her wrist. Evidence, Mason thought, of Jefferson's extreme generosity. Or gratitude. He introduced her as Bunny Foster.

'Bunny,' said Betsy, eyeing the slender, young woman as she sat down at the table, feeling rather like an inflated blimp by comparison. 'Hopefully you weren't baptised that.'

Bunny smiled. All teeth and red lips. 'Oh no, it's because I used to bounce around the place all excited as a kid.'

'She has a rather effervescent personality,' Jefferson said.

'Pleased to meet you, Bunny,' Mason said, a black, elbow-high glove reaching out to shake his hand gently.

'I've heard so much about you. I saw *Dragutin's Bride* and nearly fainted in horror.' The same black-clad fingers went to her ample bosom. 'But you're far more handsome in person than I ever imagined. Not at all like that horrible Baron. Your wife is so lucky,' she said, smiling at Betsy.

'Yes, I guess I am,' she said flatly. Jefferson's appearance at their table had been unexpected. She didn't particularly like the man. She'd heard tales of him seeing girls as young as twelve. She didn't know if any of the rumours were true, but his lecherous gaze made it true for her.

'Bunny is an actress,' said Jefferson.

'Anything we know?' Betsy asked.

Again the woman smiled warmly. She was trying hard to be friendly. 'Not yet. This is my first big break.'

Mason glanced at Jefferson. 'Really? What big break is that?'

'Bunny is being cast as village girl Anna,' Jefferson said, stubbing his cigar out half-smoked and taking out another one.

'Which village girl is that?' Mason pressed.

'It's a new part being written in, to accommodate Bunny's talents.'

Mason was acutely aware of Betsy's impassive expression. 'Yet another alteration to the script, Conrad?'

'We know what we're doing, Rick. Trust us, eh?' He puffed out clouds of blue smoke across the table; it hovered around Betsy's breasts for a second or two. 'Anyhow, just wanted you guys to meet up.' He rose from his seat. 'We got other things to do,' he said. 'Have a swell evening.'

'It's been nice meeting you,' said Bunny. 'I guess we'll see more of each other on set.'

Betsy's eyes remained frosty. 'I'm sure we will.'

'I hope everything goes well with the baby. You look so large!' said Bunny, tittering. 'I can't imagine being stretched *so* big. It must make you feel so fat.'

'I feel pregnant,' she said.

Bunny's smile dropped. 'Sorry, Miss Bellamy, I didn't mean...'

Jefferson pulled at Bunny's arm. 'Due any time now, huh?' he said, a touch of impatience in his voice. 'Anyone would think the kid didn't want to be born.'

'Any week now,' she replied. 'It won't affect the shooting-schedule,' she assured, 'if that's what you're worried about.'

'Not my worry,' he said, grinning. 'I pay other people to worry on my behalf.'

He said his goodbyes and the couple were left in peace. They ate in silence for a while. 'What was all that about?' she said at length.

'It's the way things are done, Betsy. I'm not entirely happy about it myself. Too many fingers on the script for my liking. Where is Davey, for God's sake? At least if he showed his face we could help steer things a little better. What made the last movie a success was a script largely untouched by others. Hell, Betsy, I ain't a writer. What do I know what's going to work?'

'Well everyone else seems to know what's best,' she replied. 'All we need now is a Bunny on the set.'

'You were the one looking for your big break once, remember? Give the kid a chance.'

'You like her? You found her pretty compared to me, is that it?'

'No,' he said. 'I never said that. Jeez, I'll be glad when this kid is out and we can get back to normal.'

Her knife and fork clattered noisily against her plate as she dropped them down. 'What, so now it's something to get over and done with? An inconvenience?'

'You're drawing attention to yourself, Betsy. Don't make a scene.'

'Or what, Baron Dragutin? You'll chain me up in my room and keep me out of sight?'

'Don't be ridiculous,' he said, scowling at her.

'See? That's the look you're giving me every day. You never used to look at me that way. You've changed, Rick. What happened to the happy-go-lucky socialist?'

'Even socialists have to eat. And I was never a goddamn socialist. Keep your voice down.' He grabbed her hand tightly.

'You're hurting me. Let me go.'

'Not till you promise me you'll calm down.'

She stared straight into his eyes. 'You men are all the same,' she said quietly. 'I thought you were different.'

A shadow fell over their table. They looked up to see the imposing figure of Luke Dillon, head of Prima Motion Picture Company. 'I hope I'm not disturbing you. May I join you?'

'Sure,' said Mason, releasing Betsy's hand. Her wrist remained white from his grip. She slipped it from the table to rest on her lap.

Dillon pushed away the ashtray bearing the crushed cigar and sat down. 'I couldn't help notice you sitting here. How're things with Jefferson?'

'Fine,' said Mason. 'Everything's just dandy.'

'I've not had the occasion to offer you my congratulations on the success of *Dragutin's Bride*, Rick. Or should I call you Baron Dragutin?' He laughed, but it had a way of unsettling you, thought Rick.

'He'll like that,' said Betsy straight-faced.

Mason ignored her. 'Forget the niceties, Dillon,' he said. 'What are you really here for?'

Dillon stroked his chin. 'You're astute, I'll give you that, Rick. You always were. How's Metropolitan treating you? Treating you as you deserve?'

'Treating us both just fine,' Mason returned.

'You know,' he said, leaning back in his chair, 'Metropolitan Studios ain't going anywhere. This Dragutin thing is just a flash in the pan. They're always going to be a struggling, two-bit outfit. Conrad Jefferson will always be an asshole.'

'Two-bit, huh? Takes one to know one, Dillon. It's a fact that you hate the man for something he did or did not do when you were partners at Prima in the early days. But that hasn't stopped you wanting to get your fat paws on Metropolitan, has it? That would rub Jefferson's nose in it real good, wouldn't it? And so what's the next best thing? Poach his latest stars. That's low, Dillon.'

'There you go again, Rick! What a guy!' He bent forward, his elbows on the table. 'Let's cut to the chase, huh? Prima could give you a better deal, give you both bigger and better opportunities than ever Metropolitan can. I'd make it worth your while to break contract with them; my boys will mop up any legal trouble that it stirs up. One day Prima will be the biggest outfit in Hollywood, and you'd be a sap for not being part of it. What do you say?'

Mason mirrored Dillon's posture, looked straight at him, his expression serious. 'What do I think? I think you're a heap of shit, Dillon. Think I'm going to forget how you treated me? How I was dragged from this very club and had the shit beaten out of me by your goons? Well I won't, so you can take your deal and shove it up your big fat ass.' He picked up his napkin, wiped his mouth. 'Go fuck yourself, Dillon,' he said, loud enough to be overheard at nearby tables.

Dillon's gaze was icy for a moment or two, and then he smiled broadly. 'Fine, Rick, have it your way. You could have been big. Both of you.'

He rose from the table, straightened his jacket and then strode away. After an awkward few seconds the inquisitive diners went back to their meals.

Betsy's eyes narrowed. 'Why did you say a thing like that to him?'

'Because I could,' he replied, putting his napkin onto his lap again.

'You knew he'd be here, didn't you? That's why it had to be tonight. You were hoping he'd come across.'

He glanced at her, gave a tiny smirk that twisted his lips. They looked so cruel, she thought.

* * * *

24

A Horrible Day

Another rite-of-passage, he felt, was moving into one of the mansions up on Whitley Heights. Designed by the architect A. S. Barnes, he could have afforded it with his inheritance alone, but money was flooding into his account in insane amounts. Things might be looking up, but he knew there were many new possibilities and he'd only just begun to scratch the surface. The problem, he thought, lay in his agent. Rick Mason called Victor Wallace over to the mansion with this in mind.

'Swell joint!' Wallace said, taking the cigar Mason handed him. 'Got a pool, too?'

'Got two,' said Mason.

He whistled. 'When you consider where you were and where you are, eh, Rick?' He lit the cigar from a black marble table lighter. 'Shouldn't smoke these by rights,' he admitted, looking at the smouldering end of the cigar. 'The doc says I gotta lay off them; says they're no good for my health, but hey, it's a raw deal when a fella can't celebrate once in a while!'

Wallace had done well through Mason's success. He was looking good on it, too. Less haggard around the gills.

'Thing is, that's why I called you over, Victor.'

He caught onto the no-nonsense tone immediately. 'Business, eh? OK, what's eating you, Rick? I've known you so long I can read you like a book. Betsy's pregnancy giving you a hard time? Sure, it's not always an easy time for the dames, but hell you're gonna be a father pretty soon. Any day now. You figured who's gonna be godparents yet? Me, I've never been a godparent, but if you're looking...'

'Victor, look, don't take this wrong, but I've got to let you go. We have to part ways.'

His mouth hung open for a moment. 'You're pulling my leg, right? I mean, I fought to get you fixed up with Metropolitan...'

'I know that, Victor, and I'm grateful. But I'm moving into an even bigger arena now. Bigger than you can handle. It's obvious.'

'Well it sure ain't obvious to me,' Wallace said, tossing away the cigar. 'And you're forgetting we've got a contract.'

'I can buy you out of that, Victor. We can end this amicably...'

'Bullshit!' he burst, standing up and hitching up his pants. 'I thought we were friends, Rick. We go back a while now. It ought to count for something.'

'Like you said yourself, it's business.'

'You think you can buy anything with that goddamn money of yours? Well you can't buy me. I'll fight you every step of the way.'

'You can't afford it, Victor. Sit down, let's talk this through.'

'To hell with you, Rick. To hell with you. Betsy was right; you've changed. You ain't the guy I used to know. What happened to you, Rick, to poison you so quick?'

Suddenly Mason was flooded with guilt at seeing Wallace's distraught, betrayed face. He wanted to back down, take everything back, but he'd climbed so far up this particular tree there was no way he'd ever be able to climb back down. Wallace slapped his hat on, and without saying another word he left the house, slamming the door behind him. A servant came rushing into the room, his dark skin shiny with moisture.

'Is everything alright?' he asked. 'I thought something was wrong.'

'Nothing's wrong!' he fired, actually feeling something was completely wrong but powerless to do anything about it. He remembered the conversation with Betsy in the diner, the first time he met her, about the black waiter, and he looked up at his servant. He was perpetuating it. He was still the white master and this man was still his black servant.

'Are you happy?' he asked the servant.

'Happy, sir?'

'Damn you!' he shouted. 'Are you happy?'

The man looked uncomfortable with the question. 'Yes, sir, I'm very happy,' he said without feeling.

'Go away!' Mason snapped. 'Get the hell out of here and leave me alone!'

He slumped down onto the sofa, his head in his hands. What is becoming of me, he asked? What is becoming of me?

Three days later he picked up a call to say that Victor Wallace was dead. Heart attack. Stress, said the doctor. Told him to ease up and he didn't take any notice.

Mason was profoundly upset, sent along the biggest wreath he could lay his hands on when it came to the day of the funeral. Made sure Wallace's wife had plenty of money to live on and told her Victor was more than an agent; he was a close friend. By all accounts, Wallace hadn't told her about his meeting with Mason. She remained ignorant of it and that caused him more pain than he thought he could feasibly bear.

'There's always a price to pay,' Betsy told him cryptically as they walked away from the graveside. A few photographers took the opportunity to snap pictures. Dressed completely in black, he didn't look too much different to Dragutin, he thought bleakly.

They'd been back at the house a couple of hours when Betsy took a call from Davey.

'We've got to go to him right away,' she urged Mason.

'Why? What's the matter?' he replied dully. 'I'm not in the mood. I've just been to a funeral, you might have noticed.'

'Davey's in trouble,' she said, grabbing her coat. 'Are you going to drive me or not? I can't drive in this condition and I'm not asking the chauffeur. This is a private matter.' She groaned. 'Hurry, for God's sake!'

'What kind of trouble?'

She didn't answer and he followed dumbly, his mind numb. She slammed the car door shut. 'Put your foot down!' she said. 'I've got to get to him fast.'

'Where are we going, Betsy? Hell, I've no idea where the man is hanging out.'

'He's got a small place in Owensmouth, San Fernando Valley. I'll direct you – just drive!'

She fretted the entire way. Mason was surprised when they entered undeveloped scrubland. The area had been bought by the Los Angeles Suburban Homes Co around seventeen years ago. Houses were being thrown up, the area changing rapidly, but they'd travelled to the edge of the developments and taken a detour down a dirt track into the middle of nowhere. It ended at a run-down wooden shack.

'He's been living here all this time? In this dump?'

'Pull over! Pull over!' she said, throwing open the car's door before the vehicle had stopped.

He shouted out a warning. 'Careful – you'll fall over and do some damage.'

A muscular black mongrel dog barked viciously at them, lunged at Mason's feet as he passed and was hauled back by a length of rusted chain. It coughed and resumed its barking. Betsy was at the door, trying the handle but it was locked.

'Break it down, Rick!' she cried. 'Quickly!'

The fear and urgency ablaze in her eyes told him not to argue. He put his shoulder against the door, but the hefty timber refused to budge. The frame eventually splintered on the third attempt and the door fell off its rusted hinges and landed on the wooden floor of the shack sending up a cloud of dust.

In the gloom he saw a chair turned over on the floor, and above it a dark shape jerking and kicking. Davey was hung by his neck from rope fastened to a hook driven into wooden ceiling joists. His eyes were bulging from their sockets, his tongue forced out of his mouth like a fat slug, and his skin was turning blue.

Betsy screamed. 'Get him down, quick!'

'Knife!' he shouted, pointing to a blade on a table next to a loaf of bread. She handed it to him as he lifted the chair, stood it up and set Davey's feet on it. He took his weight and slashed at the rope, hacking manically till Davey fell limply to the floor, taking Mason with him. Betsy tore the rope from around Davey's throat, the man gasping and clutching the red, sore-looking band around his neck.

'What are you doing?' she sobbed. 'Davey, what are you doing?'

'I can't take it any more, Betsy,' he said hoarsely, his words hardly intelligible. 'I've got to end it. I can't live like this, knowing what happened. They're coming to get me, Betsy!'

'Who's coming to get you?' Mason asked. 'What's he talking about?'

'They're getting close, Betsy,' he said, beginning to cry. 'I don't want to sit in that chair. Don't let them take me…'

She cradled his head, stroked his hair. 'They won't get you, Davey, I promise.' Tears ran down her cheeks. 'Help me get him over to the bed, Rick,' she said.

They Hauled him to an iron bedstead, its springs screeching as it took his weight.

'What's he talking about?' he asked. He noticed a couple of empty hooch bottles. 'He's as drunk as a skunk,' he said. 'He doesn't drink…'

Eventually, Davey settled down, appeared to drift off to sleep. Betsy left him, took Mason's arm and led him outside to the porch. 'There's something you need to know,' she said, choking on her emotion.

'No kidding. What's going on, Betsy? Who is out to get him? And why would he want to try and kill himself?'

There was a decrepit old bench on the porch. Betsy cradled her swollen midriff as she settled herself slowly down onto the aged seat. The Sun was looking to set soon.

'It's been a horrible day,' she observed. 'First Victor's funeral, and now this…'

'Is Davey in trouble?'

Her eyes looked into his. 'We're both in trouble, Rick. We're in big trouble.'

* * * *

25

Justice

'In the beginning there was just Davey, our pa and me. Never knew my ma; she either died tragically or ran off with another guy, depending on how pa was feeling. We were brought up in a Wisconsin shack not unlike this one. Worse than this one. Except it was home. Whenever I think of home I think of that shack. Mean and dirty, but it was the only home I ever had and better than some people lived in. At least we weren't sleeping rough on the streets. Not yet.

'My real name isn't Betsy Bellamy, but I guess you already knew that,' she said. 'I was baptised Margaret Harvey, and Davey's name is Peter. Peter Harvey. Anyhow, turned out pa was put away in jail for stealing a car and killing a man. Crazy, really, because he'd never driven a car before, lost control almost straight away and ran it into a guy. He didn't mean to kill the man, but they put him away for murder, because he was a hothead and one time pa and this guy had some kind of big argument over a dog and pa had threatened to kill him. He was drunk and never meant a word but they were looking to make an example of someone and pa was unlucky enough to be that example. They gave him life. Well, they were looking to put me and Peter into some kind of home. I'd be about nine, Peter eleven, and we sure didn't intend getting split up so we decided to get the hell out of there real quick before they tried. That was back in '11. Pa, we learned, got a knife in the gut for being the hothead again; you can't be a hothead inside.

'We hit the road, travelling from place to place, town to town, wherever there was food and shelter to be found, but we always stuck together. Peter, he said he'd always look after his little sister, no matter what. He'd take whatever work he could and one time got himself a job in a repair yard, where he found he had a nose for fixing cars. Ironic really, I guess, as it was a car that got us into the mess in the first place. Me, I tried my hands at whatever I could get and generally we got by, avoiding the law, keeping out of trouble, moving on when things got uncomfortable or opportunities dried up. I found I could sing, act a little, and earned a crust with a travelling carnival for a time. Peter helped fix the engines for them. But Peter got on the wrong side of the carnival owner and at the next town he had him framed and arrested for petty theft. That's where he got a record, spent a few months behind bars and that was the end of the carnival. The carnival's where I got a taste for acting, found out I could hold an audience. Only good thing to come out of it.

'When Peter got out we hit the road again, and washed up in Louisiana a few years later. I was sixteen, got a job at a hotel. Peter wanted to join up for the war, but they turned him down because of his age and because he had a record, so he answered an ad for a handyman and mechanic, to help around a guy's house and drive and look after his two cars. The man turned out to be a writer by the name of John Saunders who'd bought himself a farm but knew nothing about farms, lived in a big house all by himself except for a maid who came in once in a while to keep the place clean. He'd made his money from a series of plays he'd written before the war but hadn't had much success since. He was working on a new play that he thought would revive his fortunes. Peter was the happiest I'd seen him in a long while. He helped around the old farm any way he could, and kept Saunders's cars on the road, every now and again driving the guy wherever he needed to get. Seemed back then we could start to think about getting a life for ourselves. We rented a quiet place a mile away from Saunders's farm.

'Then one day Peter plucked up the courage and showed Saunders a piece of writing he'd been working on and, surprised at his latent talent, sort of took him as his pupil. Over the next year Saunders taught him how to hone his craft, lending him books, reading what he'd written. They became close friends. Or so I thought.

'Up till then I'd never met John Saunders. Never been to the house. Peter hadn't mentioned me – it was our rule in the early days when we might have been taken back to Wisconsin as kids, never to mention each other, and the rule stuck. He told Saunders about me, about my acting in the carnival and how good I was and Saunders asked to see me in private one night. He seemed an OK kind of guy. Older than I imagined. He told me he was writing a new play, that it was almost done and he was looking for someone to play the lead. He gave me pieces to read, said he was impressed. Asked me to come back the next day, a Sunday.

'I went along, expecting to read some more. But he locked the door, grabbed me, threw me to the floor and...'

Mason touched her arm. Her body was trembling, her face contorted by emotion as she stared down at the rotting wooden boards of the porch. 'Betsy...' he said. 'What did he do?'

She blinked rapidly, a jaw muscle twitching. 'He raped me.'

'Oh my God,' Mason breathed, his fingers tightening around her arm. She pulled her arm away.

'He raped me. He was like a savage beast. Threatened to kill me. I thought he would. Afterwards, I went home, tried to scrub myself clean, but Peter took one look at me and knew something was wrong. I eventually told him. He flew into a rage and stormed out of the house. I ran after him, telling him to come back, that we'd call the police. But he wouldn't listen and I couldn't catch him.

'When I finally got to Saunders's house I heard a woman screaming, and Peter came running out. He ran up to me, grabbed me by the wrist. His hands were covered in blood. The maid was standing at the door screaming that there'd been a murder; that John Saunders had been shot with his own gun. I asked Peter what he'd done, but he didn't answer, he dragged me away and we ran. We left everything behind and ran away from that place. We've been running ever since.'

Mason had his head rested in both hands, his fingers massaging his skull. 'Christ, Betsy, why didn't you tell me any of this before?'

'How could I? I love you, I wanted you, and if I'd told you any of this you'd have dumped me and who could blame you? I wish I'd never sat down on that trunk with you and got to talking. It wasn't supposed to happen like this.'

'I love you, Betsy. You're carrying my child. Shit, this is one hell of a mess.'

'What are you going to do?' she asked, her eyes moistening.

'I don't know. I've got to think.'

'Your career will be ruined if this ever gets out. I'm sorry, Rick.'

'Yeah, I can see the headlines now – investigated by the law to find out what I knew, dumped by Metropolitan because of the damage done to them. It doesn't look good.' He groaned. A sound came from inside the shack and Betsy got up to investigate. He was left alone with his troubled thoughts. The dog lay watching him, chained to its post. You can never escape, he said to himself. You and me, buddy, we're fastened down good and proper.

Betsy came out, sat down beside him. 'He's asleep. I nearly lost him, Rick. And it's all been my fault, for ever getting him into this mess in the first place, then for staying here with you when we should have moved on. He got word from the repair yard he worked for that the law had been sniffing around looking for him and it's been screwing up his mind thinking he could be caught any minute. But he's stayed here for me, because he knows how much it means to me, and it's all been too much for him.' She winced and clutched her midriff. Adjusted her position on the seat to make it more comfortable. 'Maybe we just ought to go.'

'No, don't leave me, Betsy,' he said, his breathing shallow. 'We've got a kid coming, a family of our own. I never had a real family.'

'What about Peter, about what he's done?'

'Davey. You only ever call him Davey from now on, because that's who he is now. We'll make sure we'll find somewhere he'll feel safe. What he did he did for you, because you'd been brutally raped. He was protecting his sister. The man, this John Saunders, deserved to die. You'd have stood no chance against Saunders's word in a court of law – a pair of drifters from outside the area testifying against a respected writer. Your word against his. Where's the justice in that?'

'So you're not going to turn us over to the cops?'

'No way. We've got too much going for us. I'm not going to let a dead slimeball ruin it for us.' He put his arm around her shoulder and she gasped in pain. 'Are you okay, Betsy?'

'If they ever found out you covered up for us…' she said, her eyes screwing up.

'They won't. What's wrong?' Mason looked down to see a puddle forming on the bench. 'Jesus, Betsy, your waters have broken! It can't be happening now!'

'Tell that to –' She sucked in a breath. 'You've got to get me to a hospital, Rick, right away!'

'What about Davey?'

'I told him he was safe. He's sleeping things off. You can call back and check up on him for me after you've got me to the hospital.' She struggled to her feet. 'Guess all this excitement was the kick it needed, huh?' She gave a tired smile.

He helped her to the car. 'Don't you worry, Betsy,' he said, 'I'm going to take good care of you. You're safe with me. Just you make sure that boy of mine is okay.'

'Boy?' she gasped.

'Boy,' he echoed, his eyes narrowing with determination as he climbed behind the wheel. 'My son.'

* * * *

26

The Devil Rises

There was a crowd of people outside the studio gates, waving hand-painted placards, the security guards looking jumpy. Rick Mason's car drew up and the people surged forward to surround it; the vehicle came to a sudden halt as if it had driven into a thick swamp. Fists began to hammer on the windscreen, the hood, a sea of angry, twisted faces peering in and shouting at him.

'What the hell is going on?' he asked of the driver.

'Don't know, sir,' he replied, a touch of nervousness in his voice. 'But I don't like it. Want me to back away?'

The guards were shooing away the crowd, the studio gates beginning to open to let the car through. Mason caught sight of the writing, mostly emblazoned in red, on the placards.

DEVIL WORSHIPPER; BAN DRAGUTIN'S BRIDE; SHAME! SHAME! SHAME! RICK MASON, SATAN'S MOUTHPIECE and so on.

'That directed at me?' Mason said incredulously. He was totally taken aback by this kind of reception. He flinched as a couple of eggs hit the car's windscreen and smeared the livid, hateful faces, making them even more grotesque. 'Who is this crazy bunch?'

The car managed to squeeze through the gates which were slammed shut after it. The crowd rammed up close against the metal bars, the guards powerless to do anything about it, overwhelmed by sheer numbers and manic determination. A few more eggs flew over the top of the gates after the car but missed. Mason asked the driver to stop so he could get out. The boiling, hissing crowd were about twenty yards away.

'What is wrong with you?' he shouted.

The chant of 'Devil, devil, devil,' floated angrily over to him.

'You're all nuts!' he responded. 'Look at the state of my car!'

He didn't see the young woman run out from behind a stack of scenery a few yards to his left. Too late he realised she had something in her hands that she was about to throw. He brought up his arm to shield his face. A wave of red paint washed over his head, arm and shoulders. He gasped in shock, spitting out the vile stuff that had gotten into his open mouth.

'Devil!' she shouted. 'You're the devil's advocate! Metropolitan is in league with the forces of darkness!'

Dripping with paint, he strode over to her and struck her hard across the face, leaving a bright-red smear on her cheek. 'Bitch!' he said. 'Don't you know who I am?' He struck her again, this time with his fist and the woman collapsed to the floor.

Two guards hurried to his aid and dragged the woman to her feet. 'We got her, sir!'

'I'll kill you for that!' Mason snarled.

The driver came over and put a restraining hand on his shoulder. 'Leave her, sir, she's not worth it. This way. Get this filthy stuff off you.'

'Devil's advocate!' said the woman, spitting out blood. The guards brusquely bundled her away.

Mason stood there, resisting his driver's pulling, the red paint dripping off him. Hell, what have I just done, he thought? I've struck a woman. I've never done that before, never felt such a rage. If the guards hadn't come along when they had...

'Sir,' the driver urged. 'Ignore them. They're religious freaks, that's all. Twisted religious freaks.' He encouraged Mason to move on leaving a blood-red trail of footprints on the yard floor.

'I heard about the ruckus,' said Conrad Jefferson, coming round from behind his desk. He shook Mason's hand.

'You need better security,' Mason complained. They'd found a fresh set of clothes for him, but their fit was far from perfect. 'Who are they, do you know?'

'A religious protest group,' said Hal Bremner from behind him. He was pouring out a drink. He held it out. 'You look like you need one,' he said, sitting down on a sofa. 'These little incidents have been springing up all over the country, organised, we think, by a right-wing religious organisation called The Church of the Holy Reckoning. Mainly they're targeting the Metropolitan-owned chain of theatres, trying all sorts of measures to get people to boycott them.'

'What have they got to complain about?' said Mason. 'It's only a movie, in heaven's name!'

'In heaven's name,' Jefferson joined. 'Very apt. It's more than just a movie to some people, Rick. It's stirred up one heck of a hornets' nest. Metropolitan's come under heavy fire recently for producing a movie that encourages sadism, bloodletting, the torture of women, drug-induced rape – there's a growing list. Some of the smaller theatres are refusing to screen *Dragutin's Bride*. We're corrupting the young of the United States, apparently. We're also the harbinger of doom, death, destruction, even another European war in the not-too-distant future. All baloney, but useful baloney, eh, Hal?'

'Sure. The movie is dividing opinion. The mailbag for Dragutin is growing daily, from young women in particular. You should read some of that stuff, Rick; there are some real sick broads out there.' He grinned.

Jefferson joined Bremner on the sofa, invited Mason to sit down opposite. 'Thing is, the bluenoses at the National Board of Review are sniffing round us again, and we don't know yet what that means for Dragutin's Bride. I've been pulling strings there again with the connections I've got, tried to oil the wheels, but truth is they're going to be keeping a close eye on the next movie that's for sure. But what it does do is give us a hell of a lot of publicity. Our press agent is having a field day with it all!' He poured a drink for himself, noticed Mason hadn't touched the glass Bremner had given him. 'Still not a drinker, Rick?' he asked, shaking a bottle of malt.

Mason downed the hot liquid in one go. Coughed a little.

'You broke that woman's jaw,' said Bremner.

'Shit, no!' said Mason.

'Shit, yes. But we can smooth that over as much as we can. You've got to keep out of trouble, though, Rick. If this gets in the press it could cause you lots of bother. We're hoping the woman's religious convictions can be bought.' He took a big swig of alcohol. 'Why'd you do that, Rick? Smack a woman in the mouth?' His eyes were steely.

'Never mind the broad,' Jefferson interjected. 'Let's get down to *The Devil Rises*, shall we?'

'So that's the official title, is it?' said Mason. 'That little crowd of bible-thumpers out there will love that one when they hear it.'

'How's Betsy, Rick?' said Jefferson unexpectedly. 'And how's the baby – what're you calling it?'

'Edward. Eddie,' said Mason. He looked from Jefferson to Bremner and back again. 'The baby's doing just fine. Betsy's not so good yet.'

'How are her legs?'

'She can just about walk on crutches, but it's a slow process.'

'Sounds like she's had a bad time,' said Bremner. 'Having a kid can be bad enough, but to get an infection like she did...'

Mason sighed, rubbed his eyes. He felt so damn tired all the time. 'Yeah, whatever it was affected her legs real bad. She thought she was paralysed at first, but thankfully that's not the case. The doctors don't rightly know what it is yet, what's actually causing it. Someone even said it might be in her head, you know, the trauma of childbirth and all that...' He studied the two men closely. 'What is it you want to tell me?' he asked. 'I can see by your faces you're cooking something up between you.'

'Thing is, Rick,' said Bremner, a glance from Jefferson his cue to talk, 'we can't afford to go behind on the shooting-schedule. We borrowed heavily against the movie to help finance it and we've got interest piling up every day we lose, and we're already pushing things back as far as we can to accommodate Betsy and this pregnancy. Now there's this other thing with her legs. You get what I'm saying here?'

Mason's jaw hardened. 'Spell it out for me, just so I'm sure.'

'We have to drop Betsy from the production.'

'It's her part. You can't do that.'

'Yes we can,' said Bremner. 'Her contract allows us to do it.'

'So who will you give the part to?'

'Bunny Foster,' Bremner replied.

'Bunny? I've seen her tests. She's OK but she's not a patch on Betsy, and she doesn't even look the part. She's all tits and teeth.'

'Tits and teeth are what the paying public want,' said Jefferson. 'You know that. They aren't paying to see Shakespeare. Look at it from our point of view, Rick; we have to move fast on this or things will get out of hand.'

'You drop Betsy and you'll have to drop me!' he fired.

'Fine,' said Bremner. 'Then we'll drop you, too.'

'I think you're forgetting I made Baron Dragutin. He's me. The movie is my movie. I've got shares in Metropolitan that says it's my movie.'

'Wrong,' said Bremner icily, putting his glass down loudly. 'You're an actor, Rick. If we want, we can put any guy we like into that damn mask, behind that makeup, and the audience won't know the difference. They pay to see Dragutin, not you. As for your shares in Metropolitan, if this company goes down your shares go down with it, and if we don't begin shooting soon we'll go down as fast as the bloody Titanic.'

'I am Dragutin, you slimy bastard!' Rick said, rising angrily from his seat and aiming a fist at Bremner's eyes. 'You can't easily take that away from me and give it someone else!'

'You threatening me, Rick? Planning to smash my jaw like you smashed that woman's? Go ahead, you do that. Do that and you're finished, not only at Metropolitan but in Hollywood. We can see to that.'

'I'll kill you if you did, Bremner!' he growled.

'Now, gentlemen, let's not be too hasty,' Jefferson said. 'We have a movie to make and all this talk of killing one another don't help matters any. Sit down, Rick,' he said. 'I said sit,' he asked more firmly. Rick hesitated, then lowered himself to the seat. 'We have to drop Betsy, OK? OK, Rick? You got that?'

Mason conceded, nodding slowly. 'Seems I don't have any choice in the matter.'

'Seems you don't,' said Bremner.

'Don't push it!' Rick said.

'Great, we've got ourselves a deal,' Jefferson enthused. He raised his glass. 'To *The Devil Rises*!' he said.

'*The Devil Rises*,' Bremner muttered.

Mason didn't say a word.

* * * *

27

Flaming Hell

'Where's my son?'

Rick Mason tossed his coat at the coat stand and missed.

The nanny, an elderly-looking woman, skinny as a rake, was carrying a mound of white towels. 'He's in the nursery, Mr Mason, fast asleep. I've just come from there,' she explained. 'Do you want me to bring him out to you?'

He shook his head. 'No, thanks. I'll go in and see him. Don't go waking the kid. He hardly sleeps as it is.' He tried to force a smile but it wouldn't come. 'And Betsy? How's she?'

'The same, sir. In her room. The doctor is with her, the one she called in.'

'Is she still refusing to see the child?'

The nanny nodded uncertainly. 'Some mothers find it difficult to bond with their babies. She's just going through a tough patch. She'll get better in time, you'll see.'

She left Mason to go about her business and he went upstairs to the nursery. There was an elaborate wicker crib in the room's centre. The smell of fresh paint hung in the air. Lemon-coloured walls. Model planes hanging from the ceiling which had been painted to look like a sky full of rolling white clouds. He went over to the crib. The crown of the baby's head was just visible above the woollen blankets. A mass of dark, tufty hair. He could smell baby. Soft, warm, inviting, drawing him closer like the smell of fresh-baked bread or coffee. He stroked his son's miniscule, perfectly formed ear and smiled as he stirred beneath his feather-soft touch. Hell, Eddie, what have you been born into?

He heard a door open and went out of the nursery to see the doctor standing out on the landing, his Gladstone in his hand. Doctor Lombard was a gentle-looking soul, middle-aged, balding, expanding paunch, a voice of clinical calmness amidst the madness, Mason thought. Betsy would have nobody else but Doctor Lombard. Heaven knows where she dragged him from, but he appeared to be a good old fella.

'How is she, doc?'

The doctor smiled his familiar easy-going smile and fastened his bag. He indicated with a flick of his head that they walk down further down the landing, away from the bedroom door. 'She's still the same. I'm more than a little concerned for her. She still maintains she can't walk, has taken to using the wheelchair she insisted on.'

'She can't walk or won't walk?'

He shrugged. 'I can't find anything physically wrong with her. The infection she had has healed, and I can't see why it would cause this kind of intermittent paralysis. In my opinion, it is in her mind.'

'What's causing this, doc? She has barely seen her child since he was born.'

'Has she suffered some kind of trauma recently?'

'In what way?'

'Anything so emotionally upsetting that it might have an effect upon her mind?'

Mason averted his gaze, thought about the horrific moment they came across Davey hanging from the ceiling.

He shook his head. 'I can't think of anything. Will she get better?'

'Oh yes, I'm certain of it, Mr Mason. In time. All things heal with time.' Fuzzy grey eyebrows descended into a frown. 'If you don't mind me saying, Mr Mason, you don't look too good yourself. Are you feeling ill?'

He pumped out a humorous laugh. 'Feeling like shit if you must know. Truth is, I don't feel good. Strange thoughts, weird feelings; and I'm so tired all the time, and angry. Getting angrier.'

'Only natural, Mr Mason. It's stress. You exist in a pressured environment.' He opened the clasp on his bag, took out a brown bottle of pills. 'Here, take two, twice a day, with water, and avoid alcohol – though I know that's not a problem for you. My advice is for both of you to take things easy, rest up. Enjoy being parents and bask in what you have together.'

'Do you believe in curses, doc?' he asked out of the blue.

'Curses, Mr Mason?' Doctor Lombard shook his head. 'Curses do not exist. People have made such things up over the years to account for those events we cannot, or do not wish, to acknowledge as random acts over which we have no control. It is the human condition to seek to rationalise, to explain, even if the explanation appears irrational. Is that what you think is affecting you and your family, Mr Mason? Seriously? You've had such good fortune recently, have you not? Wealth, marriage, a successful movie, a son – if that is a curse then there are many who would wish it cast upon them!'

Mason did his best to return Lombard's smile. It was a pale imitation. 'You're right; it's stress. I need to lie down, take it easy. Thanks for the pills,' he said, rattling the bottle.

'Take them,' he insisted. 'Two tablets, twice a day remember. I'm coming back in a few days to check on Betsy. I'll be checking on you, too.'

Mason bade the doctor goodbye and knocked lightly on Betsy's bedroom door. She'd taken to sleeping in a separate room now. That pained him greatly, but she needed the space, he thought. He entered. The drapes were drawn, the place washed in something like twilight.

'Hi, honey. How are you?' he said.

Betsy was in bed, propped up on a mound of pillows. There was a bottle of pills on a bedside cabinet at one side, the wheelchair at the other. Mason swallowed hard, his chest feeling heavy, his head beginning to hurt again. The pain rarely seemed to go away these days.

'Have you checked on Davey?' she asked. Her voice sounded distant, lost in the gloom.

'Yeah. He refuses to leave that damn shack of his. But he says he's OK and not to worry about him. I've made sure he's got plenty to eat, fresh clothes. What a pair you are!' he said lightly, but it didn't draw a change of expression from her. 'Babe, I've got something to tell you...'

'If anything happens to Davey I'll die.'

'He's fine, Betsy. Nothing bad is going to happen to him. How are your legs?'

'They won't work,' she said flatly.

'Are you sure? Doctor Lombard says he can't find anything wrong with them.'

'Are you saying I'm making this up?' Anger lit her voice.

'No, of course I'm not saying that. Calm down. He said maybe it was some kind of trauma that caused it.'

'What does he know?' she said, turning her head so she didn't have to look at him.

'If you can't walk, they're pulling you from the picture, Betsy,' he said, sitting on the edge of the bed, needing to reach out and stroke her hair but feeling as if his hand had turned to lead.

'They can't do that!' she screeched. 'I'm Dorottya! That's my part!'

'I told them that, but they haven't got a choice...'

'Did you fight for me, Rick? Really put up a fight for me?'
'Sure I did.'
'Like hell! I know your game – you want to keep me locked up here, in this horrible mansion, in this gloomy old room, like he did with Dorottya.'

'You're rambling,' he said shortly, his heart heavy. 'You're not well.'

'Not well, like Dorottya, eh? She pleaded with Franz Horvat, didn't she? Asked for his help. Told him she was being kept a prisoner, being drugged, and all so Dragutin could make sick plans for having a son. A son of the devil!'

'You're talking crazy, Betsy.'

'Am I? Am I really? Are you drugging me, too, Rick, is that why I can't walk? You want to keep me locked away here, make everyone think I'm going crazy.'

He rose from the bed. 'Betsy, listen to you. You're not talking sense. Something's happened to you and I don't know what. You can't even look at your baby – our son! What's gotten into you?'

Her pretty face contorted into something grim, almost monstrous. 'It's you, can't you see that? It's Dragutin, he's got a hold on you. You were the one to let him in, wouldn't let him go. You let him take control of you.'

'That's sheer drivel!' he burst. 'Stop talking like this, Betsy; you're frightening me.'

She reached out across the bed, grabbed a newspaper and threw it at him. 'Look at that, Rick! You broke a woman's jaw! My Rick would never do something like that!'

He scanned the article. The woman had gone to the press after all. He put a hand to his head. 'I don't know how to explain...' he stammered.

'So who's next? Me? Is that your plan?'

He threw the newspaper aside. 'I need you to be a mother to our child, that's all!' he shouted. 'The kid needs a mother! Christ knows, we both never really had one of our own. Do you want the kid growing up shackled to our troubles?'

'It's too late for Eddie. The kid's already cursed...'
'I'm not listening to this, Betsy,' he said.
'Where are you going?' she said shrilly.
'Out.'
'To see Bunny Foster?'
'What?'
'You've been seeing Bunny, admit it. She's getting my part in the movie, right?'
'I haven't been seeing anyone.'
'First she becomes Dorottya, then what? She becomes your wife?'

He left the room, slamming the door behind him, his chest heaving. Once downstairs he poured a glass of water, took the tablets the doctor had given him, his head pounding like someone was laying into a corrugated-iron roof with a pickaxe.

He drove his car aimlessly for a couple of hours, then as the Sun sank down he headed into downtown Los Angeles, cruising the speakeasies and gin-joints till he found a place he could lose himself in a game of high-stakes back-room poker and drink himself senseless on illicit hooch.

Game over, a few hundred bucks lighter, he was invited to stay a while by an attractive brunette that reminded him of Betsy. She took him by the hand upstairs to a dingy little room that stank of cheap perfume and female sweat, sat him on the bed and made him watch whilst she undressed before him. He stared dolefully, his head swaying, feeling as if razors were slashing through the soft, pink flesh of his brain.

The woman's bare breasts were two inches from his face.

'You're that Dragutin guy, aren't you?' she said huskily, her blood-red lips glossy, wide and enticing. He nodded. 'You want to tie me up? You want to get rough with me? I don't mind if you get rough.' She kissed his neck, bit into it with her white teeth. It left a red welt. She began to unbutton his shirt, ran a soft hand over his chest. She pressed her breast against his lips. 'Bite me,' she insisted. 'Put me in your mouth and chew me. Eat me up, Baron Dragutin.'

He kissed the soft, resisting mound of her breast, took her nipple between his teeth and clamped down hard. She moaned gently, like the final breath of the dying, he thought, and then she tossed her head back, arching her slender throat.

The next instant he had his hands fastened around her neck, pushed her back onto the bed. Her eyes were closed in pleasure, her lips a perfect scarlet circle of wet velvet, her mouth a deep fleshy tunnel that beckoned him inside.

Then her eyes were opened wide in horror, her pink tongue sticking out from between her lips. She croaked out a strangled cry of alarm, her arms and legs beginning to thrash wildly on the bed covers, as if she were swimming in a sea of soft cotton. He pressed harder, ever harder, feeling her flimsy neck beneath his clawed fingers that dug deep and cratered her white skin.

He felt elation. He felt his blood coursing hot through him, down into his fingertips that glowed with the heat. He wanted her to die. He wanted to feel her body crush and crumple and her frail life extinguish beneath him. He wanted to kill her.

Then he released her, looking at his hands, shocked, as if they didn't belong to him.

'Oh Christ, what am I doing?' he said pathetically. He looked down at the woman who was gasping for breath, grasping her throat, trying to talk. She regarded his with abject terror, scrabbling over the bed, away from him.

He grabbed his coat, ran out of the bedroom, down the stairs, out the door and into the street. He paused to suck in the fume-filled air, began to sob uncontrollably. He rubbed his eyes, his sweat-drenched temples. His head was ablaze. He regained his breath before buttoning up his shirt, wiping his nose on his sleeve and staggering over to where his car was parked.

But before he could reach it the vehicle exploded in a giant fireball that threw him backwards so that he crashed against a storefront wall. The windows beside him shattered and he was showered with shards of broken glass. Burning fuel fell like tiny, writhing demons all around him. Then, with his eyes filled with a sickening vision of flaming hell, he blacked out.

* * * *

28

Monster-Guy

Two officers from the LAPD took a statement from him as he lay in the hospital bed. He was still feeling groggy from something the doctors had slipped him. They'd had to stitch up a deep cut above the eye, caused by flying metal from the exploding car and which they said had come close to taking out his eye. He was bruised all over from the fall, but he was grateful just to be alive. They insisted he stay there a while longer, just to be on the safe side, but he was already desperate to get his clothes on and get out of there.

'It was a bomb,' said one of the officers.

'Someone deliberately set out to kill me?' Rick Mason said incredulously.

'We received a message that it was members of the Church of Holy Reckoning who planted it. We contacted one of their spokespeople who strongly denied all connection to it. He maintained they are non-violent. A wad of their protest leaflets was found at the scene, which seems to corroborate the call. Could be a rogue protestor taking it a little too far. The bomb was too big, though, too sophisticated for it to be one guy, we think. Whatever, you were lucky you weren't sitting in the car at the time otherwise we'd still be picking up tiny pieces of Baron Dragutin off the sidewalk.' He chuckled, realised Mason wasn't amused. 'Did you see anyone loitering near your car?'

'No, can't say I did.'

'What were you doing in that neighbourhood anyhow, Mr Mason?'

'I needed to take a stroll,' he said abruptly.

'Maybe in future you should stroll someplace safer.' He rose from the chair at Mason's bedside, put his cap back on. He handed Mason a piece of paper and a pencil. 'Would you mind, sir?'

'Mind what, officer?'

'It would be real swell if you could give me your autograph. My wife, she's crazy about you. Don't know what she sees in that ugly son-of-a-bitch Dragutin, but all the same...'

Mason obliged and handed the officer his pencil and paper. 'Do you think you'll catch whoever planted that bomb? They might want to try again.'

'We'll do our best, sir,' he said with scant assurance. 'Like I say, better if you stay away from districts like that, eh?' He winked knowingly.

I've got to get the hell out of here, Mason thought, but the sedative they'd given him kicked in and he fell asleep in spite of his best efforts to fight it and stay awake.

When he arrived back home the following day there were many relieved faces there to greet him. Betsy was there too; she'd been brought downstairs and was sitting in her wheelchair. Her face was pale and anxious.

'I thought you were dead,' she said. 'The police told me you'd been blown up by a madman.' She began to cry, sending away the two servants who stood by her side. She held out her hand and Mason grasped her delicate fingers. 'What's happening, Rick?'

'Just some religious nuts, that's all. The police say they'll get them soon.'

Her head nodded towards the large plate-glass window that looked onto the swimming pool beyond. A tall well-built man stood with his hands behind his back. 'I don't trust the police,' she said. 'I've heard so many stories about them being corrupt. They could be in on this.'

'I don't think so, Betsy…'

'So I hired someone…' She waved and the man opened the door and stepped inside. He was pushing thirty, maybe, all muscle, meaty paws for hands. He wore a no-nonsense, narrow-eyed expression. 'This is Warren Sykes,' said Betsy. 'He's going to be our bodyguard.'

'We don't need a bodyguard,' he protested.

'Yes we do. You were nearly killed yesterday, and until whoever planted that bomb is found and arrested we'll need someone to watch over us. To watch over you. Please, Rick, for my sake. For Eddie's sake.'

'He eyed the man. 'Are you any good?'

'Ex-military, sir. Years in the field. Your wife has my references if you wish to see them, sir.'

He sighed, shook his head. 'That's OK, Sykes,' he said wearily. 'Welcome to the war zone; the devil on one side, God on the other.'

'That's not funny,' said Betsy.

'You should be caught in the middle,' he returned. 'It's hilarious!' He waved the man away. 'Go away and do whatever it is bodyguards do,' he said.

'Yes, sir,' he said and went outside again.

'Keep him close by you,' Betsy insisted, her eyes imploring.

'You've changed your tune haven't you? One minute I'm not to be trusted, the next you're looking after my skin. I don't get you.'

'I still love the man I married,' she said, spinning the wheelchair around and rolling away from him. 'He's not altogether lost,' she added. 'Not yet...'

Had Metropolitan's press agent got hair he'd have been tearing it out, Mason thought.

'This is getting out of hand,' he opined. He had a number of newspapers laid out in front of him on the desk. Other people looking similarly harassed shared the large desk in the centre of Metropolitan's conference room, sharp-suited men that Mason had never seen before. They all looked like they'd been up all night, their tired eyes all focussed on the press agent. 'First the broken jaw, then the increase in protests, and now a goddamn bomb. I'm not a miracle worker; there's only so much I can do to make a positive out of a negative.'

He looked close to having a breakdown, Mason mused. Welcome to the club.

'OK, so I admit it was wrong to go socking that woman, but I didn't cause the protest, and it was my life that had been on the line when that bomb went off. Why aren't the papers concentrating on that instead of hounding me?'

Conrad Jefferson had been sitting quiet at the head of the table, watching proceedings and puffing hard on his cigar, the third of the meeting. 'Well you gotta think of something!' he boomed suddenly. 'It's what we fucking pay you for! Scram and get me some good news for a change!'

The man scooped up his papers and scurried from the room. Jefferson scowled at one of the suits sitting in front of him, a sign for him to speak.

'It's a crucial time, Mr Jefferson, for both the new movie and for Metropolitan Studios. The backers of *The Devil Rises* are getting edgy with all this negative publicity mounting up. We've got a couple itching to pull out.'

'They're under contract,' Jefferson observed sourly. 'Let them try.'

'Neither can we afford a series of protracted legal battles, sir. Metropolitan's shares are falling and the shareholders are also getting edgy.'

'Fuck the shareholders. We should never have floated the goddamn company. OK, so I hear all that.' He turned to Mason. 'What have you gotta say?'

'I hear it, too, but I'm not sure what you want me to do about it.'

Jefferson wiped his tired eyes with a handkerchief. Hal Bremner was there amongst the suits, eyeing Mason. 'We have to pull the plug on Dragutin,' Bremner said.

Mason couldn't believe what he was hearing. 'You can't do that.'

'Makes sense to cut our losses,' Bremner continued.

'Mason's right,' Jefferson cut in. 'We can't do that. We've got too much riding on this movie, including our reputation. We've invested too much up front in the production to quit now. It would ruin us for sure. Hell, this damn production has been jinxed from the beginning.'

'Cursed,' said Bremner wryly.

'Funny,' said Mason. 'Look, if I have to pump even more cash into this I will.'

'If this movie goes ahead then I'm quitting,' Bremner said, the bombshell causing an explosion of complete silence around the room. 'I've got my reputation to think about, too. Mason can flash all the cash he likes, but my career is more important than that of a two-bit actor.'

Mason sprung to his feet. 'Cut the shit, Bremner!'

'I wish I could,' he returned, 'but that's proving difficult to do.' He pushed back his chair, rose calmly from the table and made for the door. 'We'll talk later, Conrad, in private,' he said.

Jefferson called the meeting off to give everyone time to cool down. A woman – one of Jefferson's army of secretaries and administrators – came looking for Mason.

'There you are! I've taken a call from your wife. Can you call her back first opportunity you get? She says it's very urgent. And she sounded more than a little panicky, Mr Mason.'

He thanked her and she found him a private office where he made a call, asked the operator to be put through to his house.

'Betsy,' he said wearily, 'what's wrong?'

'I've been trying to reach you for ages!' she said agitatedly. 'I was told you were in a meeting. Rick, I had a call from Davey. He sounded real bad. I'm scared he's about to do something crazy again. Please can you run out to his place and check up on him?'

'It's been one hell of a day, Betsy,' he said. 'Can't this wait?' Her sudden, shrill voice at the other end of the line told him it couldn't. He hung up, went out and told the secretary that if they called the meeting again to tell Jefferson he'd be late.

He popped a couple of the pills the doctor had given him, his head feeling as if it was about to explode and set off for Davey's shack. Along the way he found he kept watching other cars to see if they were following him, scanning the sidewalks to read the expressions in people's faces. Someone out there wanted him dead, blown to smithereens in God's holy name. What a fucked-up world this was, he thought bleakly. This entire thing with the bomb had him spooked real bad.

He saw the black plume of smoke billowing into the sky from some distance back and didn't think much about it till he realised with horror that it was coming from somewhere down the track that led to Davey's shack.

Cautiously he turned off the main highway and pointed his car down the narrow track. He saw two police cars first, in the distance, and immediately pulled over to one side. Mason walked a little way down the track, keeping under the cover of trees, till Davey's shack came into full view about a quarter of a mile away.

It was partially engulfed in flame which was being beaten out by a couple of guys swinging blankets. The fire had spread to a mound of car tyres, which had caused the dense black cloud of smoke. He saw an ambulance, men in short white coats entering the shack.

Headed towards him was an old man, his face blackened by smoke, his watery eyes rimmed red. He had a coat draped over his arm.

'I say, buddy,' Mason said, stopping the man, 'what's going on down there?'

'I was out in the field,' he said, 'working on the ditches. Then I see this smoke, coming from the old Cooper place. Some careless hobo, I thought, or kids fooling around with matches. But when I get close and look through the window I see a man lying on the floor and he's covered in fire. So I try to get into the place, managed to beat some of it out. Some cops saw the smoke and came snooping around, they told me to get out of there. I did, but not before I heard one of them get all excited.'

'Excited over what?'

'I heard him say they found papers in there, a wallet, things like that. He said the guy in there was someone called Peter Harvey. Turns out the stiff was a wanted man, a guy who wasted someone in Louisiana.'

'He was dead?' he said, his legs going weak.

'Sure was. Black as charcoal. Poured gasoline over himself and set light to it. That's what they said.'

Mason put his hand to his spinning head. 'No...' he gasped, struggling to breathe.

The old man squeezed one eye closed and stared at Mason. 'Say, aren't you that monster-guy? The one from that movie?'

'No, you must be mistaken,' he replied.

'You sure look like that monster-guy.'

He ignored the old man. He looked to the shack and saw the two men coming out with a stretcher. There was a body on it, covered with a sheet. He groaned and went back to his car, started the engine.

The old man came up to the car, grinning a toothless grin. 'You sure are that monster-guy. I knew you were! I said to myself, Jesus, that's the monster-guy! You can never escape!' he said, laughing. 'Ain't that what you say? You can never escape!'

'Get out of my fucking way!' said Mason.

'You can never escape!' he called again, a cloud of thick dust being thrown up by the car's speeding tyres causing the old man to choke and put his hand over his mouth.

* * * *

29

A Short Memory

'How is she?'

Doctor Lombard's face was grave. He closed the bedroom door. 'She was showing signs of slow improvement, but I'm shocked by what I see. What happened to cause her such distress?'

His tone was flavoured with accusation, which caused Rick Mason to shake his head and look down at the carpet. He knew what had brought about this sudden relapse. The news of Davey's death had come down on her fragile emotions like a sledgehammer. She'd been inconsolable, screaming and lamenting like some forlorn banshee. Nothing he could say or do could calm her down. He rang for the doctor at once.

'She's depressed, Mr Mason. Her nerves so shredded, her mood so low that I truly fear for her safety. We should really move her to a hospital where we can keep a watchful eye on her.'

'She doesn't want that,' he said. 'All she wants is to be cooped up in that damn room.'

'And you are certain you know of nothing that might have tipped her over the edge like this?'

He desperately needed to tell him, to tell someone, but he knew he could not. He was helpless. 'What can I do to help her?'

'I've given her strong sedatives to help her sleep. I'll be prescribing a course of medication to help manage her mood. All you can do for now is look after her. Keep an eye on her, watch out for signs that she's sinking any lower.' He put a hand on Mason's arm. 'You look shocking still, Mr Mason. Are the tablets I gave you helping any?'

Mason shrugged. 'I dunno. I feel terrible. My head… I feel like I'm losing it.'

'It's only to be expected with everything that is happening to you.' Doctor Lombard reached into his leather bag. He handed Mason a bottle. 'These are stronger than the others. Try them. Same dosage.' He noticed how Mason had trembled as he took the bottle from him. 'Please, for your own sake, Mr Mason, get some rest. I'll be back first thing tomorrow to check up on Betsy, but if you need me urgently you know where to reach me.'

'Thanks, doc, you've been a big help.'

'I suggest you employ a private nurse to take care of Betsy from now on till she gets well. I have a good one in mind and can leave details.' He was escorted by Mason to the door. 'The life of a Hollywood star is not always what it is expected to be, eh, Mr Mason? There are unseen prices that must be paid in return for fame.'

As Lombard drove away Mason saw Warren Sykes striding towards him, the bodyguard holding a wad of paper in his hand.

'I've increased security at the gates,' he said. 'I've put a man on them at all times. I've looked at perimeter security and there are places your walls might easily be breached by an intruder, so I'm installing lights and barbed wire in some areas, though I'd be happier if you'd allow me to build some of the walls a little higher. I've got a man with a dog patrolling the mansion grounds from 9pm to 5am. We can extend that, of course.'

'Is all this really necessary?' said Mason.

'You were nearly killed, sir. That's reason enough. I'm just following your wife's instructions on additional security.'

The man was like a machine, Mason thought. As serious as a notice of foreclosure. 'You fought during the war, that right?'

'Yes, sir.'

Mason licked his dry lips. 'You kill anyone?'

'Yes, sir. Plenty.'

'You get some kind of pleasure from that, Sykes?'

The two men locked eyes, but Mason couldn't read what lay beyond the man's steely orbs.

'I was doing my job, sir.'

'Still, did you enjoy killing even though it was your job?'

'Some guys did,' he said.

'And you?'

'I'd rather not talk about it, sir.' He bent to his papers. 'I'd like to go through this list of proposed changes with you, sir, at some time.'

'Fine, later.'

'We'll soon have this place as impregnable as a castle,' he said.

Mason studied the man's face for a smudge of irony but found nothing. As Sykes walked away Mason turned to look up at his mansion. He'd never noticed how the place resembled parts of Castle Dragutin back in Slavonia. A pared-down version maybe, but the ghost of it was there. Had something deep inside him chosen it with that in mind?

He went back inside, checked on Betsy, who lay fast asleep in her bed. The nanny was feeding his baby boy. He'd barely held the kid himself. What was he afraid of? Why daren't he touch him?

He ran a cold glass of water in the bathroom, swallowed a couple of pills. Next he filled a basin full of water, ducked his head into it and held it there until he couldn't hold his breath any longer. He raised his head, looked into the mirror over the basin.

The leering, distorted, skull-like face of Baron Dragutin stared back at him.

He yelled out in shock, jumped away from the basin and slipped on the tiles, his back hitting the wall behind him. He lay there, gasping for breath, his wet hair plastered down over his forehead, dripping water into his eyes and blurring his vision. He staggered to his feet, cautiously looked in the mirror again, his heart crashing against his ribcage.

His reflection was normal.

He swiped a hand over his face, rubbed his eyes. 'Oh, Jesus!' he said breathlessly.

Without drying his hair he dashed out of the bathroom, threw on a jacket and went out to his car.

'Where are you going, sir?' said Sykes.

'None of your damn business!' he yelled.

'I'm being paid to watch you, sir.'

'To watch me?'

'To make sure no one does you any harm.'

'Trust me, they can't do any worse to me.'

He drove away, noticing that Sykes was getting into his own car with the intention of following him.

He drove aimlessly, his mind in a whorl. First Franz Horvat, then Victor Wallace, now Davey. So many deaths. Was there really a connection, or was he trying to find one that wasn't there?

Somehow he ended up at the gates of Metropolitan Studios. He didn't acknowledge the wave of the guard as he drove into the yard. He parked the car and wandered around the various stages, watching blankly the comings and goings of a busy studio. Movie-making at work. This had been his dream once upon a time. A lifetime ago. Now it was a nightmare that he couldn't wake from.

He made his way to stage number three, where they were constructing some of the interior sets of Castle Dragutin. They were impressive. Based on his own recollections, the rooms were so real he could have been standing inside Castle Dragutin back in Slavonia.

Outside they'd been building the exterior walls, which would be used in external shots along with the subtle use of matte paintings to increase its size up on screen. They now had to be done on a back-lot instead of filming on location as they had intended. The precarious financial situation kicked that into touch. All the same he was mightily impressed by the sheer size and scale of the work, staring up at the massive circular towers, the many windows studding the realistic plaster walls.

'Scary, isn't it?'

He turned to see a woman standing there behind him, following his gaze to the high castle walls.

'Bunny, I didn't see you there,' he said. She looked different without all the makeup and fancy clothes he'd seen her in when accompanied by Jefferson. Her face was almost childlike in its wonder.

'I thought I'd come and have a look around the set. See where I'd be working. Seeing it on paper is one thing; to see it with your own eyes is quite a different thing. Now I feel the enormity of it.'

'You'll be fine,' he said unemotionally.

'You don't like me, do you, Rick?'

'I don't have an opinion either way.'

'I admire you,' she admitted.

He laughed hollowly. 'That I find hard to believe.'

'It's not your fault, all this that's happening out there. You were brilliant as Dragutin.'

'Hollywood has a short memory, Bunny. Always remember that.'

'Is your wife any better?'

'I'd rather not talk about it.'

'I'll bet she hates me, too.'

'That's OK. She hates me as well.' He found he couldn't stay angry with her. 'You have to take your chances in life when they come along, Bunny. Nobody blames you for that, least of all me.'

'Can I ask you something, Rick?'

'Fire away.'

'Would you mind if we spent some time together, going over our lines? I'm more than a little nervous. It would help immensely.'

He eyed her uncertainly. 'I don't know, Bunny…'

Then she laughed in embarrassment. 'Oh no, I didn't mean that! I'm not that kind of girl!' She held up her hand, showing Mason an engagement ring. 'I'm getting married in a few months time. I just wanted to go over some lines with you. It would be a big help, settle my nerves. I've got this meeting coming up with Hal Bremner and I admit the man scares me half to death.'

He laughed, too. 'Sorry, you must think me a sap. Sure, Bunny, that sounds like a swell idea.'

He couldn't remember laughing like that in a long time.

* * * *

30

Poor Kid

He awoke and was instantly gripped by wild panic, sitting upright in bed, his heart racing and his chest as tight as if someone had placed metal bands around it and was squeezing them hard. His entire body was drenched in sweat, his hair dripping with it, as if he'd been in the fiery grip of a raging fever.

He didn't know where he was. He was entombed in almost total darkness and he couldn't get his mind to focus. For a disturbing moment or two he didn't know who he was, and the panic welled up within him even stronger till he was on the verge of screaming out in fear.

Then he saw the outline of the window, the heavy drapes, and with that objects in the room floated out of the gloom, came together and started to make sense. The whole resolved itself from some overwhelmingly dreadful black cave of death and despair into the familiar surroundings of the spare bedroom.

He gasped thankfully as the loose ends of his brain tied themselves neatly together and he released a pent-up breath.

Rick Mason sank bank down to his pillow. It was wet with sweat so he sat back up again.

'You damn fool,' he said to himself, combing fingers through his damp hair, across a damp forehead. 'What's gotten into you?'

He threw the covers off him, swung his legs over the side of the bed and rubbed his eyes. His head hurt like blazes again, as if someone had poured broken glass into his skull and cocktail-like was giving it a good shake round. His mouth felt as dry as the desert soil.

Mason made out his crumpled clothes cast unceremoniously into an untidy mound on the floor. His shoes had been kicked off, one by the drapes, the other by the side of the bed. He frowned, because he couldn't remember undressing, getting into bed. His eyes narrowed further in thought, as if trying to squeeze out the relevant memories. Then it came to him that most of yesterday was a blank. There was nothing there and nothing he could do would bring it back.

He found himself getting panicky all over again and he rose from the bed, aware that he was naked, the sweat on his body cooling and causing him to shiver. He went over to the drapes and pulled them open slightly. The Sun was up. Looked like mid-morning approaching noon. It was unlike him to sleep so late; he was an early bird, but he guessed from the way he felt he was coming down with something. And tired – hell, he could hardly put one foot in front of the other. He'd talk to the doc when he came round to check on Betsy. Maybe he'd give him a shot of something. He couldn't afford to fall ill with shooting about to begin soon.

He went to the bathroom, checked himself out in the mirror, and was even happy to see his own haggard, bloodless face staring back. 'You look like shit,' he said, splashing water onto his hot face. He took a warm shower, washed away the sweat smell, still concerned that the events of the day before were still locked away in his skull somewhere. But he put it down to the fever he was obviously running.

From the wardrobe he chose a clean set of clothes, and as he did so he was washed over by a great sadness. They reminded him he had to sleep here, in a spare room because of Betsy's worsening condition, as if it were a physical sign that their life together was unravelling, being torn apart and he was powerless to prevent it.

He dressed, then bent down to pick up the pile of discarded clothes from the floor.

That's when he saw the blood.

A small patch of it, about an inch in diameter, soaking into the woollen fibres of the carpet. He put a finger to it, brought it up to his nose to smell it. Yes, it was blood, a definite metallic tang. He examined the jacket and saw splashes of blood on the sleeve, even more of it on the white of his shirt front.

He dropped the clothing in horror, stepped back from it. There was too much of it to be a cut, and anyhow, there wasn't a mark on him. It wasn't his blood, that was for sure.

'My God!' he mouthed 'Oh, my God!' He stared at it for a minute or two, not knowing what was happening, what to do. He walked around the pile of clothes, his head in his hand, trying to rationalise what he was seeing. An animal, perhaps? Had he hit something with his car last night on the way home – a dog, maybe? On the way home from where? This is crazy, he thought; I can't remember last night!

His attention was snagged by a cigar box on his bedside cabinet. He'd not noticed it before. He didn't smoke cigars himself; it was a silver box he kept downstairs, filled with cigars that he kept for visitors. What on earth was it doing up here, he thought?

Not knowing why, he felt escalating trepidation as he took the cigar box and flipped the lid.

He dropped it with a gasp. It hit the floor, and a white finger fell out of it, rolled briefly over the carpet and lay pointing accusingly at him.

'Oh Jesus!' he said, backing across the room to the door. When his breathing settled he crept slowly back, bent to his haunches and looked at the finger.

Mason immediately recognised the ring that it still bore. It was Bunny Foster's engagement ring.

He fell to the carpet, his legs unable to support him, the finger but two feet away from him.

'This can't be!' he groaned. 'It's impossible! It's not happening, none of it is! I've got a fever – I'm seeing things. It's not really here.'

But it didn't melt away. It remained, along with the blood on the carpet and on his clothes. His mind became a seething storm of crashing thoughts. He banged a fist against his temple. 'Remember, damn you! Remember!' But he couldn't, and with memories of how he'd nearly strangled the woman in the bedroom, he was faced with the terrible truth that he had done something horrific to poor Bunny Foster.

A full half hour passed as he sat in a semi-trance, then, almost automatically, he got a handkerchief, picked up the finger with it, feeling his stomach heave at the touch. He put it back in the cigar box and shut it away in a drawer. He did the same for the pile of clothes. But the patch of blood on the carpet regarded him like a red satanic eye. He needed to clean it away, he told himself. There had to be a rational explanation for all of this, but he still needed to get rid of it.

That makes you guilty, his other self told him; wanting to hide the truth.

Guilty of what? I don't know what's happened. It could all be nothing.

Nothing? There's a woman's finger in a cigar box in one of your drawers. Call that nothing?

He took aspirin, composed himself and went out to the landing. Nobody was around. He went downstairs and found a set of keys and returned to lock the bedroom door. He'd make sure the maids stayed out of the room till he could clean it up, sort things out.

Betsy was laid in bed. Mason paused at her door, the patch of light falling from the doorway onto his wife's sleeping figure.

'Help me, Betsy...' he said.

He went to her. Her face on the pillow was at peace. She looked beautiful, he thought. He loved her from the moment he first met her, and it cut him up dreadfully to see her like this. He could have saved Davey for her. He should have tried harder.

Her eyes flicked open. They were blank, as if dead. Then she screamed and lashed out with her clawed fingers, catching him on the cheek. He jumped back from her and she sat up, pulling the blankets protectively to her chin.

'Get away from me, you beast! Help me! Help me!' she screamed again.

Mason put out his hands. 'Betsy, it's me, it's your Rick,' he pleaded. But it only caused her to scream out all the louder.

A maid, alerted by the shouting, dashed into the room. 'What's wrong, sir?' she asked worriedly.

'He's a monster!' Betsy shouted. 'Get him away from me!'

Mason hurried from the room. 'Call Doctor Lombard!' he ordered the maid 'At once. She's ill.'

Downstairs, he poured himself a large drink. As he was downing his second the phone rang. He ignored it, poured another, sat down, his head and shoulders slumped forward. A knock came at the door. Warren Sykes was standing there.

'You Ok, sir?' asked the bodyguard. 'You look – '

'It's none of your fucking business what I look like!' he fired angrily.

'The studio is trying to contact you, sir,' he said.

'I don't want to talk to the fucking studio. I'm busy.'

'Bunny Foster's been found dead. She's been murdered.'

Mason dropped his glass. It shattered on tiles. 'When?'

'Last night. I don't know the details exactly, but they say she's been cut up real bad, like someone's tried to drain all her blood as if she was a pig.'

'No...' he said shakily.

'All hell has broken loose down at Metropolitan, sir.' His eyes narrowed. 'You're bleeding, from your cheek, sir.'

He put a hand to his face. Felt the tiny sting of pain. 'Betsy did it, just now.'

'Betsy?'

'Do they know who killed Bunny?'

'No, not yet. The police are swarming all over Metropolitan, though.' The phone rang again. Sykes looked from it to Mason. 'You want me to get that, sir?'

'Get the hell out of here, Sykes,' he snarled, and the sudden flaring up of anger took them both by surprise.

'Sure,' said Sykes.

Mason picked up the receiver and put it to his ear, the stem of the phone clutched in a shaking hand. 'Yeah?' he breathed into the mouthpiece. He listened in silence. 'Yeah, OK, I'll get down to the studio as soon as I can. Yeah, it's tragic. Poor kid...'

Mason drove down the winding path from his mansion to the main gates. He called the guy over who was manning the small hut Sykes had installed.

'Morning, Mr Mason,' he said. 'What can I do for you?' His eyes were drawn to the scratches decorating Mason's cheek.

'You keep a log of who comes and goes here, don't you?'

'Sure do, Mr Mason. Every visitor, every car, date and time. Mr Sykes' orders.'

'Can I see the log, please?'

The guard went to his hut, brought out a grey ledger which he handed to Mason. With trembling fingers, Mason flipped the pages till he got to yesterday's date, his finger travelling downwards till it got to his own name and car registration. Time out was given as 1.20pm. Time in as 2am.

'Everything OK, sir?'

'Were you on guard last night?'

'No, sir. That will be Joe. He finished his shift at 8am this morning; that's when I came on duty.' He reached for the book.

'I'll keep this, thanks,' said Mason.

'All yours, sir,' he said, smiling and giving a salute as Mason drove away, the ledger on the seat beside him.

* * * *

31

The Sacrifice

'This is a *crisis*!' hollered Conrad Jefferson. 'What I need is constructive dialogue, not schoolyard mud-slinging! Let me tell you something; nobody here smells any better than the next man, because we're all in the shit!'

The conference room was deathly quiet after that. Someone shuffled paper. Even the paper sounded nervous. Someone said, 'We didn't need this, Mr Jefferson. This is real bad news.'

'You think I need to be reminded of that, you blithering moron?' Jefferson chomped on his cigar, found it distasteful and tossed it across the room. His face was almost puce coloured in parts, and he looked like he'd been ragged by a dog.

Someone else felt brave enough to speak. 'We need a final decision on the movie. One way or the other. We've held off too long already.'

Jefferson scanned the room full of suits. He singled out one of them for his steely gaze. 'As head of finance tell me like it is, and don't even think to dress it up with any fancy bullshit.'

The man bit at his lower lip for a second. 'As you are well aware, shares have been precarious to say the least, falling as fast as a whore drops her underwear. Bunny's murder has leaked out and cranked up the uncertainty in the company. Once it hits the markets tomorrow Metropolitan shares are in for a tumble that will make the walls of Jericho coming down look like a kid stepped on his toy building blocks. *Bride of Dragutin* was always going to be a risky venture which we all know the studio needed to succeed, as Metropolitan couldn't sustain its run of feature productions and was fast running into financial trouble. Thankfully the movie exceeded expectations. In order to capitalise on *Bride*'s success we moved fast to get a sequel into production. We've ploughed a lot of the profits from *Bride* into the sequel, as well as raising significant money off the back of it from a number of key backers. Thus far, all good and well.

'Unfortunately, we couldn't predict everything that has happened. The increase of negative feeling towards the movie has grown steadily, and in particular towards Rick Mason himself, which has rubbed off on Metropolitan. Nor could we have foreseen the murder of one of our actresses, and the fact people are even saying it is a copycat murder, influenced directly by *Bride*, which adds another distasteful and complicated layer to the entire thing.

'Financially speaking, we have both our own and our backers' money tied up in the sequel, a great chunk of it already expended on production costs. We've got some of the largest sets we've ever built standing ready to use out on the lots, and as you know it's like a train that's gathered up a head of steam and already heading down the track, difficult to stop and turn around. In short, we've already spent a fortune on this which we'll never get back. Then, on the other hand we have such a strong swell of public resentment turning against us that people are already falling out with the entire Dragutin product and may not be in the mood for the new movie when it's released. It's likely the film will flop, even if we manage to get it past the censors, which are already waiting like a bunch of hungry sharks to rip it to pieces.

'So, no bullshit; if I had to play devil's advocate I'd say that this will bring Metropolitan close to bankruptcy, shares crash, the board gives a vote of no confidence, the vultures would swoop in – forgive the predator metaphors – and fight amongst themselves to initiate a takeover.'

'Over my dead body!' Jefferson burst angrily. 'The way I see it we still ain't got a choice. We have to make the movie. Production costs have been immense, everything's lined up and ready to start rolling, like you say. We just can't call a halt now. Pulling out at this stage would shove us into bankruptcy for sure. Our investors will sue us for every cent we have and those same vultures would take everything I ever worked for. We have to keep this thing running. You ain't telling me anything I don't already know. What I need is something to make the pain easier to bear.'

'Forgive me for asking,' said the head of finance, 'but is a big part of the problem here the movie or Rick Mason, because they're not the same thing.'

'Go on.'

'Ditch Mason and you ditch a big part of the problem. A lot of the gripe has been levelled in his direction. It's him, not necessarily the movie, that's been targeted by those religious nuts – they didn't bomb Metropolitan, did they? They hit him. Nor have they tried to take it out on you, or the producer or director. The police have already said there may be a connection between Bunny's murder and the religious protestors. Why don't we play up that aspect? When we deal with the press we subtly emphasise how it's Mason the public are falling out of love with, and it's this that has given rise to the religious protests, and eventually led to Bunny's death. We deflect public disquiet away from Metropolitan somewhat.'

A murmur went around the room and Jefferson eyed his head of finance. 'He becomes the scapegoat, that what you're saying?'

'It wouldn't solve everything but it will help. Drop Mason from the movie. Make it loud and clear that you're making a big sacrifice here, bowing to public opinion. If Mason kicks up a fuss, which he surely will, you can always make out you're doing it in his interest, privately and in public, too. After all, his life was put in danger because of the movie, and you don't want another death on your hands do you? Pay him off, whatever; it's peanuts compared to losing the company. If he kicks up a stink we stick to our guns by insisting it's in his own and the public interest. If he fights it further he risks turning people even more against him, because he obviously doesn't have the public interest at heart. You come out of this squeaky clean, public faith in Metropolitan's integrity restored and the religious nuts getting their pound of flesh into the bargain. They'll be back, of course, but by doing this you can at least get on with the production.

'Let's face it, Mason's become a liability we don't need, and even his wife is reportedly going nuts. They're dragging you down, Mr Jefferson. Cut them both free and let them sink so Metropolitan can float. It's a small price to pay and personally I can't see many more options.'

'I don't know,' said Jefferson after thinking it over for a few seconds. 'It's a risk. Mason is the star whether we like it or not. In spite of those loons there are still thousands of women that want to see him up there, not some cheap stand-in...'

'Which makes it an even bigger sacrifice by Metropolitan.'

He blinked slowly, his eyebrows working their way ever downwards. 'Ah fuck it!' Jefferson said. 'Have my legal-boys look at it and draw up something watertight.'

* * * *

32

A Black Rage

Rick Mason studied the police officer warily. They were sitting in a small office at Metropolitan Studios, hurriedly vacated so that preliminary interviews could be carried out and statements taken. Mason found it impossible to stop his hands from shaking, so he put them beneath the table, clamping them onto his thighs. His vision was blurred, his eyes beginning to water.

'I won't keep you long, Mr Mason,' said the officer. 'As you can see, we're asking a lot of the people at the studio a lot of questions.' He glanced at his notes.

'What exactly happened to her?' said Mason.

'She was murdered, sir,' he returned flatly, flicking paper, licking the tip of his pencil.

'That much is blindingly obvious. How, when? More importantly, why? She was a decent woman...' He felt his words trying to choke him.

'For obvious reasons I can't go into too much detail, sir. But safe to say she was found dead in the bathroom of her apartment this morning by her maid. She was cut up real bad.'

'Rumour has it she was found in the tub, her wrists and throat cut, as if to drain all her blood...'

The officer looked up. 'Gossip gets around Hollywood faster than in any place I know, Mr Mason.' His eyes narrowed. 'Are you feeling OK, sir?'

'Must be coming down with something.' He managed a misty-thin smile.

'I'm a big fan of yours, Mr Mason,' the officer admitted. 'You scared the hell out of me and my girlfriend.'

'Thanks.'

'Seems like you've got another fan who likes you more than most.'

'What do you mean?'

'Although we didn't see any of it in all its gory detail up on screen, you and I know the manner of Miss Foster's death is very reminiscent of what happens to a young woman in *Dragutin's Bride.*'

'Are you implying someone's actually copying what Dragutin does in the movie, doing it for real?'

The officer didn't like the blunt end of his pencil and took out a small penknife to whittle away at it. 'Wouldn't be the first time someone thought they were a Napoleon, or a Julius Caesar, a George Washington, or maybe now a Baron Dragutin...' Satisfied, he put his knife away, Mason watching the small movements intently. 'Miss Foster was at the studios yesterday.'

'Nothing unusual in that; she's making a movie here.' He realised it sounded curt. 'Sorry, like I said, she was a good woman.'

'You were here yesterday, too, which as you point out, is not unusual. Did you see her?'

He couldn't read what was going on behind the officer's eyes. He grew nervous. Hesitated. Tried to swallow but his mouth went dry. 'Yes I did. We met at the castle set and talked.'

He nodded. 'Yeah, that's what I've been told. Someone saw the pair of you. Why'd you meet?'

'She just happened to be visiting the set same time as me and she then said she wanted to go over the script together.'

'Did you? Go over the script, I mean.'

'Yeah. We found a quiet corner of the studio and sat for a while.'

'How long is a while?'

'Two hours maybe.'

'Then what?'

Mason's memory was getting foggy at this point. 'She said she had to go. She was meeting Hal Bremner, I believe. She appeared to be nervous about the meeting.'

'Nervous about meeting Mr Bremner? Why was that?'

'She said he scared her.'

'In what way?'

He shook his head. 'Just that type of guy, I guess. Abrasive, you know.'

The officer nodded. Made notes. 'What time did you part?'

'I dunno. Maybe three, three-thirty – I can't be certain.'

Again the police officer nodded. 'That tallies with the security guard at the gate. She left the studios at four-fifteen precisely. You've no idea if she saw anyone else before seeing Mr Bremner? Or did she mention anyone else she was seeing after meeting with him?'

Mason said no, she didn't mention anyone. He was relieved he hadn't left with her; he simply couldn't remember what happened after the reading of the script. It was all a terrifying blank. 'Sorry, I can't help you there,' he said.

'Did she seem troubled by anything?'

'Nervous at making the movie, but quite the opposite really; she was excited at the prospect. It was her big break.' He felt a grey wash of sadness engulf him as he said it. 'And she was getting married soon. She showed me her…' He trailed off. Pointed to his finger.

'So let's get this clear; you never saw her with anyone, either before or after you met with her?'

'No, officer. I didn't see her with anyone.'

'And when did you leave the studio, Mr Mason?'

His chest began to tighten. 'I can't quite remember. Some time after, I guess.'

The police officer singled out a sheet of paper from a small pile he had on the desk. He ran his finger down a list. Mason began to sweat. 'This is a copy of the gate log from yesterday. You left the studio at six-ten in the evening.'

'Six-ten,' he echoed. It was no use; it was still a black hole, a fearful void. Any moment the officer was going to ask what he did next and he hadn't the faintest idea. All he knew for certain was that he had a pile of bloodstained clothes and a severed finger at home. He sucked in rapid breaths. He should confess to it. He needed to tell him what he'd found, tell him about his memory blank…

'Thank you, Mr Mason,' the officer said, closing up his notebook and tidying the sheets of paper. 'We'll be in touch if we need to speak again. I'm sorry this had to happen to Miss Foster; I know you liked her. But the world is full of crazy people and things like this happen.'

Mason sighed heavily with relief. 'Do you reckon there was some kind of motivation, like robbery?' he fished. 'Isn't that the usual motive?'

'The officer paused, gave him the once-over with studious, careful eyes. 'The only thing missing of any value is her diamond engagement ring,' he replied. He thought about what he was going to say next very carefully. 'Plus her finger with it,' he added. 'I've seen too much to know that robbery wasn't the motive. This is one sick mother we have here. And a movie it ain't. Thank you for your time, Mr Mason. I've got others to see now.'

Mason wandered down the corridors of Metropolitan Studios in a daze, vaguely aware of people moving around him, the odd-one greeting him, seeing a few more uniformed police officers who he astutely avoided, and he made his way to the exit. The receptionist at the main desk called him over.

'Mr Mason, your agent is looking for you.'

'I'll give him a call later,' he said dully.

'He's here,' she said, and pointed to a sharp-faced man who rose from a seat and dashed over to him.

'Where have you been, Rick? I've been trying to get hold of you.'

Mason looked at him. He missed Victor Wallace dreadfully, and to rub it in this new guy had been shit. Hurt was piling up on hurt. 'I've been busy,' he said.

He grabbed Mason by the arm and led him away from the desk. 'They're dropping you from the movie,' he said. 'I found out half an hour ago.'

'That's impossible!' he said 'It's my goddamn movie!'

'They've done it. Nothing you can do, Rick.'

He clutched the man's shirt and put his face close to his. The agent's eyes balled up in fear. 'You weak, little man!' he said. 'You let them do it! Victor would have fought for me!'

'Well I ain't Victor!' he said. 'And there's nothing you can do about it. Any of it. You've only yourself to blame!'

Mason pushed him away. A strong urge to punch the man in the face rose like a geyser inside him and he struggled to put a heavy lid on the building pressure. 'Nothing I can do? Well we'll see about that!'

He dashed away across the highly-polished wooden floor, burst into Jefferson's office, the secretary behind the desk rising on seeing him.

'Mr Mason...' she said uncertainly.

'I want to see that swine Jefferson!' he roared, stomping to the door of his office.

'He's not in. I can make an appointment for you.'

'Fuck an appointment.' He tried the handle on Jefferson's glass-fronted office door. It was locked. 'I know you're in there, you two-faced, lying bastard!' He rattled the door.

'He's out, Mr Mason,' the secretary said, picking up the phone.

Mason ignored her, put his shoulder against the door, threw his weight upon it. The door frame splintered and the door flew open, the glass splintering. The woman shrieked at the noise. But the office was empty. Mason spun on his heel to see Hal Bremner telling the secretary to calm down.

'You're behind this!' Mason cried, a black rage boiling up, flushing his cheeks.

'Are you drunk?' Bremner said. 'Get the hell out of here, Mason, or I'll get someone to throw you out.'

In an instant, Mason threw himself on Bremner, bowling the man to the ground with the impact. The secretary screamed as the two men rolled kicking and punching on the floor.

'I'll fucking kill him!' Mason roared. 'I'll kill the two of you!'

Two uniformed security guards piled into the office, dragged Mason off Hal Bremner, who put a hand to his bloodied mouth. 'You're finished, Mason!' he said. 'Get the fucker out of my sight!'

Mason resisted, thrashing madly, but the guards had him pinned down real good. They hauled him out of the office.

* * * *

33

A Creature of the Night

They said they weren't going to press charges for assault and criminal damage, because they knew they had him where they wanted him. He'd made it all the easier for them to dump him.

Rick mason didn't know how it had happened. One minute he remembered being interviewed by the police officer, then a vague idea that he'd spoken to the woman behind the desk at reception. The next he was being sat on by security guards in Conrad Jefferson's office. He'd suffered a blackout again. But his bruised knuckles, his painful shoulder, told him he'd done something drastic. When he was fully briefed on his actions he was both dumbfounded and alarmed. It had happened again. The rage had built up, had taken over him, swamped his very being and smothered his normal self.

Normal self? What was that? He didn't know who he was anymore, what he was becoming. He was fast losing control, and something else was gaining the upper hand. He feared that he would relinquish control fully.

Eventually he was driven home. A bristling wall of newspaper reporters was standing in front of his mansion gates, clamouring for a comment, pointing cameras. He cowered away from their attention, wanting to seek solace in the darkest corners of the vehicle.

He was relieved to get inside and close the doors on the madness outside. Madness outside? He grimaced; he wasn't so sure he could escape the madness. It was everywhere.

He went to the bedroom, opened the drawer and looked at the clothing again. He left the cigar box closed; he couldn't bring himself to lift the lid. What was the point? The finger would still be there, pointing to his screaming guilt. He'd murdered Bunny Foster and he'd go to the electric chair because of it. Or maybe he'd get off because they'd think him mad, his only defence being he was possessed by the evil spirit of his dead father, the results of a pact with the devil. Then he'd spend the rest of his days locked away in some lunatic asylum, with all the horrors that brought. Or he ended this right now. Take a pistol, put it to his head. Blow his fucked-up brains out...

He closed the drawer on the gruesome reminders and padded along the landing to Betsy's room. Strange how he now called it that, the room they used to share not so long ago. He looked down on her sleeping form.

His eyes were drawn to a small medicine bottle on the bedside table. He lifted the brown bottle; liquid sloshed inside. He didn't recognise the bottle or its label, had never seen it before.

'Betsy,' he said quietly. She didn't respond. He touched her shoulder, shoved her gently. She appeared to be so deep in sleep it was almost as if she really was drugged.

The thought stuck like a thorn in his mind. He looked closely at the medicine bottle again, unscrewed the cap and sniffed the contents. A bitter smell. He pocketed it and went to the bathroom.

'What are you doing to me, you sick bastard?' he said to his reflection in the mirror over the basin. 'You're dead. Leave me and my family alone…'

'Mr Mason! Mr Mason!' The maid was calling upstairs. 'There's a blacksmith here to see you.'

He came to lean over the banister. 'What do you mean a blacksmith?'

'That's what he said he was, sir. He says he's got a parcel to deliver to you directly, not to anyone else. He won't leave it with me.'

'I haven't ordered anything from any blacksmith,' Mason said, descending the stairs. But a man was standing impatiently at the door, a wooden box in his hands. 'What do you want?' he asked; he noticed a truck parked outside with the name *Benny Fortune, Blacksmith* painted in faded yellow letters on its side.

'It's what you ordered,' said the man. 'We made it for you.'

'I didn't order anything to be made. What is it?'

The man took a sheet of paper. 'You sure did, sir,' he said, waving the paper. 'This is yours. I was told to hand it to nobody but you.' He pushed the box at Mason and he took it. The man planted the piece of paper on top. 'Sign here, please, Mr Mason.'

He did so. 'How much do I owe you?' he said mechanically.

'You already paid in full.' He fingered his cap in mock salute and went to his truck.

Mason carried the box inside. It was weighty, rattled with something metal. He prised off the lid.

Packed out with straw he saw a length of chain. Bemused, he lifted it out. He dropped it back inside when he realised what it was.

A leg-iron and chain. Like the one Franz Horvat had described that had been used to keep Dorottya a prisoner in her room in Castle Dragutin.

'She won't wake, doc,' said Mason.

'How many have you had?' said Doctor Lombard, nodding at the glass of spirits in Mason's hand. It was dark outside, and Mason was sitting all alone without a single lamp burning. Lombard went round flicking on switches, lighting the place up.

'Not nearly enough,' he replied. 'It's Betsy – I can't wake her up.'

'I'll check on her.'

'Doc, what is this you've been giving her?' He held up the brown medicine bottle.

Lombard came closer, peered at it. 'That's not one of mine,' he said. 'I don't recognise it at all. Where did you get it?'

'I found it by Betsy's bed. You didn't prescribe this?'

He shook his head firmly. 'Not at all.'

'Are you able to test what's inside?' His voice was slurred, his head fogging up but not as fast as he'd like.

'It would take time, but I can, if you wish. Why?'

'I think it's some kind of sleeping drug.'

'A drug?'

'I think it's being used to keep Betsy ill. That's why she can't walk. That's why she's not been herself.'

The doctor's expression grew serious. He used his handkerchief to take the bottle from him, uncapped it and took a sniff. 'Why would anyone want to drug Betsy?'

Mason raised his glass. 'Now there's a question!' Then his face fell sombre. 'I'm not myself, doc.'

'You haven't been yourself for some time, Mr Mason.'

'No, you don't get it; I'm not myself!' He laughed hysterically and found he couldn't stop. Then he began to sob. 'What kind of a man orders leg-irons to be made for his wife?'

'You're drunk, Mr Mason,' he said, taking the glass off him. 'And you are far from well. Come, let me take you to your room so you can lie down.'

Meekly, he let Lombard lead him upstairs. Outside the bedroom door Mason bade him check on Betsy. 'I love her, you know, doc,' he said. 'I don't care about all this…' He waved loosely at the ceiling. 'Money, fame, it all counts for nothing in the end. I'd do anything to go back to when I first met her, before I ever heard of Baron Dragutin.'

'Take a tablet, lie down,' he insisted.

'Sure, doc. You've been good to us.' He paused in closing the door on the doctor. 'I miss Victor Wallace,' he said. 'He was like a father to me. A real father, not like…'

'You're upset and the drink is doing the talking for you. Rest up.'

'Yeah, sure,' he said. 'Everything will be fine in the morning. All back to normal. People that are dead will be alive again and people who should be dead will be dead.'

'Sounds fascinating,' said Lombard, smiling, closing the door on Mason. He went across the landing to Betsy's room, taking the medicine bottle out of his pocket and checking it over.

For a long while it seemed he existed in a place between wakefulness and sleep, where shadowy creatures crept from the far recesses of his mind to gnaw at him; where he swam in a thick sea of warm blood that he swallowed, breathed up his nose and made him choke; where the land turned to a carpet of severed, writhing, shivering, crawling, slug-like fingers.

Something dragged him from his torment. Something that pricked his exhausted mind awake. He lay there on the pillow in the pitch-black room. Staring up to where the ceiling should be, the ghosts of his nightmares playing out on it briefly before being torn to shreds as consciousness swept the remains of those grotesque images into the far reaches of his brain.

But then Rick Mason's nightmares came vividly to life again.

A shapeless black shadow launched itself out of the dark and his breath was knocked suddenly from him as something heavy landed on his chest. He raised his hands to fight off the creature of the night, opened his mouth to scream out in alarm, but something soft was stuffed over his mouth, pressed hard against his nose. He struggled wildly, thrashed his arms and legs as the cotton wadding threatened to smother him.

Then his world began to smudge like fingers being dragged over a charcoal sketch. He grew tired, weak, his thoughts a ragged mess of frayed beginnings and loose ends that didn't make any sense.

The face that was close to his was lost in the darkness, but he could smell cigarette smoke on its breath.

He lost feeling in his fingers that gripped the arm which pinned him down. His hand slipped away as his world crumbled into dust and was blown away into the furthest reaches of a cold, empty universe.

* * * *

34

Never to Move Again

He fought to prise his eyes open, his lids so damn heavy, his thoughts refusing to come together into anything meaningful. The first sensation was that he felt he couldn't breathe, something stuffed deep into his mouth that threatened to choke him; and everything was hellishly black.

Rick Mason sought to spit out whatever it was filled his mouth, needing to shout, to scream, but his lips were unable to move. Neither could he move his hands.

Was he dead?

He tried to regain control of his breathing, to stem the sheer terror that threatened to engulf him.

No, he wasn't dead. But he was in a heap of trouble, that much was for sure. His mouth had been gagged, and a hood of some sort had been thrust over his head. His hands had been tied above his head to something solid that didn't want to budge, so that he hung there like a pig from a spit. The weight of his body caused pain in both outstretched arms. It became apparent that his legs had been tied securely too. What the hell was going on, he thought?

Then the hood was ripped off his head, causing him to start. He blinked, hardly believing what he was seeing.

He was in a dimly-lit stone-walled room, the walls glistening wet and slimy-green in places. A tiny slit of a window was embedded into one of the walls, beside this a series of rusted chains fastened by iron hoops to the wall. When he looked up, however, he discovered there was no ceiling; high above him was a dark void, barely visible rafters criss-crossing through it. It soon began to dawn on him exactly where he was.

Incredibly, he was being kept a prisoner in one of the newly constructed movie sets for *The Devil Rises*. It was Baron Dragutin's dungeon.

A scuffling sound from his right made him look round. He saw a man, his fat upper torso naked, arms also tied above his head, which was covered by a hood, crudely made out of coarse sacking. His feet were bare and bloodied, his trousers muddied and torn.

Both men were strapped to a frame made from metal scaffolding poles. The man by Mason's side was tugging at his bonds, tiredly, as if he'd been at it some time and his strength was flagging; his white, sweat-drenched flesh rippled with the sharp movements.

Mason became aware of someone else standing behind him. The sound of metal against metal, metal against stone. He tried to turn his head round to see who it was, but he couldn't twist far enough.

The man at his side was groaning pitifully. Almost whimpering.

What is happening to me, Mason thought? His anxiety rose hot again. This doesn't make sense. None of this is real.

He fought against his bindings. The scaffolding rattled but his bonds remained secure.

'Easy there, Mason,' said a man's voice behind him.

Mason froze. He recognised it at once.

Warren Sykes stepped round to Mason's front, bent down between him and the other stricken man. He placed a long knife on the stone floor, and next to it two pairs of pliers. Satisfied, he looked up, regarded Mason with moon-cold, dispassionate eyes, then he took a pistol from his coat pocket, checked it over, put it back. Mason thought it looked ex-army issue.

He pulled desperately at his fastenings again.

'Don't do that,' warned Sykes. 'It's not going to get you anywhere.' He went over to the half-naked man. 'Want to see who you've got for company, Mason?' He ripped the hood off.

It was Conrad Jefferson.

The man's eyes were billiard-ball-wide, panic-stricken. He flinched when the hood was removed, as if he'd been burnt, his chest ballooning in and out.

This just wasn't real, Mason thought. It was as if he were still caught up in a dreadful nightmare from which it was impossible to wake.

Sykes came back to stand directly in front of Mason, staring unflinchingly deep into his eyes.

'I'm going to take this gag off you,' he said. 'But don't even think of shouting out for help. In the first instance this entire stage has been soundproofed. Personally, I don't think talkies will take off, but they sure did me a favour. Hell, a bomb could go off in here and I'll bet no one would hear it. Secondly, you so much as make a murmur and I'll send my fist so deep into your stomach that it'll snap your backbone. You got all that?' Mason nodded dumbly. Sykes untied the cloth that held the wadding in his mouth. Next he pinched out the wadding and dropped it to the floor.

Mason coughed, gasped for air, and screamed out for help.

Sykes landed a balled fist into Mason's unprotected stomach and he crumpled in pain. He vomited and struggled to draw breath.

'What did I tell you?' said Sykes. 'Why is it actors find it so difficult to take direction?' He gave a grunt of a chuckle at his own little joke.

Mason, his eyes watering, shook his head, as if trying to shake away the madness. 'Sykes, what's going on?'

Sykes went over to the knife on the floor, bent slowly down and picked it up; its blade appeared cold and icy-blue in the dim light. Sykes twirled it before his eyes. 'You know, Mason, I gotta admire your father.'

'My father? You're crazy, Sykes. He was a monster. In God's name, what are you doing with that knife?'

He saw Jefferson's gaze was transfixed by the cruel blade, his flabby body glossy like a large white seal. He glanced over at Mason. There were tears in his uncomprehending eyes.

Sykes ran a thumb down the sharp edge of the knife. 'Some people find pleasure in sex, some in food, some in fine wines. Some find it in pain and in death. Ever seen a man die, Mason?'

He shook his head. 'Let me go. Set us both free.'

'I've seen a hundred different days to die,' he continued. 'Bullet, bomb blast, bayonet, grenade, knife, strangulation, drowning. Ever think it strange that there is only one way to enter life and a hundred ways to leave it?' The blade drew blood and Sykes studied the bubble of red sitting on the end of his thumb. He put his thumb into his mouth to suck off the blood.

'You're my head of security!' he said. 'What the fuck is going on?'

'Ironic, eh?' he said. He sized Jefferson up.

'Are you after money, is that it?'

'Got my money, thanks.' Sykes prodded Jefferson's exposed stomach and the man shuddered. 'People don't realise how tough the human skin is, or how thick. It can quickly blunt a knife, which is why you have to make sure it's good and sharp to start with.' He placed the back of the knife on Jefferson's stomach. 'I'm going to skin you alive,' he said. 'First I'll make a long incision across here...' He drew the blade across his flesh. '...all around you. I'll warn you now that the pain will be almost unbearable. Perhaps you will faint. That will be a good thing for you, because I will then take these pliers and I will peel the skin upwards, as if I was taking a vest off you. A thick, fatty, white vest. If you are lucky you will stay unconscious. If you are doubly lucky you might have a heart attack and die. And when I have stripped the skin from you and have let you suffer for a while I will take my gun and I will put a bullet through your head.' He turned to Mason. 'You see, your father is such an inspiration to me!'

'You're mad, Sykes! That's inhuman! Look, you can have money, lots of it. You don't have to do this!'

'Yes he does,' said a voice from behind him. 'Sykes, just get on with it. We haven't got all night.'

'Betsy?' said Mason disbelievingly. He was totally shocked to see her step in front of him. She wore a long black coat, a black hat whose brim bathed her eyes in shadow. 'You're ill – what are you doing here? Christ, Betsy, is this some kind of sick joke?'

'Ill?' she gave a crackling, humourless laugh. 'I'm an actress, Rick. I act. It's what actresses do, when they're given the chance.'

'Betsy, I don't understand! Look, you're not well, you don't know what you're doing!'

'Yes I do, Rick. I know exactly what I'm doing.' She motioned for Sykes to begin.

Jefferson shook his head wildly, yanked at his fastenings, but all to no avail. Sykes placed the sharp edge of the knife against the man's stomach. Blood started to dribble from the cut. 'Hold still, you old fool, or you'll ruin my line!' said Sykes. He dragged the knife across the flesh, pressing down deep. Jefferson's head tilted back, his eyes screwed up in agony, his screams stifled by the gag. 'Not too deep,' said

Sykes clinically, almost to himself. 'Don't want to split open your stomach now, do we?'

Blood splashed onto the stone floor at Jefferson's feet. He juddered, then his head went limp, chin resting on his chest as he passed out.

'Hurry up, Sykes!' Betsy urged.

'I like to take my time over these things,' he replied curtly. 'Like I did with Bunny.'

'You bastard!' Mason cried. 'You killed Bunny Foster? Betsy, what the hell have you gotten into?'

Sykes stopped, stepped back a little to admire his handiwork. He pushed a finger into the foot-long gash on Jefferson's stomach. 'This should come away nicely,' he observed, gripping the flap of skin between a bloody index finger and thumb. He moved forward, brandishing the knife again.

A loud retort rang out and Sykes lurched sideways. He dropped the knife, his hand going to his upper arm, turning to see where the bullet came from. As he turned he reached inside his coat for the pistol, aimed it quickly at the shadows and managed to let off a single round before another bullet ripped through his chest.

He hung there for a moment, then slumped to his knees, dropping the gun into the pool of blood that had run down from Jefferson's gaping wound. With a sickening gurgle, Warren Sykes fell face down onto the floor never to move again.

A figure emerged from the shadows, a smoking gun held out before him in two shaking hands.

'Don't even think about running, Betsy,' said Davey. 'I swear I'll use this on you if I have to.'

* * * *

35

Silent

'You're dead!'

Davey advanced, bent cautiously down to Sykes. He shook his head dolefully. 'It's lucky for you that I'm not dead, Rick,' he said, picking up the bloody knife from the floor. Covering Betsy with the gun, he began to slice through Mason's bonds.

'What are you doing?' Betsy cried, her hands out before her, pleading with her brother. 'Don't do that! Don't set him free!' then her voice plunged to one of rage. 'I said stop it!'

Mason's hands fell free and he rubbed them together to restore life to them. Davey ignored her strident demands, and his gun still pointed at her. 'Stay there!' he said to her. 'This has got to end.' He handed Mason the knife. 'Cut Jefferson down and see if you can pack something into that wound to stop it bleeding.'

Conrad Jefferson was coming round, a pathetic groan rumbling deep in his throat. Mason cut him down and he lay in a puddle of his own blood.

'We can still do this,' said Betsy. 'You don't know what you're doing.'

'For the first time in years it's very clear what I'm doing,' Davey replied, his expression grave.

'What's going on, Davey?' Mason asked, tossing aside the knife and grabbing Jefferson's shirt that had been dropped a few yards away.

'Everything that's happened has been leading up to this,' he replied. 'To murder Conrad Jefferson and frame you for it.'

'Stop it!' Betsy warned, taking a bold step closer. Davey stiffened, waved her back with the gun.

Mason was shocked. 'To murder Jefferson? Why would Betsy want to do that?'

'She's got her own personal reasons, but someone's got an even bigger one. Luke Dillon of Prima Studios. He's the one behind it all.'

Mason removed Jefferson's gag and he sucked in air. He wrapped the shirt around the wound. He was losing a lot of blood, but he was fully awake now, listening to what Davey was saying.

'I know there was no love lost between Dillon and Jefferson,' said Mason, 'but to want him dead?' He turned to look at Betsy. 'I don't understand.' He didn't recognise her face anymore. She stood like a stranger to him.

'True, they hate each other,' Davey said. 'Dillon wanted revenge for his long-standing grievances. And what better way than to take away Jefferson's company, to ruin the man. He's been trying for years. He knew Metropolitan had been struggling recently, but the Dragutin films were in danger of resurrecting the studio's fortunes so he was scared he'd never get his hands on the company. And you giving him the public cold shoulder only incensed him more. He hated you after that, Rick.

'The Dillons have some very nasty connections with the Los Angeles underworld, which is partly why Jefferson parted company with them in the first place. You'd never guess who they've got in their filthy pockets. Politicians, police, a raft of powerful people. Somehow, Luke Dillon got to know that I was wanted for a murder back in Louisiana.' He stared at his sister. 'With his police cronies working for him he was privy to all sorts of information, and I figured that's how he found out about me being in Hollywood, in hiding, on the run. He contacted Betsy and me, we had a private meeting with him. He told me he could fix it so that nobody would be coming after me ever again. But it came with a steep price tag. If we didn't go along with what he had planned he'd turn me over to the cops and he'd use his connections to make sure I went to the chair. Told me Betsy would be sent to jail as an accessory to murder. The options were pretty slim, so we agreed to go along with what he told us. Thing is, I believed he found out about me by accident, that my dear sister here was an unwilling accomplice in it all, that she was even doing it for me, to protect me, to save my life. But that's not quite the truth, is it?' He waved the gun at her.

'This is not the time or place,' she said. 'Think about what you're doing...' she said.

'What a sap I've been. I never thought you'd use me, too.' He frowned, his jaw muscles stiffening. The gun was shaking. 'Luke Dillon told us he could fix it so that I'd be found dead, the hunt for Peter Harvey called off. In return he wanted Betsy to bring down Jefferson, and in his eyes he would settle for nothing less than Jefferson's murder, finally allowing him to get full ownership of Metropolitan Studios.'

'You're a fool!' she said. 'You've spoiled everything for us! We could have had so much!'

'You had everything!' Mason fired. 'You had me, money, a baby...'

'I didn't have everything,' she spat angrily. 'I was being forced out, dropped by the studio and you didn't care at all. I saw what they were doing early on. Everything I ever wanted, to be a star, was going to be torn up before my eyes.

Did you seriously think I'd be satisfied with being your simpering little wife, a mother? A nobody?'

'I would have helped you,' he said.

'It's no use,' said Davey. 'She's blind to it. And nothing gets in the way of what she wants, isn't that true, sis? She'll even kill for it. She has already killed for it.'

'Liar!' she cried.

'It wasn't me that killed John Saunders, was it? Come on, sis, stop thinking about yourself for a change and spill the beans. Rick is owed that much.' He waited a moment. 'No? Then let me spell out what really happened in Louisiana. You tried out for John's play, but he didn't want you because you weren't right for the part. He tried to let you down gently, but you wouldn't have that, would you? You killed him for that.'

'He was a filthy, degenerate animal!' she said, her eyes livid, her cheeks and neck flushing with rage and frustration. 'He was a sick man and he deserved to die! He raped me!'

'You've said it so often you're even starting to believe it yourself. That's not true though, is it? You know that can't be true, because of who he was. You tried to blackmail him, didn't you? Because of what you saw.'

'He was sick! You were both sick!'

'He was my lover,' said Davey quietly. 'I loved him.'

'Stop it!' she said, putting her hands to her ears. 'I don't want to hear that! It's obscene! It's vile!'

'You discovered us together, in bed. I know that because John told me he thought he saw you at the door. You weren't supposed to be there at his house, but he also told me how you'd been desperate to get the part in his play and had turned up a couple of times begging to be taken on. But now you had something you could use against him, didn't you? Let me tell it as it probably happened, shall I? You went back to him and tried to blackmail him, threatened to tell everyone about his preferences for men. You were hoping he might think he could be ruined. But he wouldn't take the bite, would he? He refused to go along with it, told you to go away. But you wouldn't let it rest, you took his gun which I told you he kept in his desk drawer. You threatened him again. But he didn't respond and you shot him dead.'

'I was perfect for that part!' she said. 'He knew that.'

Davey shook his head. 'And you'd kill a man for that reason? For nothing more than that? I'm ashamed of you. For so long I wanted to believe what you told me, about you being raped. You're my sister; you wouldn't lie to me, I thought. You wouldn't use me in that way.'

'So it wasn't you who killed him?' Mason said. 'She told me...'

He turned to Mason. 'I know what she told you. But it's a lie. She came to me in distress, Rick. So cut up, her dress ripped. She said John had raped her. Said he was dead, that she'd shot him in self defence. Concerned, I went back to his place. It was true. I found him on the floor, his chest covered in blood. I picked up the gun that had killed him. I don't rightly know why. I looked down at the man I loved, and didn't want to believe how he could betray me and attack my sister. I was torn.

'Then the maid came in for her afternoon shift, saw me there and screamed. I ran out of the house, still holding the gun, which I threw away into the bushes as soon and I realised I had it in my hand. I believed you, Betsy. I believed every word. I was willing to take the rap for you – it was me they saw, me they were after, me that would have gone to the chair, because I wouldn't turn you in, wouldn't ever admit it was you who killed him. That's how much I loved you.

'But recently it's dawned on me what you're really capable of, and forced me to confront the truth about what really happened in Louisiana. I think I knew, really, but I didn't want to know. I wanted to believe you. But all this with Dillon made me reconsider everything. Now you'd use Rick, too, to further your own selfish ends.'

'I thought you loved me, Betsy,' Mason said, his eyes beginning to flood with tears. 'I truly loved you...'

'What does love matter?' she said. 'Love gets you nowhere in life. Love is a means to an end.'

'I'm as much to blame for what's happened to you, Rick,' said Davey. 'OK, so I could say I didn't have a choice, Dillon was blackmailing us to go along with his plans. But I went along with it to save my own neck. My suicide attempt wasn't real. Betsy and I arranged it so that you'd come into the shack at the same time I kicked away the chair. We even placed a convenient knife there so you could cut me down fast. It was to make you think it was me that was in that burning shack, that it was my body they'd found burned to a crisp, a man who had already tried to commit suicide once and this time had succeeded. In truth it was Dillon who arranged it. The man they found was some dead hobo or other. Dillon also arranged it so that the body would be identified by the police as the late Peter Harvey, wanted for murder in Louisiana. I was to disappear, make a life elsewhere free from looking over my shoulder. What I didn't know was how it was that my sister had approached Dillon to cut a deal.'

'Can it, Peter!' she said. 'Don't listen, Rick, he's lying!'

'Luke Dillon didn't just happen to find out about me, about us; you went to him. It was you who came up with the entire thing, to get me off the hook, frame Rick for Jefferson's murder, and all so that you could have your stardom and he could have his revenge on Mason and Jefferson. You were in on it together.'

She had her arms folded about her, shivering. She looked much smaller, as if she were gradually fading away. But her eyes still burned with fury.

'I thought you were ill,' said Mason, emotion drained from him. 'I thought I was going mad...'

'That's exactly what they wanted you to believe. You were being drugged, slowly, day by day, something that was making you more aggressive, gave you severe mood swings, a hallucinogenic. Doctor Lombard was on Dillon's payroll. Lombard and Betsy worked together to make you believe you were under the Dragutin curse, even making you think you might be turning into him. Punching that woman that day, that wasn't you, it was the early effects of the drug. And you willingly took more tablets from Lombard without question. Believed everything he said about your wife. And why should you even think to question it?

'Dillon even funded some of the religious protests so that the movie, and you, would be discredited. Then the bomb under your car – that was arranged by Dillon, too, partly so that you'd not question taking on a new head of security to protect you and your family, partly to draw negative attention to the new movie. Warren Sykes here,' he said motioning with the gun to the dead man, 'is not ex-military but an ex-con. The men on your mansion gates are all part of the deception. They've even created false logs of your movements to and from the mansion, ready to use in evidence against you. Truth is, when Bunny was murdered you were home, drugged to the eyeballs. It was Sykes who murdered Bunny Foster, making it look like there was a Dragutin copycat killer on the loose, and he planted her bloodied clothes and severed finger in your room to make you think you did it. But he was careful not to lead the police directly to you. Not yet. You see, they wanted something else first. The plan was to make it look like you'd gone off your head; you killed Bunny and then went on to kill Jefferson. Finally you turned the gun on yourself. No one would even think to question it. All the evidence pointed to you. Christ, it was so good you even believed you were under a curse yourself. The jury would find out how you'd gradually flipped, drugged your wife like Dragutin drugged

Dorottya – the bottle you found and gave to Lombard was planted there; it had your prints all over it and would be used as evidence of how you kept Betsy under sedation. A nice final touch was for them to order leg-irons. They'd thought of every little detail that would point to you as the murderer.

'With Jefferson's death, the new movie in big trouble, Dillon would manoeuvre ownership of Metropolitan, especially when Betsy sold the shares you owned in the company to Dillon. And in return, Betsy would get everything you inherited and a lucrative deal with Dillon promising her long-term contracts and stardom with the new Metropolitan Studios. A grateful Luke Dillon would set her up for life.'

Mason rose from Jefferson and went over to Betsy. His hands were covered in blood. 'Is this all true, Betsy?'

'You believe all that?' she said. 'You really think I am capable of something like that?'

'We had so much going for us. Was it really worth killing someone? For all this plaster crap?' He waved his hand at the towering set. 'It's all false. None of it's real. It doesn't last. It can never last...'

Her expression softened, and for a flickering moment the woman he fell in love with shone through her mask of hate. 'I'm still your Betsy, Rick...' she said.

'You would have had me killed...' he said.

'Don't listen to her,' said Davey. 'I tried to warn you about her, Rick, but you wouldn't listen...' he said. 'I tried to protect you from her...'

'You mean you wanted him for yourself!' she snapped. 'That's why you're doing this. Why don't you tell him?' she said coldly. 'Go ahead; tell Rick what you really feel.'

'What do you mean?' asked Mason.

'Don't believe anything he's saying, Rick. He's the one who's sick. John Saunders corrupted him!' Her eyes steeled.

'He loves you,' she said acidly. 'Can't you see that? Davey is in love with you.'

Mason turned to Davey, whose head was shaking as if emotions ran through him like an electric current.

'Maybe I do. Maybe I just don't want to see you do this to Rick,' said Davey. 'It has to stop here. You're twisted. You've let crazy ambition and greed blind you to everything that's good...'

'It's all lies,' said Betsy. 'You have to believe me, Rick. He'll stop at nothing to have you for his own. It's not love, it's a travesty!'

'What do you know of love?' Davey said quietly. 'You've stamped all over it.'

'You love me, don't you, Rick?' she said, stepping closer. 'You still love me. I can see that in your eyes. Don't listen to him. He's the one behind all this. You can't trust him.'

Mason shook his head slowly. His mind was in turmoil. He wanted to reach out to her, to hold her close again, to forget all this ever happened. And for one brief moment he was powerless to resist her, as he had always been powerless before her, and lifted his hand to hold hers.

Swiftly, Betsy bent down to the floor and scooped up the gun Sykes had dropped. She pressed the end of the barrel hard against Mason's stomach and pulled the trigger. He staggered backwards, falling over. And as he fell he saw, as if in slow-motion, Betsy raising the gun to fire at Davey.

A scarlet rose bloomed at her throat, and her mouth, framed by her bright-red lips, spouted silent words. She let the gun tumble from her hand, putting her fingers to the wound, staring at the wisps of smoke spiralling from Davey's gun. Then her eyes glazed over and she dropped down into a heap.

Mason felt an intense, fiery pain engulf him. He stared at the high, fathomless ceiling. A face hovered into view.

'Rick!' said Davey, his voice wavering. 'Rick, stay with me!'

But already the pain was subsiding, replaced instead by creeping, comforting warmth. He turned his head to one side. Betsy's sightless eyes were fixed on him.

'Betsy…' he whispered.

Something shimmered in the darkness behind her. A lone figure came briefly into focus, seen as if through a summer heat haze.

It wore a military uniform, decorated with gold braid and silver buttons; its face appeared to be the white porcelain mask of Antinous. No sooner had Mason fixed it in his sights than it vanished. He became afraid.

Davey's voice was fading. The light dimming. His face was nothing more than a pale blob floating in a starless night sky.

Then Rick Mason's world fell silent.

Printed in Great Britain
by Amazon.co.uk, Ltd.,
Marston Gate.